T0290324

KNOLL

STEPHEN HILLARD

KNOLL

THE LAST JFK CONSPIRACIST

A Novel

SELECTBOOKS, INC.
NEW YORK

The book is a work of fiction. The characters, dialogue, places, and events that occur
are either products of the author's imagination, or if these are based on real places,
events, or people, they are used in the text fictitiously.

Copyright © 2017 by Stephen Hillard

All rights reserved. Published in the United States of America. No part of this book may be
reproduced or transmitted in any form or by any means, graphic, electronic, or mechanical,
including photocopying, recording, taping or by any information storage or retrieval system,
without the permission in writing from the publisher.

This edition published by SelectBooks, Inc.
For information address SelectBooks, Inc., New York, New York.
First Edition

ISBN 978-1-59079-421-0

Library of Congress Cataloging-in-Publication Data
Names: Hillard, Stephen, author.
Title: Knoll : The Last JFK Conspiracist / Stephen Hillard.
Description: First edition. | New York : SelectBooks, [2017]
Identifiers: LCCN 2016040976 | ISBN 9781590794210 (hardcover)
Subjects: LCSH: Kennedy, John F. (John Fitzgerald),
  1917-1963--Assassination--Fiction. | United States. National Security
  Agency--Fiction. | Conspiracies--Fiction. | GSAFD: Mystery fiction. |
  Suspense fiction.
Classification: LCC PS3608.I43834 K63 2017 | DDC 813/.6--dc23 LC record
available at https://lccn.loc.gov/2016040976

TEXT DESIGN BY PAULINE NEUWIRTH, NEUWIRTH & ASSOCIATES, INC.

Manufactured in the United States of America

10 9 8 7 6 5 4 3 2 1

While a work of fiction, much of this book is based on true facts. It follows closely a very real set of people, circumstances, and events that occurred in North Louisiana in 1963. The dedication is thus a natural. To my father, Dean Crandall Hillard, who left with me a legacy of questions and inspiration. And, of course, to the fictional world of Junction City, which lies but an imagined half-parallel from the real city of Grand Junction, Colorado, where I had the good fortune to live in an especially formative moment of my life.

Stephen Hillard
Grand Junction, Colorado
February 2017

knoll (\\'nōl\\):

 a small, rounded hillock; to sound a knell,

 as to give forth a mourning or warning

 sound; an advantaged perspective for

 targeting an individual (post-1963).

PART ONE

VOICES

"Three can keep a secret if two are dead."

—Sign in the office of Carlos Marcello (1962)

"*Quo vadis?*" ("Where are you going?")

—Peter to Jesus on the road exiting Rome
(apocryphal Acts of the Apostles)

CHAPTER ONE

A CANYON EVENT

Colorado slick rock country. Dawn.

Salt Creek winds through a slot canyon cut between a thousand feet of vertical red sandstone cliffs.

Two vans, green and bearing the logo of the Colorado Department of Parks and Wildlife, proceed cautiously along the narrow dirt track that competes for a share of the streambed. They traverse the creek, meander in and out of the veins of sunlight, dodge newly fallen rock, and progress toward the only entry to the ovoid-shaped valley up ahead.

The six sunglassed men in the vans scan the canyon through open windows. They are dressed in false uniforms, carry false IDs, and yet, in fidelity to their trade, bear expert tools of stunning lethality. In the air, a hundred feet above the road and a quarter-mile ahead of them, their Parrot-4 survelliance drone is hovering like a guard dog on point.

Their mission is singular. No warrants. No Miranda warning cue cards. They have shovels.

High above them, an intermittent track, an old mining burro trail, clings to the sheer cliffs. It is invisible save for scattered wood and metal debris that a century of sun and weather has transformed into the same colors as the cliffs. It leads to a mine that wormholes a score of man-size borings into the porous Kayenta Formation. In three of these borings sit stacked cases of dynamite, easy to procure in this country, armed with electronic, sequentially initiated blasting caps. The caps, despite a century-plus of development, remain testy, subject to sparks, pressure, heat, shock, electromagnetic interference, and the wild cards of Fate. They are the jokers in a bomb maker's deck.

The mine is known to only one living man, who spies it now in a spotting scope from five miles across the valley. The man's eyes shift to his laptop screen. An eagle's view of the two vans from his RS-Searcher drone loitering high above the canyon walls.

The data for his devices is via satellite, and thus picks up a half-second of latency, which is of no importance today. The encryption is his invention, superior to TOR, absolutely unbreakable.

The Searcher watches the vans pass a rock topped with an "X" made of weathered tree limbs. They slow to a hard turn on the streambed. The man's fingers, adept at screens and keyboards, mouse the cursor to a gray button sitting lower right. He double-clicks the button.

The report from the explosives rockets down the canyon walls, reverberating back and forth. The first van slams to a stop. The passengers look upwards as the initial debris-fall blocks the road. The cliff face, vast and implacable, leans out and over them. The sunlight is swept away by its deep shadow. The slow-motion fall, as if a cosmic crowbar peeled off a slab of canyon, defies comprehension and only their reflexes pull their unbelieving eyes away before they, their drone, and the entire lower canyon, are buried.

Sealed, the man at the computer thinks as he binoculars the mushrooming dust cloud and waits for the sound wave.

CHAPTER TWO
THE BEGINNING

Campaign rally for Representative Gary Ochray, 38th District of Texas, August 20, 2014.

"My assistant, Banner McCoy, has the mike. Banner, please . . . yes over to the gentlemen there. Thank you."

"Test. [thump] [cough] Yeh, here. I got a question. Congressman, seein' as yer on the Intelligence Committee and what not, if y'all so damn smart, catching Obama (laugh) . . . I mean . . . Osama and all, why the hell cantcha pump up your little spy factory and figure out just who in the *hail* shot JFK? [applause, whistles] You gotta lot of honest Americans here, taxpayers and voters, everyone. Fact is they lived his death and the story dies with them. They deserve a straight answer to pass on to their grandkids. 'Fore another generation grows up and doesn't care. We'd all take kindly to a straight answer."

"I agree. I have sponsored an appropriation to get exactly that accomplished. Consider it done. Next question."

CHAPTER THREE

BANNER—
TWO YEARS LATER

July 10, 2016

PRESS RELEASE VIA SPYFLOW.COM

My name is Banner McCoy. I am in territorial waters of a country that does not have an extradition treaty with the United States. I work—worked—at TCC, the Texas Cryptological Center in San Antonio. My NSA identification number is tcc-49387-4b.

I did not defect. I fled.

Before he squirrelled away the biggest trove of top secret information in history, and boarded that fateful one-way flight to Singapore, Edwin Snow warned me, "If you're going to do this, the first rule of survival is to get *very public, very fast*. Make your elimination too costly. *Then* try to hide. But don't count on it."

In case my disappearance is being investigated by cold-case hobbyists someday, here is a list of some distinguishing characteristics: DOB: 6/10/1988, blonde and blue-eyed, 5'8" (I was a fair volleyball player), red birthmark on right calf, butterfly tramp-stamp tat on my lower back, all four wisdom teeth intact due to growing up without a dental plan.

My project at TCC was called "KNOLL." Its stated mission in the black ops appropriation was "to utilize all available resources to gather evidence and resolve questions regarding the assassination of [JFK]."

That's a lie.

Its real mission is to destroy any remaining evidence of a conspiracy.

I also know what can happen to people like me.

I have with me certain files. They are encrypted with IGT. Should harm befall me, it will activate their release.

I'm not a terrorist. I'm true-blue, apple-pie, gun-loving, cry-at-the-national-anthem American to the core.

And just so everyone knows. I still have access to the Glass Box.

CHAPTER FOUR

"BUS"—
JUNCTION CITY, CO

The framed State-U diploma hanging on the wall behind me bestows a law degree:

Columbus William McIntyre

That's me. I'm considering murder.

That's because for the first time in my life, and on my last day as special prosecutor in Junction City, Colorado, I am accused of corruption.

Eating my Cheerios this morning, I'm oblivious, but one headline and two phone calls today are about to put a ninety-degree turn on the course of my life.

As I ponder my first real crime (I mentally hesitate there, but move on), I'm sitting at my desk, the journeyman's workbench of my legal trade. I'm proud of it. The auctioneer's gavel came down at my outcry bid of $200. Right on the steps of the failed Sentinel Bank of Junction City. RIP 1883–2012. The desk belonged to the bank president, now departed from this fair city.

I lean back, let out a breath, and survey the self-congratulatory accoutrements in my lawyer's lair. Indulgent wood paneling, photos and certificates on the walls, a frame holding a yellowed, hand-typed letter to the House Un-American Activities Committee from Dalton Trumbo, blacklisted Hollywood screenwriter and Academy Award winner. In one corner is a glass case of arrowheads and other artifacts gathered from jaunts in the jumbled canyons bordering this sprawling green valley.

In the opposite corner leans an ancient mesquite fencepost. It is entangled in a rusty Gordian knot of barbwire. A weathered sign hangs askew on the post. "Dude Stomp," the lettering sunbleached long ago.

Next to this is a battered credenza on which rests an array of family pictures. My mother (Woolworth's lunch counter uniform), my two grandparents (she is aproned and holding pies; he is shirtless and pitchforking hay onto a horse-drawn buckboard). Between these are my three kids, Jessica, Scott and Stephanie, at signature stages of growing up. I slow my gaze and linger on them, contemplating the stories they tell— pumpkins, princesses, volleyball, Pop Warner football, proms, first hunts, graduations. Now they are scattered across three time zones that are not mine. In the foreground are recent pictures of the growing entourage of grandkids.

I reflect, as always, that I haven't seen kids and grandkids enough. These days any trip to visit them must first pass through a hellish gate guarded by my newest wife. Even a birthday gift becomes a matter of grim negotiation. I shrug.

Hidden in the back are two other items, perhaps related. One, to complete the generations thing, is my only framed picture of my father. The other is a different artifact. Something I recently acquired from a client. It is a rare four-rotor German Enigma machine. Pristine condition. The device with the supposedly unbreakable code used by the Nazis in World War II.

My eyes lift and there looms, of course, the obligatory wall of law books. I haven't opened one in years. Everything is digital these days. Which occasionally makes me a bit paranoid. If I pull up a file on my computer, who else knows what I'm reading? Old-time, low-tech, hard copy print is, I fancy, still untraceable. But so *yesterday*.

At this moment I could care less about cybersecurity. I am staring goggle-eyed at our local hard copy, low-tech newspaper. The 60-point headline on the front page shouts:

Prosecutor McIntyre Shields Leaker, Favors Own Interests

The "Leaker" in question is a group of activists who call themselves "Leaks 2.0." They are a lesser version of WikiLeaks, existing in the cloud and trading in the gathering and dissemination of information. Governmental and private information.

No doubt, money had changed hands in lots of directions. Some of the disclosed stuff was internal memos and emails about Shale County projects, some of it career-mauling scandal, some of it just damn juicy gossip. But who said it was a crime?

Well, in this case the Colorado legislature did, in a midnight bill last year that made trading in stolen proprietary information for profit a class three felony.

Based on its breadth, I believed the law was unconstitutional, so I refused the indictment. For that stand on the First Amendment, I am today's headliner.

My *own interests*, as the article howls, is ownership of a digital encryption company called, oddly, I-Gig-Tam, Inc. IGT. I took it, along with the Enigma Machine, in payment for legal services from a local geek who was ditching his connected life and moving off the grid. To my knowledge, IGT has no business operations and no revenues, but it owns two patents for an obscure encryption technology. Plus, a handful of weird-looking thumb drives. The owner left me these with a note, tailored to his estimate of my IT capabilities: "These USB drives are plug-and-play. They upload to IGT. Call it 'in the cloud,' Bus, you ignorant doofus. In fact, never mind. Just contact me, if you can, and I can explain this stuff. You know where to find me. Richard."

"Where" is a remote, twenty-square-mile valley, with only one road in. It is called "Sinbad," in reference to a sailing ship etched high on the canyon walls. By the conquistadores, the mash-up legend says.

In any case, a bunch of hedge funds—patent trolls really—have made lucrative offers for IGT. I disclosed these before accepting the job as special prosecutor. Nonetheless, the article breathlessly unveils the implication that I must like Leakers because they make my "Secrets Business" more valuable. A stretch, but so be it.

I can visualize my seething anger, like the antique boiler in the basement of my Victorian house on a subzero day. Flames in the firebox casting a red glow that pulses on the brick wall. Acrid steam hisses. You can feel the pressure building. A rivet adjusts with a metallic "pang." Then another. Almost like a . . . knock.

I look up and see Carrie Williams, her knocked hand holding open the door, the other holding some papers.

She is, I observe, one classy woman.

She's also my new law partner, so that compartments my thoughts. Old lessons flash through my head and I correct my vision to a purely professional lens.

She is the only black lawyer in a town with less than one percent African-American population, a town where, until recent years, "diversity" was begrudging, given to lip service, and pretty much meant "Latino" only.

If Carrie saw those barriers you'd never know it. Her real distinction was simple: she was very, very good. I know because I lost cases to her. Cases I should have won. Over the past decade she'd built her solo practice from divorces and DUIs to a solid litigation caseload with local businesses as clients. The best kind: paying clients. When a big case needed local counsel, she got her share of the calls. Maybe more.

So, looking ahead, perhaps seeing myself in public office, I recently lured her into my growing little firm.

She holds up the papers. It looks like a court order. "Summary judgment. The Benson case." She pauses to see if that registers. I acknowledge with a chin up and questioning eyebrow. "Our favor," she says. She starts to go, turns and says, "Buck up, cowboy," before closing the door behind her.

Leaving me back in that steaming boiler room.

I snap a lead pencil in two.

Vance, you editor prick. This is below even you.

Vance Tilson, owner of the *Junction City Monitor*, is my imaginary victim. Even now, I see him dead-center in the cross-hairs of a night scope. The one I occasionally use for coyote hunting. My finger paused . . . so-o . . . ready.

Being a gutless wonder, he had his editor call me last night. The guy was evasive, asking for my comment on "the IGT story." I declined. I'd learned *that* relevant lesson as a young lawyer. Years ago, I'd tried to help some impoverished Indian tribes get recognition for their land claims in Colorado. They'd been massacred in 1865, their aboriginal homelands near Denver stolen, the survivors run off to a desolate rez in Oklahoma. They wanted two acres to build a casino to help break the iron cycle of eight generations of poverty. I indulged my mouth, said that the magnificent glowing dome of the Colorado State Capitol (where, by the way, I'd worked the year before as a law clerk for the Colorado Supreme Court) was made of "stolen gold." The *Denver Post* crucified me. I learned Mark Twain's axiom the hard way: "Never pick a fight with someone who buys ink by the barrel."

Now, when it comes to the press, I keep my mouth shut.

Next month is the deadline to file for the Shale County primary election. I planned on running for district attorney. A modest organization has coalesced around me, even fabbing up an Obama-style poster in red, white and blue, me with the scowl appropriate for the gravity of the prosecutor's office. It reads:

Get Aboard with BUS!
Columbus McIntyre for District Attorney
Son of a Murdered Cop

A bit over the top. Recognition of my nickname would be spotty. Worst is the line at the bottom. The thinking perhaps that even the political left in this county likes this sort of cred. Anyway, most people around here never knew that small footnote of local history. I nixed the poster.

Perhaps the whole thing was too political to begin with. So why do it? Another notch on my professional gun handle? Yeah, sure. Maybe even a stepping stone to a judgeship on the state appellate court. Some kind of cosmic redemption? *For what?* my shrink always asks.

That particular answer is locked away. The gate keyless. The secret safe.

With today's headline, political aspirations are moot. I make the first of those two phone calls. Taking a breath and blowing it out, I dial up my rival, James Cressen.

I can see him clearly, my former law partner. Both of us aged lions that have fed on legal carcasses on this western Colorado plateau for decades. Public defenders at first. Then private practice. His stint as a district court judge. Me as a trial lawyer. That's where the jealousy eased through the door of our friendship. I envied his clear, sober, analytical view of the world. He maybe envied the modest pile of dough I'd made. And the plum selection as special prosecutor when conflicts over Leaks 2.0 froze up the engine of local government.

Jim, seeing my number on his direct line, picks up. He starts the conversation, saving me from stumbling.

"Sorry, Bus, just hang in there. The world has a short memory. People will forget by tomorrow."

"Not for me, Jim. I'll pass on this ride and you'll win easily. You got my support."

Jim will be a great prosecutor. He's worked the defense side, knows the tricks and respects defense counsel. He's tough as nails when he makes up his mind.

We endure the beeps of other incoming calls, say our goodbyes, and promise to meet soon for lunch.

I have lost plenty of times in my life—trials, divorce, investments—with the scars to prove each one. This one stings because I never got to start. But it is, in the end, the result of an open, if unfair, press. I like things transparent. Let the truth play out.

Except in the back rooms of my own life. As I'm about to learn, that's what the next call is about.

It is from Rick Van Pelt, detective at the Junction City Police Department. We'd played side by side on the football team at Shale High so long ago.

"Bus, sorry about the paper. Bunch of crap. What's next? You've played, win or lose, in every legal game around here."

I deflect. "Thanks. Jim'll be a great prosecutor. Convict all those perps you're catchin'."

Rick hesitates just a moment, then gets to the point. "Look, this is about something else. I just got a file. An old file. We were cleaning out the evidence storeroom, someone noticed the name. Your dad's name. About his murder. Bus, you there?"

I'm not. Rick's office is across the street, on the second floor of the City-County Building. I am already past the Doric columns that front that building, through security, and quick-stepping up the stairs to see him.

He is standing in his office when I get there. Gray at the temples, a bit jowly, but still that fast, compact body shape that was vintage pulling guard. The guy who played at my left side as I snapped the ball.

He had followed in his dad's footsteps, becoming chief of detectives within a year of Rick Senior's retirement. Where his father was small-town and low-tech, Rick is a next-gen officer, in tune with forensics, schooling several weeks a year over at the CBI lab in Denver. My eyes involuntarily snoop his desk. I'm a fair reader of upside-down print. A framed certificate for a course in "Cold Case DNA" sits in his mail stack. The bottom line: the guy's got one helluva nose for the truth. Not someone you want on your suspect ass.

Fine by me. He is good, and a friend.

"You didn't want that thankless job anyway, Bus." He holds out his hand and we shake. "Do what you're good at, suing those *heartless bastards* out there."

Rick can mimic a litigator's affects, including mine, to a T. He isn't being cynical, just picking up on the one really big case I'd won, where a juror had sent me a note after the trial echoing the words I'd uttered in closing argument (and been admonished by Judge Slawson for), "My client thanks you for letting us bring justice to these (long pause and my condemning finger pointed straight at them) . . . heartless bastards."

The bastards happened to be some of the city fathers, sitting on the board of Sentinel Bank, Junction City's oldest, most esteemed and now liquidated bank. Corners were cut, books cooked, secrets revealed (some say courtesy of Leaks 2.0, but that was never established), a scandal uncovered and, at my hands, they paid big right out of their jeans.

The biggest loser was a man named Hydee Thomson, a local rancher and developer. A gruff puffery who prided himself on his conservative civic image and yet left a long trail of questionable deals and busted partnerships. He specialized in shifting assets to companies owned by the venerable, untouchable Mrs. Thomson.

The result, before I came along, was that he'd never been tagged with a loss.

Unfortunately, although their pockets were lightened, Hydee and the rest survived. And so, I've come to appreciate, my public office fortunes in this town have distinctly limited prospects. The Special Prosecutor position is going to be it. The news article today is just a warm up.

I think about the nice thing with having a little f-you money: you can say those words and mean it. So, as I stand in Rick's office, I've resolved to forget public office and stick with being a gunny in the local trial bar. The fact that I have notches on the handle of my legal six-shooter still works in this little Out-West town where great-grandfathers saw the whole Ute Tribe run out of the county and the bank over in Delta robbed by Butch Cassidy and the McCarty Gang.

So I will reflexively fall back on my roots. Poor side of the tracks, armed with a legal shingle. I'll try cases and scare the hell out of the Establishment.

Maybe warm up my hardly ridden Harley. Hell, maybe even write another book.

Coming down the hallway just now, I'd fussed with the usual crowd, some folks shaking hands in conversation, some avoiding my eyes. The calendared, pedantic details of my life still hovering about me.

Shrink appointment at eleven. Cleaners. Get coffee beans for Mary.

Now, I'm standing in front of Rick, and he is about to change all that. He gestures to a table.

On it is a file, manila cover, maybe half an inch thick, looking dog-eared and ragged with time. It is watermarked with coffee stains. A pink post-it, obviously new, sticks out. My dad's name is on the cover:

Dean McIntyre, Personal

Next to it is a blue, cloth-covered three-ring binder. It is full of dog-eared pages.

"Cleaning out the back part of the evidence room. Part of your dad's files. When he worked dispatch. Before he left."

The last words drift off, acknowledgment that my old man left the Junction City Police Department after falling off the wagon. It was right after my mother died. He pulled it together again after that and took a job as the only cop in a scruffy little town named Lowena. It was west of Junction City, forty miles from the state line, straddling the main road to Utah. His last job.

Funny, Rick and I were not just ex-high school jocks, we were connected in another, weird way. We both got into plenty of trouble, sometimes together, while our dads were in law enforcement. His, the hard-nosed detective. Mine, the police dispatcher that heard everything, felt the pulse of Junction City, and directed the tentacles of the cops up and down its maple-lined streets.

Now here we are: cop and lawyer.

What is in front of me, however, isn't a memory. It is a hard artifact from a bygone time that I've tried to erase from my consciousness. I haven't been able to do that, of course, but my shrink says I am one of the most "walled-off" people she's encountered.

Rick is talking. "I looked at these. Cold case stuff. They were scheduled for shredding till someone recognized the name. Most of it is just personal, but I put a sticky on the inside. Carbons of a note from the day-shift dispatcher to your dad, after he'd gone out to Lowena. I'm giving them to you to look at. Just keep them intact for a while."

He's thinking something, but isn't telling me. I'm not sure how to react. In the end, I thank him, and scoop up the materials. I vaguely hear him reminding me as I leave about our upcoming showdown at the Police Benefit basketball game.

■

I walk from the City-County Building to the parking lot next to my office. I sit in the cocoon of my car. I hold the stuff in my lap like it is dynamite. Opening this is not going to be simple. Not at all. The file and the binder might hold innocuous fragments—old shopping lists, my mom's obituary, who knows. Or it might be bones that would have to be rolled all over again, their pattern revealed.

I flip open the binder and see maybe a hundred pages of text typed out on notebook paper. I do a quick thumb-through. The flick of pages releases the faintest mist of name-brand scents, each an evocation of my old man—*Old Spice aftershave, Lucky Strike cigarette smoke, Seagram's 7 whiskey, Loss, Regret, Secrets*. The pages themselves are in no apparent order. What I see is a mental image of the man, pecking on his old Remington portable at our duplex unit where we lived in Junction City when I was a kid. I realize where I got the instinct to write things. Here's the first entry in his journal:

October 6, 1970

   It was Thursday and I got a call from a friend
working front at the Junction City PD. A man had
come in, asking about me, seeing if I still worked
there. The man showed a legit-looking ID. May be
real, maybe not. Said he was a private investigator.
Dallas. The friend said that he looked off. Tall,
thin, shades, ponytail. Southern accent. A redneck
country boy. As a private dick, he was a fake.
   The hillbilly already had half or more of the
facts: knew I'd been five years with the PD,
knew I founded Bridge House, a rehab shelter for
alcoholics. Save the other alkies and save myself.
The man from Dallas didn't know the latest chapter,

that after my wife died, I stumbled badly, that I'd
taken a job as a small-town cop out at Lowena, last
gas stop before the Utah state line. The PD didn't
tell him either.

But the stranger would figure it out.

Being tailed creates a feeling. It had been years,
but I felt it now. An old but familiar buzz in the
spine, a worry that steals what little rest you can
muster.

Not since I'd run, not just because I was sick of
the vice and the secrets and the next hacksaw night
manager gig. I ran because I realized how deep in
the shit I was with the Little Man. Jumped on the
white line and headed west from Louisiana. Stints
as hotel night clerk. Amarillo, the Herring, Santa
Fe, the La Fonda. Then on to little Junction City,
tracking down the wife and kids that'd fled there
the year before.

Now I am the one being tracked.

I look at the date again. A week before he was killed.

Time slows and I walk backwards through the text, like treading
upstream in a slow-moving bayou. My feet touch things I don't
want to know about, things I have scrupulously avoided thinking
about for decades.

I jerk and slam shut the binder as a colleague, my new junior
partner, Enrique Escamilla, honks cheerfully as he drives by. *2-E* or
Tooey for short, he is a computer geek with Latino tats to shame
any homie. His arms are full-sleeved with intricate ink. On one
arm: jaguars, the Mayan calendar, Olmec signs, the tri-color with
eagle and snake. On the other: a mustachioed Pancho Villa with
crossed ammo belts next to a sombrero'd and otherwise naked
que linda senorita. Like me, he went to law school in Boulder and

clerked for the Colorado Supreme Court. The difference being that a street-wise guy like Tooey, genius or not, would never have gotten the breaks I got back in the day. He's gonna be good.

He often pimps me about my own puny tats—a sort-of scorpion on one arm, on the other my cryptic tag sign. "You get those smudgy things in jail, cholo, like with a Bic pen?"

He is gone and I reflect on the fact that my tag-sign is an image my father used to draw. The most visible of a lot of marks from him.

I take a deep breath. I still have the manila file on my lap. I open it again and this time the first item is a loose newspaper clipping someone had ripped out of the *Monitor* and just stuck in there.

Of course, I'd read the same article long ago.

Officer Slain Near State Line

JUNCTION CITY, AP OCTOBER 10, 1970.
Dean A. McIntyre, an officer with the Lowena Police Department, was killed by gunfire early Friday morning. The incident occurred while Officer McIntyre was alone at a roadblock on Highway 50, approximately one mile from the Utah state line. Investigators for the Shale County Sheriff's Office said that a number of roadblocks had been established in the county Thursday night. This was in response to information that several armed suspects were fleeing west after a series of drugstore burglaries in the Aspen area. A Sheriff's Office spokesman said Officer McIntyre had requested backup at 3:00 a.m. His body was discovered

by Sheriff's officers who arrived at the remote
location at around 3:45 a.m.

No arrests have been made.

Officer McIntyre is survived by his children,
Alice and Columbus, in Junction City, and his
stepson, Gene Wray Kochrek, in Bossier City,
Louisiana.

————

I fidget in my seat like a leery animal, then flip through the little
binder again. None of it jumps out until I pick the words "Bossier"
and "Dallas."

A handwritten note, unmistakably his scrawl, is at the bottom of
a page. I ponder the artifact, its simplicity, a voice so direct I can see
and hear him. As if he is taking a deep breath, clearing a smoker's
cough, then eyes up level and saying . . .

*For what I did in Dallas, they will find me. Carlos Marcello, his
lapdog Mike Maroon. That prick Louie.*

Carlos Marcello? I vaguely picture a short, surly Mafioso from
New Orleans. Scowl. Big cigar. Popular on the Crime Channel.
Frequent cameos in the lineup of JFK assassination suspects. His
picture always in black and white.

The other names? Mike *Maroon.* That's too rich, like a Beagle
Boy or a Dick Tracy villain, maybe a minor character in Gotham
City. *Louie?* No idea.

I turn the page. Someone else honks. I glance at my watch.
"Shit!" I fumble with the car keys, and exit the parking lot like a
rocket.

CHAPTER FIVE

LOUIE

Calagero Minacori, aka Carlos Marcello, aka the Little Man, is two decades dead. He wears a natty, going-to-court suit, broad forehead framed by gassed-back, graying hair. He looks over at Louie. *So I'm dead. Fuck you.* Like it's nothing. He leans back, his scowl softened by introspection. He lets a ghostly swirl of cigar smoke meander upwards, like an eddy in a lazy bayou. It gathers in the car's headliner, a stinky gray halo. A silenced Walther PPX9 rests between them. The patient enforcer.

"Louie," the dead man drawls in a high-pitched, Sicilian-Cajun accent, "you nice talent, you know. Still a fuckin' *sa-vant.*"

Nice, the way he says it. That slow, New Orleans, tomato-salesman mishmash.

Louie Diamond nods at Marcello, long-departed kingpin of the Louisiana-Texas Mafia. Louie pockets the heat, eases out of the car, the door closing like silk on velvet. He carries a briefcase and disappears into the rumbling sea of idling rigs that island the truck stop known as Natchez Wheels. The sound of his boot heels echoes away.

It is hot. It is humid. It is night.

It is North Louisiana.

CHAPTER 6

BUS—AMALIE

You'd think psychologists were on psychological time, but they're not. Amalie Adams is a stickler for her schedule. She goes by the clock, and I am ten minutes late. With her encouragement, we jump in with both feet.

We get through the newspaper headline, my ditched election plans, my swerving career. I lie, something I do a lot with her. Probably because seeing her is my wife Mary's idea. Amalie probes about my disappointment on the run for DA. I pretend it's no big deal. Maybe I'm not even pretending. It's already feeling like old history, like looking in a rear-view mirror.

Given what's happening today, I decide to break our brittle mold. I share with her a few elements of the truth, what I'm really thinking.

The story comes out like this: certain experiences never die until you do. From the moment they happen, every minute you exist is marked by another erratic beat in what you do, who you think you are.

What happened to me in 1963 in Bossier City is still there, unresolved, marking its strange off-rhythm tempo in my guts. Like a heart murmur of the soul.

I was fifteen when someone killed JFK. They say that, for my generation, it was a loss of innocence. For me, it was a sea change. Within two weeks, my mom suddenly fled my old man, Bossier City, everything. She uprooted us from our shitty, air condition-er-less little apartment in a poor white trash housing project, piled all of our belongings into an ailing Rambler station wagon and, almost penniless, drove west.

I had two hours' notice to say my goodbyes. They were still adjusting the Eternal Flame and planting the grass at the JFK Memorial when we arrived in Junction City.

It was the kind of quiet, nowhere place you go to if you are scared. If you never want to be found.

Looking back, there was a lot of emotional wreckage going on, but in all the tangle, I hardly suspected my little catastrophe was anything other than an All-American Dysfunctional Family Blow-Up. That, of course, was the itch. JFK, our flight to Junction City, my old man's murder. A litany of disparate tragedies, or, just maybe, a connected array of bitter stars. A constellation perhaps bearing greater meaning, its signs and portents mysterious and still unread.

As I'm talking, my mind feels like my old man's GI Timex. As if I'd just re-wound it after decades of neglect. The gears are meshing, the balance wheel oscillating. I'm thinking.

The only picture I have of my old man is a faded, off-color five-by-seven relegated to the rear of my office credenza. He's in his Junction City PD uniform, a dun-colored Stetson set jauntily on his head, standing next to a squad car. I review what—amazingly little—I know about him.

He was born in 1925, adopted "within the family," the quaint euphemism whispered in the south to cover up certain kinds of young ladies' indiscretions. He didn't exactly gel with his adoptive parents. They sent him off to military school at nine. He never came home. At nineteen he was a war hero. North Africa, Salerno,

Monte Cassino, and that little Italian town named after Saint Peter. *San Pietro*. The Keeper of the Keys.

The saint must indeed have kept them, because my old man went through life keyless.

At twenty-five he was a fully-blossomed initiate in the old school of alcoholics: hard-working, steady-drinking. As in around the clock. This progressed to intermittent benders and lost weekends, life settling into a see-saw pattern of big plans, failures, deep rage and deeper remorse. The remorse was the scariest, the sound in the voice of a man who knows he is lost. It would last about half a day, like an unwatered flower in the hot Texas sun.

The long, slow-mo downward spiral went on for years. You might think booze is liquid, but it's not. For him it was a relentless, grinding, steel-toothed machine. My mom and three kids were caught in those metal gears that ground up everything that fell into that neon-colored, whiskey-smelling maw.

Amalie interrupts somewhere in here, "Think of it as a movie. Tell me the scene, what comes into your heart and mind when you talk about him."

Of course, that's the crunch isn't it? You reveal your heart and you're exposed. Say what's true, what's deep inside, and the walls could suddenly collapse, revealing The Jeering Crowd. Your once-sympathetic listener and all the world, smirking, laughing, pointing at you, hands-held-over-mouths in derisive guffaws. Imbue the words with your heart, take them from the loneliest of places, the place where you cry, and you leave unguarded a secret gate.

So I decide not to reveal the scariest image of my old man. In that image I see his ghost, like in a shattered haunted-house mirror, as I dance barefoot through his left-behind fragments. There is a particular glistening shard. It shows a sweltering Deep South summer night. My old man, decorated WWII vet credited with six known kills, drunk, raging in the kitchen. He is wearing only worn and yellowed tighty-whities, his skinny frame crouched grotesquely, deftly shifting his weight. He brandishes a butcher knife expertly, tip up, so that you know he can use it. He is spitting guttural curses in GI-German. He threatens to gut my mom, my brother, me. Only it's not us. His glittering eyes don't see us. He is confronting those three Waffen-SS officers. Once again and forever, he is cornered in San Pietro, in that bombed-out Italian church.

During 1963, that star-crossed year, as the booze closed in on him with its vicious vice grip, he was night manager at the Captain Shreve Hotel in downtown Shreveport, Louisiana. I remember he moonlighted at a place called the Countryside Motel across the Red River in Bossier City. Based on things my mom would say, things I heard, I suspected he was a low-level gofer for the Mob in Dallas and Bossier. What I knew was that in his heart he was a doomed outsider who marched to the bebop, hepcat beat of a different drum.

I sometimes hear that drum.

Oh man, I think, *the bricks in the wall are tumbling down now. Gotta get my feet under me. Protect those locked rooms.*

"You know who Dalton Trumbo is?" I blurt this out to put Amalie off-balance, and because, suddenly, it just fits.

"A writer?"

"Not just *a* writer! *The* Academy Award–winning, local-boy-makes-big screenwriter. He wrote *Spartacus, Exodus,* two books about this little town." I'm dancing now, deflecting, relishing putting her back on her heels. "He was blacklisted in Hollywood, spent ten months in the pen for his beliefs, for refusing to testify to the House Un-American Activities Committee. He grew up six blocks from here." I let that sink in, then keep going. "I met him once, here in town. His last movie was *Executive Action,* starring Burt Lancaster. About a conspiracy to kill President Kennedy. Pulled from theaters all over the country. Ironically, the *Monitor,* where he'd been a cub reporter, refused to advertise it. I was at the last showing at the Canyon Theater. For some reason, Trumbo was in town. He showed up and, bold as hell, walked to the front of the theater and started ranting, saying, 'This film is being shut down because it is too close to the truth. The key witnesses are being eliminated, forty or so, so far.' Afterwards, being sort of anti-government myself, I went up and told him he was my free-speech hero. He was approachable, talkative, a movie *writer*, not a movie *star*. What he said blew me away: 'I have clues. I'm pretty damn sure they will lead to who *they*, at least some of them, are someday. I'm going to follow them. When I find out, I'll reveal the whole damn blockbuster truth!'"

I look up. Amalie is staring at me, her notepad and pen laid down to underscore a *very* serious moment. "Bus," she says, "this thing with your past, it's got to get to some resolution."

She's right, and I know it. I realize I'm at that something's-gotta-give moment. I'm *so there*. I have nothing to say.

"OK, what about the *flashbacks?*"

Ah, my curious affliction.

She waits a further moment, watching me, testing my demeanor evidence.

Like most lawyers, I regard myself as a good poker face and an expert-in-waiting on everything. Failing that, I'm a good bullshitter. On this topic, despite her quasi-medical degree, I'm on even terms with Amalie.

Starting with the weighty depth of a Twitter feed and a Wikipedia article, I've come to view my "acid flashback" phenomenon as susceptible to hard science. I tell myself that my disturbing, and fortunately intermittent, sense that reality is only a thin veneer over a more profound and flowing universe is based on pure pharmacology. Lysergic acid diethylamide, LSD, if ingested in large doses, collects in the central nervous system, especially the spinal cord. Like a virus, it can lurk there, inert for decades, and then, for reasons unknown, release. Old acid heads call this the "free ride."

Sometimes it's comical. *Wow, that sure is a shiny toaster.* More often it's a deep unease, a peeking under the edge of this false world.

As to her question today, I fudge.

"Nothing much for a couple of months. Last time, I think it was just late-night pecan pie and Nyquil."

I'm more than fudging. I'm brushing her off and she knows it, but our hour is over. That stickler schedule.

She's closing up her notebook, removing her glasses, signing off. "Oh, one last question," she says. "Are you still having the dream about the Enigma Machine?"

Shit. I blow out a breath. That is one sorry can of worms. I never should have mentioned it.

"No problem. Dream never came back." I lie as tinky-tinky music plays in my head. A distant Rod Serling, Cheshire-cat grin above a black suit and narrow tie, intones:

> *Meet attorney Bus McIntyre,*
> *Once a practitioner on Planet Earth.*
> *About to answer a summons*
> *To the Twilight Zone.*

I say goodbye, politely cancelling my regular follow-up appointment.

The thought comes to me that I'm going to need more help than Amalie can possibly conjure up in her little notebook.

CHAPTER SEVEN

BANNER—WHO I AM

Spyflow.com

My security fields leak. They are discrediting my press releases, bricking my social media platforms.

Worse than being hacked, they are geolocating me.

Which means I'm now a physical target.

So here's how I'm going to survive: I'm going to talk.

Call it a *Good Girl's Guide to What to Do When Your Government Is Spying on You.*

Some of the things I'm going to tell you in this blog you may not believe, may not *want* to believe, but they lay out my creds. And sure as hell will give the agency pause before actualizing my elimination.

So, just to get it straight, so there's no question who it is they are trying to find, here is a little more on who I am:

Banner Crandall McCoy, daughter of a retired fireman in a small Texas town. I am East Texas simple. "Getting along" has never been my strong suit. I have four brothers, all football linemen on our little high school dynasty of 8-man state championships.

I went to UT in Austin, BA in Political Science, 2010; MS in Computer Science, 2012. I interned for Congressman Ochray from 2010 to 2012. He sits on the House Intelligence Committee. He got me my job at the NSA.

My shift supervisor at TCC is Allen ("Double-Dis") Bernsmith.

I met ES, aka Snow, courtesy of Uncle Sam. We both attended the Wiretapper's Ball in 2011. More on that later. We were both vetted by ISIS. Not the Sunni caliphate. The acronym is for the government contractor that did high-security screening. All things considered, they did about as good a job as airport security on 9/11.

This is published through a blog that has previously been established as a bona fide journalistic venue. Accordingly, its sources are protected by the First Amendment, and cannot be revealed by court order. Of course, my former employer doesn't need warrants, orders, or courts. It simply takes.

I am going to start revealing the real 411 on JFK's murder.

I'd do it all now, but I know the limit. Better than they do. I'm going dark for a while.

CHAPTER EIGHT

BUS—TRIPS

You might as well know the real story about my mental affliction.

I've had these . . . experiences on and off for decades, since my first, last, only megadose of LSD. Well, OK, along with a few supplemental trips. Anyway, that first time, I was nineteen. That Moment is a whole other story, as they say, but over time these recurring, flashback echoes have been distracting enough. One particularly bad version came on years ago, as I was driving through the mountains at night. The drivers of passing cars were transformed into disturbing, garish masks, hitchhikers were dangerous puppets jerked by cosmic strings. Anyway, after that, I went to a clinic over in Denver. Kept it quiet, like maybe I had some loathsome disease.

They did all sorts of tests. Blood, spinal fluid, x-rays, MRIs, CAT, Rorschachs, polygraphs, interviews by highly educated people wearing white coats. They worked down a list: drug interactions (no), tumor (no), infection (no), schizophrenia (no). Charles Bonnet Syndrome? That one I remember because of the cool name. The victim sees scary faces. It's a visual thing associated with eyesight deterioration. "No" on that one too.

Eventually they get down to the two final possibilities. Maybe, they grumble, there really is such a thing as an "acid flashback." Not just the caricature of Duke in *Doonesbury*. The clinical literature, they say, is sparse and inconclusive. The theory centers on the unique ability of lysergic acid diethylamide to stay chemically intact and linger in certain cells, until released by trauma or stress. It would help if it was anointed with an acronym. It would get instant respectability. Like "Yeah, he's suffering from AFS (Acid Flashback Syndrome)," or "He's got an evident case of PL (Psychedelic Latency)."

In the strange epistemology of language, acronyms pose as little truth engines.

That diagnosis being long unrecognized by science and therefore unavailable, they get to the last one. The main psychiatrist comes in, gray flecks in his coiffed hair. He talks awhile about the lack of answers, then speaks with solemn reserve about, since, well, I'm Episcopalian, and that's close to being Catholic, well (nervous cough), would I like to know about exorcisms?

I walked out. That was ten years, six serious flashbacks, and zero exorcisms ago. Now I go to my flashbackers support group. A bunch of old acid heads. Like vets of some obscure war. Perhaps the US invaders of Grenada or the cavalry regiment that chased Pancho Villa across the border after his raid into New Mexico. We sit around, tell war stories, and commiserate about our unrecognized malady.

We meet in the basement of the Episcopal Church. There, by pointless ritual, we pretend to anonymity, go by pseudonyms. Mine is Tashtego. Yes, I've got a soft spot for Melville. We sit around in a circle of folding chairs. We talk in a guiltless version of AA. Guiltless because there is no "wagon" to fall off of. Lately we call ourselves the Leary-Thompson-Garcia Society. Our black humor motto: "Hell, sit back and enjoy!"

Somehow it came up last year that I'd written a book. After that, they're all over me, pushing me to write another one—better yet, a reality show proposal featuring all of us. Sort of *Duck Dynasty* meets *Acid Heads*.

A book? (I pretend you ask.) So, I did write this book entitled *Mirkwood*, a novel featuring J. R. R. Tolkien as a character imbedded in an urban fantasy. It didn't get shortlisted for the Booker. No Book Channel interview.

But it caused a stir. Following a cease-and-desist letter from the Tolkien estate, I decide they picked the wrong country lawyer to push around. Litigation ensued, things went viral, the *Hollywood Reporter* and London *Guardian* ran stories, and it became a cause célèbre for First Amendment rights. I stopped counting web comments at over fifty thousand. It made an Amazon best seller list, won a national award, and got published worldwide in Spanish. I fly to LA and pitch it. It gets picked up by Hollywood. I luck out and get a great producer and cowriter. A bigger book deal emerges. TV Project rep'd by CAA. Who knows from there? "Development Hell," they say.

So not the greatest writing chops, but enough to fake a conversation.

Anyway, back to flashbacks.

At the last meeting, someone handed out a grainy, over-faxed, two-page article from an obscure pop medicine journal that usually delves into the properties of obscure seeds. It was about selective serotonin reuptake inhibitors. Now, finally, that sounds like progress. SSRIs. Yes! That's the answer. Most of us learn to manage it. A few, the old acid vets, have, if you will, never come back. They reside still in that "other side," the place beyond the rainbow, the moon, the stars. The fount where the Higgs-Boson is burped into the cosmological awareness. The place of Far-Outness.

Meanwhile, back on Earth, I pretty much just cope. Like an old cowhand, I resolutely, calmly ride with my brand.

Except when the Enigma Machine fires up in my dreams. Here's how it goes: the dastardly machine in my office suddenly lights up, clicks and clacks, and receives messages. I pull out a code book with a big Kriegsmarine symbol and a swastika on the cover. I methodically set the rotors. I decode the message. It is from U-417, the ace of the U-boat fleet. It is 1939. She is loitering off Halifax. She is observing a convoy being assembled. She will track the convoy across the North Atlantic, guiding the rest of the wolf pack to the intercept. The captain is waiting acknowledgement. He signs off, "Defeat England."

At Bletchley Park in Merry Ole England, the British code breakers, Alan Turing and, amazingly, J. R. R. Tolkien among them, are silently listening in with me. They seek to locate and destroy the submarine.

I end the dream pondering the deep cold of big water, the deep cold of voids, the loneliness of U-417 marooned in time. Waiting . . . waiting.

I have, at Mary's insistence, seen Amalie every two weeks for the past six months. Pretended to give my soul unto the tender mercies of Sigmund Freud. Amalie has no real truck with flashbacks. She wants to disinter my body, blood, breath, brains, guts from any relation with my old man.

My old man, who now has some connection to Dallas and this guy Marcello. And murders. His and, just maybe, JFK's.

Something in all this has gotta give.

I remember I've got two weeks that are pretty open on my calendar. Tooey and Carey can handle all the pieces.

I'm teetering on the brink of something really important or really stupid.

CHAPTER NINE

BANNER—LESSON

SPYFLOW.COM

Here's a jewel I've been thinking about: the difference between an Orwellian world and ours is simple. In *1984*, the state adhered to the Whorfian hypothesis: If there is no word for it, it can't be thought. Newspeak limits words. Newspeak limits thoughts. Newspeak holds that uttering, *thinking* forbidden words is a sin.

Our licentious society goes at it from the other end.

We can say whatever we please, whenever we please, to whomever we please, by any medium we please. With one caveat: what we say, *everything* we say, is heard, monitored, compared, stored, digested, labeled and, at some point, acted upon to our detriment.

You can be prolix, but you can't be private.

That is the unforgiveable sin.

CHAPTER TEN

NATCHEZ WHEELS

It is hot. It is humid. It is night.

It is North Louisiana.

Even now, when he's dead, Carlos never accompanies his man to the job. A holdover from the old days.

Right now his man is on the job, savoring the up close and personal approach to his business.

Holding the Walther, adjusting his gloves, Louie flips open the briefcase, sets it on the ground, unzips his fly, and, on sheer whim, pisses all over the money.

The stacks of fresh bills, sealed and banker-wrapped, glisten off-green from the sodium-arc lights of the truck stop parking lot.

Louie smiles and inhales, his nostrils flaring above a thick gray moustache. *Like* The Big Lebowski, *yeah.* The scent is sharp as a scythe. A trademark, like Chanel Number Five.

Piss on the money. Make the delivery. The rest, as they say, is situational.

Five minutes later, in a shadowed cavern between idling tractor-trailers, mostly Peterbilts and Whites and an old Diamond REO, the asphalt beneath Louie's feet vibrates with the loping diesels. He notices his shadow, splayed in alien proportions against a trailer's side. Exaggerated but still him—lean, tall, baseball cap with the bill curved over hard, ponytail hanging out the back. He looks down and tries to see the narc's face as the man kneels to open the briefcase. The man—Vincent, he'd said—freezes as the tangy smell comes up. Vincent wipes his hands on his pant legs in disgust, his mouth drawing into a harsh scowl. He looks up, ready to dish out some serious hurt.

Straight into the abyss of Louie's short-silenced Walther PPX9. Aimed point-blank at his face.

Now an open parking lot in an interstate truck stop is a helluva place to do a dope deal, and come to think of it, a helluva place to invoke justice on a crooked cop.

At least the hour is late.

Louie knows that, in this business, *everything* is situational. And this feels just right. In the distance, framed by the corridor of eighteen-wheelers, looms a huge billboard. Its façade depicts an onrushing big rig. The improbable words "Natchez Wheels Truck Stop" are writ over-large in faux Santa Fe font along the side of the trailer. The truck image has real headlamps that salute intermittently with high beams as a smiling mechanical cowboy leans out the cab window and waves a giant cowboy-shirted arm. *Howdy!* Over and over. It all seems just right. The trucker cowboy presiding over the two of them. A hot, sticky night on Interstate 20, the tripwire between Dallas and Louie's hometown, Bossier City.

Vincent is still staring into the cut-out hole in the universe that is the bore of Louie's gun.

"Now . . . *Vinny*, move over there. Slowly." The barrel gestures toward the Peterbilt, like a backup man giving an eloquent nod.

The only backup Louie ever needs.

Vincent rises on unsteady legs and shambles backwards, his feet crunching on bits of gravel. Above them, June bugs buzz and whirl among the arc lights. A few splat on hot bulbs and spiral crazily down. One plops into the swampy innards of the briefcase.

Louie can see big rivulets of sweat running down Vinny's face. He inhales again and smells Vinny's fear and savors it. Last week Louie turned seventy-two. Helluva thing. And here he is, still at it.

His mind rockets back over the lost decades.

Old promises are part of this turf. Carlos is long gone, but still it had been a promise. The kind you don't forget. The Little Man used words like "omertà," but to Louie it was just redneck, hillbilly honor. Hell, the man had bribed him a parole, walked him right past the looming gates of Angola. A hard-ass eighteen-year-old otherwise destined for decades of incarceration. Carlos changed that, gave him his start, *made* him in fact. That right there was a debt, and about the only thing in his life that wasn't situational. All the rest, before and since Carlos, was just stuff—good jobs, bungled jobs, the year at Rikers, old bosses, new bosses, all stretching down memory lane to this job and this two-faced piece-of-shit narc.

And the directions from Louie's current boss, wiseass Mike Sarto.

Air brakes screech and release on a tractor a few rows over, reminding Louie that it is time to complete this deal.

He looks hard at Vinny. "Why'd you steal from *both* sides?" He pauses. "You got greedy, didn't you?"

The man, his hands halfway up in a pitiable supplication for mercy, blinks as fresh sweat rolls into his eyes. "I . . . I didn't know it was you guys. I'm sorry. I'll make it up. We can work this out together."

Louie frowns, showing himself skeptical like some scary, hairy, cross-armed Judge Judy, holding court at the intersection of Hell Street and Damnation Avenue.

"You took one helluva wrong turn, Vinny. Now you're at those famous crossroads, right here in this parking lot." Louie is warming up now. "And you better do more than just confess. You better show some goddamn penitence, 'cause my people are beyond mad. They say you gotta be . . . *punished*."

The way he says that last word, just right. He waits to let it sink in. It does.

The man squirms, his eyes darting to the trailers on either side.

"And I don't mean just chastised, Vinny, I mean giving up some fucking payment. You hear me!"

Vinny is hyperventilating hard now, like a man drowning and flailing and gasping.

"Look, Louie, I can get you inside. This whole thing. The deals. This road. All of it."

The way he says it, *this road*, with zero appreciation for this segment of I-20. Laid down on the bones of old Highway 80. This old-time freeway to sin between stuck-up Dallas and wide-open Bossier. Louie narrows his eyes. The guy isn't just at the crossroads; he is digging his fucking grave right in the middle of it. This is the fun of working close up.

"All right, so, if I let you go, you'll come back, see my boss, tell the whole story? Tell us about these new Mexican bastards?"

"Sure, no problem. You guys get it all. You take it all. All back."

"OK, Vinny, you better deliver. I'm tellin' ya. Now close up the case while I check your gym bag."

Louie steps back from Vinny as the narc bends over and snaps closed the briefcase lid. Two little lock snicks. Nice and neat.

Neat like the single silenced shot—*chummpf*—that cuts through Vinny's right parietal, sucking in his soul like a negative Big Bang, and snapping his head back and away as he crumples to the ground.

Head snap, Louie thinks. *Away from the bullet. Simple physics. Always away.*

He doesn't really see poor Vinny. Louie sees something like those famous thirty frames of the Zapruder film, the ones that capture the fatal shot. Except Louie's memory-view is closer. Through a rifle scope.

He reaches down and tugs Vinny's gun from his shoulder holster. He starts to search for a wire, but lets it go. He lifts the briefcase by its handle, leaving beneath it a little pool of pee to honor Vinny bleeding out on the asphalt.

As he walks away, the word *erratic*, lingers in his mind. Piss. DNA. Other mistakes?

Fuck it, they got no matches. Leave it as a teaser. I'm 'bout done anyway.

Louie hears Vinny's cell phone, somewhere in the man's clothing, ring a plaintive digital rendition of the old tune "Sleepwalk." Louie cocks his head. He missed the cell phone, which means he missed the wire if there was one. He keeps walking.

He has never made a cell phone call, ever, even on a throwaway burner.

He gets in his empty car and wheels through the lot. His head is full of unbidden memories, the briefcase full of fragrant money, the gym bag full of dope. He glances right. The Little Man is there again. Riding shotgun. This time he's a bit wispy, but still never to be underestimated, still dapper and commanding, still pulling strings. Always there. Always.

He's staring at Louie in that way that never, ever fails to make you sweat. He says, in that tone that *no one* ignores, "Old friend . . . you slippin'!"

Louie feels his own lips finish the sentence, the last syllable coming out with a slurred lisp.

"Let's get back to the Countryside."

As he pulls on to I-20, heading east to Bossier, Louie isn't sure who, if anyone, just spoke. A lot of the time he can't tell. Not that it matters anymore.

Turning to his left, Louie stretches his arm out the window and into the night air. The warmth flows over his arm, his dragon tattoo writhing. It all feels hot and sticky and flowing and real. He waves vigorously, in sardonic parody of the stiff-armed cowboy in the billboard.

The Little Man, a convivial companion again, says, "Louie, let me tell you a story you're not going to believe."

CHAPTER ELEVEN

BUS—TWO KINGS

After leaving Amalie's, I stick with my usual routine: head for a coffee shop. Retreat and sort things out.

Driving along, reflecting on this morning, something passes close to me. Something my memory won't tolerate, even though I've tried to dredge it up every few years. Like snagging in a river for a drowned body. Through all the mental crosscurrents, this thing, whatever it is, always drops off the snag hook just as it bulks into the glistening, warped sunlight. Briefly visible, then gone. Sinking once again into the murk.

This time the memory is skewered good. Tugging, like something alive, it approaches the surface. Some crazy kid thing I'd done just as all hell broke loose at home. Right after Kennedy got killed.

Reel this in, nice and slow, keep the hook set, separate it from all the other distractions. Concentrate.

There was this box, yes. THE BOX. We stole it and hid it in a cabin out on Loggy Bayou. My brother, Gene Wray, will remember the place. The rest is still fuzzy. The Sarto kid. The cops. The stolen car, a white '61 Chevy. Pieces for later.

I arrive, famished, at the Mesa Bakery downtown. I get an espresso and bagel, hear someone say, "Kick their asses, Bus." I look up to see, of all people, Joe Don Looney.

Not many people would recall the mercurial ex-Longhorn, Sooner All-American, first-round NFL pick and all-around bad boy from the sixties, someone my wife Mary could give you the sports trivia stats on right off the top. It's not the real Joe Don of course. This is a guy my age who sells shoes.

When he's not selling hiking boots or broughams under his real name at Benger's Shoe Store downtown, the guy I know as Joe Don will, at the Flashbackers' Club, tell you he's ridden the world hard, that he's dug his spurs deep into the flanks of the life-beast until it bellowed in rage and howled out the sounds that just might be the Last Words of Truth. I've sat through a few of his Ginsbergian, gonzo-level revelations.

Not that I'm much better. Hell, at one session I started getting into my aversion to mayonnaise. The Mayo Conspiracy. The Red China connection, all that.

Today, however, I don't have time.

I nod, he reaches out a long arm, and we do the power hand-shake, followed by a brutha's finger clasp and snap. Followed by a power fist knock. A sly wink caps it off.

It's enough to make you think you're having an acid flashback.

I move along, see other folks, shake hands, acknowledge and thank them for their support, accept the averted eyes of others, and retreat to a table in back. I flip open the binder and select another journal entry. Pretty quick, I see that it fits stories my old man used to tell about meeting bigwigs and celebrities at the Captain Shreve. Folks like John Wayne, William Holden, Patsy Cline, Richard Nixon. I peer into his words, wanting to know him, to *be there* . . .

        Ten o'clock. Friday night. I stand behind the
        front desk, knowing this was as high up as I am ever

gonna climb. Night manager at a top-line downtown
hotel. Six blocks from the red smoke-colored river,
from the dim echoes of long ago riverboat cries
and long-gone commerce at Shreve's landing. And a
world away from where I thought I'd be. Or is it?
The white line brought me here, it sure as hell will
take me away again.

They call me "Mr. Dean," and I see them come,
alert at my approach. I check the VIP room.
Everything waiting for the special guest. The man
driving in from Memphis. Storms out there tonight,
misty haints on the bayou roads, and just across the
river: endless neon, smeared and bleary along the
Bossier Strip.

I stroll down Peacock Alley to the adjoined
Washington Youree Hotel, check the party girl
action at the Sternwheeler Bar and the band at the
Captain's Room.

Instinct, a change of electricity in the air,
tells me the special guest has arrived. I rush
back to the lobby. I survey, send the doorman and
bellhop with VIP umbrellas out in the rain. I wait
at the big glass doors. The guest hustles in, wet,
goofy hat, shades. His entourage follows. I hold out
my hand. "Welcome back to the Captain Shreve, Mr.
Presley."

"Thank you, thank you very much." He shakes my
hand, takes my arm, and quietly pulls me aside.
"You're Mr. Dean, right? I understand you're the
gentleman that gets things done. I come down here
to get, well, to get back my roots. Back to where I
started, you know, the Louisiana Hayride. I'd like
to get away tonight. Get social. Get away from all

this Hollywood bull. You help me with some regular
clothes? Shit, all I own anymore is sequin suits and
pajamas."

   The King offers me a C-note, which I take to pass
on to the staff.

I stop, put the journal down gently, like it's something holy,
maybe a Dead Sea Scroll. I go get more coffee, looking over my
shoulder, watching it. I return and pick it up with two hands, an
offering from the past . . .

   Thirty minutes later it's all arranged. New
threads from Brownstein's delivered to the King's
room. A call to Mike Maroon. Private car to the
Boom Boom Room on the Strip. Then on to the Gold
Room at the Countryside. Where I moonlight on my one
supposed day off. Where I watch over how it's going
for Mr. Marcello.

   I make sure both clubs are cleared of any unwanted
clientele. Keep a few regulars, the band and the
girls. Later, his people call to say there's been
a minor disruption over at the Gold Room. One of
the reporters for the *Shreveport Gazette*, the blue-
blood, holier-than-thou rag for the city's upper
crust-who loathe the Bossier Strip-got wind that
Elvis is at the Gold Room. Somehow the reporter gets
in, his photographer flashes a couple of pics, they
get ushered out by Marcello's Doberman, guy named
Louie, with their shorts pulled up to their ears and
their noses in the parking lot gravel. Everything
gets back to normal, as in a good party.

```
     The Little Man is there. He comes out from the
back of the Gold Room and talks to the King like
they're fellow royalty. Hopes he has a good time. He
does.
     Four a.m. and the phone rings at my desk. A mumble
but I know the voice. "Mr. Dean, sure had a nice
time. Yessir, real nice time. Thank you, man, thank
you very much."
     I start to hang up when he says, "You know, they
call me the King, but there's only one King, and
that's Jesus Christ. And it's in the signs. I talked
to Mr. Marcello about it, he says, anything big, you
gotta have the spirits on your side."
     We all gots ta have dem spirits.
```

Reading these pages, my heart won't settle down. I am making a decision. The way a clock is pretty much going to strike midnight. In truth, I sense that it's way more. I'm about to do a cliff dive. At night. Into an unknown surf.

I finish the coffee when my cell rings. Mary. We always talk about now. I fold up the stuff and answer.

CHAPTER TWELVE

BUS—ABOUT MARY

Gather the strength to start again.

We all have stars that guide our destiny. Mine dictate that I succeed and fail extravagantly. I try desperately to box in that fortune, keep it within the small planetary orbit of my life, but it never works.

What I have discovered along the way is that in one particular aspect I am disabled. Not in the sense that I can't work hard, make tough decisions, kick ass if appropriate, lead (especially, I pride myself, by example). No, my disability is in the humble sense that God gave some men. I need a woman's leash, even if it comes with a choke chain collar. Either that or my feet will disengage from the ground and I will drift right off the planet. I will self-destruct.

As I have in the past.

So Mary, my current wife, is upstairs, but really she's right here. Also snared within the tensions of our bond. I sought her not because of what the tattlers might whisper, but exactly the opposite. She's five foot five and one hell of a short-leash, hard-grading presence. Seemingly made to order for me.

We've been married five years.

Now, ironically, I have to slip her leash.

I have climbed the stairs and am walking into her office, a bedroom converted into the workplace for her day job. She is an ex-English lit teacher, now morphed into a sports blogger. "Pink Stripes: TV Sports from a Woman's Perspective." People online eat it up. She starts every blog with the line "Let's talk sports, let's talk Chick." As in Chick Hearn, the indefatigable sports announcer for the LA Lakers. His aphorisms part of American sports dialect. Things like slam dunk, triple double, charity stripe, faking the flop-eroo. She makes the lingo relevant, useable to women who feel sidelined with sports talk. One hundred and fifty thousand subscribers. Ninety percent women. A demographic gold mine. Talk of a YouTube Channel. Feelers from ESPN and FOX.

When things are good, we bullshit on sports a lot. She likes to get in the groove of trash talk and sports analogies. I'm not even a close match.

Anyway, things aren't so good right now.

There is a further, upper story to this house. It is invisible. It cannot be reached by stairs. It holds observation platforms of the mind to which we each ascend at times.

Hers is a politely railed widow's watch that surveys a world of bucolic and well-ordered countryside leading down to a sunlit sea that seldom offers more than dancing whitecaps on a breezy day. Her survey will detect any disorder, any movement unplanned by her, and she will promptly, repeatedly descend to the real world to meet it with stern address.

At least, that's what I think.

Mine, on the other hand, is a battered rampart, clinging to the heights of a besieged keep. My Heorot, my Elsinore. Spread before me is a field of battle, ravaged down to distant beaches that border a tumultuous sea. Out there, vessels founder, tipping horribly with storm-tattered sails. Even now, forces rogue, inchoate, and unnamed have transcended the beach. They slouch and bellow unseen in the fog as they approach these failing walls. They are more fearsome precisely because they lurk. They are the red blood of superstition; my Grendels and great wyrms.

Secured deep within the foundation stones of this fortress is a dungeon. It is sealed. Behind its locked door, shackled to the wall, is another demon. One that never sleeps. I can sometimes see his once-familiar face as he screams my guilt.

In my life I have sometimes ventured from this beleaguered castle. Stared up at those destiny stars. Embarked on what one might describe as a great journey of knight errantry. Sometimes extravagantly successful, sometimes ending in disaster and hasty flight back to the encircling walls of this stronghold.

Now is one of those times. I will leave.

I must tell her what I've decided, however contrary it is to the restraints I've accepted. I take a deep breath. She does not take "no" well.

"Honey let's talk," I start.

She looks up at me, her dark hair pulled back to frame a pretty, perfectly oval face. Something different flickers across her features. She must be thinking this is more bad news about the article from this morning.

We had talked about it last night, when the *Monitor* called. We talked about it again this morning, right after the paper arrived and the damage was being tallied. Now she clicks her mouth and her three kelpies, whom I adopted as part of our vows, jump up on the couch with her and pile into a panting, happy mess of muzzles and tails and paws.

They, the couchful, are all looking at me.

"The *Monitor* article is bad, maybe 10 percent accurate and 90 percent dead wrong, but it's old news already. It's not what I need to talk about."

I think, in hindsight, I started off too aggressively, too arbitrarily, trying to claim a position.

She makes a move to cut me off, not sure where I'm going. She is playing our ball game of marriage with the impeccable instinct that the best defense is a strong offense.

"*Don't* you *dare* think . . ."

The dogs, sensing one of those stormy lightning-bolt moments, decamp en masse for the downstairs.

And so it begins.

After all our straw men have been mowed down and burned in roaring haystack fires, we are left with that fundamental contract that couples, in love or not, write between themselves. Ours says that, at some point, you've got to listen. I know, think I know, we are in love, but that's not what this is about. I need her to listen.

I lay it out as plainly as I can. "Things are coming together that I've got to sort out—clues, keys, clocks." She scrunches her face but I keep going. "I'm sixty-eight. That's sure to hell a clock."

She objects, telling me wherever I'm going with this, I'm full of crap, that my grandfather lived to eighty-five, "so quit whining."

"Yeah," I stop her, "but my old man was murdered at fifty, and that's what this is all about."

That works for the moment. She knows the whole story about his killing, as much as I know. Correction: knew.

I hand her the newspaper article about my old man's murder. "Check the date. Now read this. It's from a week before." I hold up the page that talks about the fake private eye from Dallas. "Just read it first."

She reads it. You can feel gears whirring. She reaches and takes the file with my dad's name on it. Anticipating I might miraculously get this far, I have moved Rick's pink sticky to an internal office memo in the file. She turns to it. It reads:

SEPTEMBER 12, 1970

Officer McIntyre of the Lowena PD requested access to the NCIC database. His queries were regarding the following subjects: Carlos Marcello, Mike Maroon, Paul Sarto, and Louie Diamond.

Six replies were received by this officer and made available to Officer McIntyre.

Copies to this file.

[scrawled in the margin: *"Bus, I searched, but they weren't here – Rick"*]

Two days later, this office received a query from the Bossier City, Louisiana, PD asking who the party was who made the informational requests. Per the open information protocol for use of NCIC, we identified Officer McIntyre as the requesting party.

She reads it, digests it, then looks up at me. She's adhering to the bedrock protocol. She's waiting, ready to listen.

I go to where a lot of women want their man to be, at least once in a while. Talk too much, lay it all out. I try to fill in the timing with JFK's murder, the file from the PD, the Carlos Marcello mob stuff. The raw mystery I can't let go.

I end with the unvarnished truth. "I've got a hole in me. Now it's uncovered. If I don't fill it in I'm gonna fall in. I'm already slipping on the edge."

She looks from me to the papers to me. Her eyes aren't glaring; they're emitting radar beams. Trying to size me up. Maybe something else. I'm too worked up to detect it. In any case, I can feel the flat "no" coming.

I'm surprised. It isn't flat. "You're not really up to a big journey, Bus. You chase this thing and you will be part of the wingnut conspiracy cult. Worse, bad things happen to you. Like King Tut's curse. This JFK thing, people get in too far, they disappear— mentally or physically. This is a real dragon, not just undressing a bunch of village elders in the courtroom."

I'm relieved but pretend I'm mildly pissed. "You through?"

"Let's just say your past *is* your dragon, Bus. You want to wake it up?"

"Look, I feel like an unfinished script."

"Cut the drama. I've had enough."

"Honest, baby, I . . . I got no . . ."

"What? . . . *arc*? *I gotta do this*." She's mocking me.

I wait till she speaks again. She picks up the TV remote, a signal this conversation is about to end. "Fine. I need alone time anyway."

That remark passes by too quick. It fails to register at the moment.

"So, how long do you need?" she asks.

Surprised, I jump to close the deal. Make it sound reasonable. Blow past any residual questions. "Ten days. Tops." I blurt out the next part. "I'm gonna take the motorcycle. Don't ask why 'cause I'm not sure I know."

For a moment, she looks like she's about to say something, but thinks better of it. I can feel her suspicions, as in does he need to go back to the mental clinic in Denver? Maybe something deeper, something hidden inside her. Maybe another round of resentment toward my kids—from my first marriage. I start to feel the acid spray of that topic, but then it stops. Whatever she's thinking, she comes out of it and zooms at me in her own way, always from my blind side. "You remember *Hamlet*?"

I'm off a step. OK, I realize, here she goes again, disguising her offensive strategy. As to the question, of course I do. She knows I once understudied for the role in my freshman year at what, for me, initially passed for college. The JC right here in Junction City. I knew the lines, and to this day thank God I never got called up.

Recovering, I ignore her bait. "I'll go to Bossier, reconnect with my brother, see the old places, track down some clues. Probably find nothing. Drink beer and eat barbeque. Come home. Mission over. That's it."

In the end, she says yes by not saying no. "We need to talk when you get back. *About us.* You really think you and that damn bike are up for the trip?"

I'm mentally packing as she talks.

I decide to start at midnight. Just that much more zaniness. Mary says she's going to bed, gives a desultory *have a safe trip.* I kiss her barely offered cheek goodbye, feel her stiffness, say all the inappropriate things a crazy man might, and go downstairs to finish packing. In the three-stall garage—a new addition styled as a Victorian carriage house—our vehicles are quietly stabled. Hers is a neat, yuppie-millennial Subaru, still shiny from the carwash; mine is a dirty F-150 4x4. My fourteenth version of the same basic pickup. I ought to be a Ford ad.

Time is moving on. I multitask between gear cabinets and my cell phone clamped between ear and shoulder. With Mary in bed, I separately call each of the kids, try to sound nonchalant. It doesn't work. I'm usually in bed by now. I tell them I'm just going to visit my brother. To them at least, I can't lie for shit. In the end, they are dubious but merciful. I assure them I'll report in later in the week. I hang up, blow out a long breath, and look up. There, next to the autos, my bike is waiting. I disrobe it, fire it up, and let the sound rumble through the neighborhood, open garage doors framing the waiting night.

I am ready, leaning on the bike, holding the journal before it gets squirreled away in the saddlebags. I'll try to read the whole thing as I go, but I can't help taking a peek now. Like a pilgrim consulting the Bible.

Sure enough, there's an unsettling but apropos entry:

```
Surely this was a night that needed rum or brandy
or a yellow jacket or maybe a cup of hemlock, for
what had been an idyll was sure to turn into a
nightmare.
```

```
     I wonder how they found me--perhaps a loose lip
and a big mouth in big "D." No matter, for the magic
has gone and reality has taken its place--still I
wonder to what end is this wrecked shell, this river
road, this peace that comes with the white line.
```

I stop. The question hangs in the air. Why did they want to find my old man?

I look at my watch, feel the flow of time like the tide signaling a ship's departure. I put the journal into the saddlebag.

In about a minute, I will begin to reverse his steps and return by that same vaporous white line. I feel, hell, am *living* my old man's desperate yearning for the empty road, for that haunting recognition of big questions that we know damn well have no answers.

My heart knows the route I'll take. Through the mountains. South to Raton. South by southeast across Texas. Descending into the borderlands of words spoken in drawls, of roadside sno-cone stands, deep-fried frog legs, tin roofs, narrow blacktop lanes through red-dirt pine forests. Hints of night mist at rural cross-roads. Lazy rivers named Trinity, Sabine, and Red. Rivers that, as I cross them, will replenish the mushmouth accent and forgotten memories of a kid raised in the South. A kid who, one late November day in 1963, saw too much.

Now, his remnant thoughts with me in that journal secured on my bike, I commune with him. We are taking together that deep-breath moment before the plunge into the hard asphalt dreams of the road.

PART TWO

TWELVE HUNDRED MILES

"'Tis sweet and commendable in your nature, Hamlet,
To give these mourning duties to your father:
. . . but to persevere in obstinate condolement
is a course of impious stubbornness;
'tis unmanly grief."

William Shakespeare, *Hamlet,* act 1, scene 2

"I, with wings as swift as meditation or the thoughts of love,
May sweep to my revenge."

William Shakespeare, *Hamlet,* act 1, scene 5

CHAPTER THIRTEEN

BUS—MCCLURE PASS AND BEYOND

Four hours of hard riding from Junction City. I am stopped, sitting astride the Harley. The night stars jump out at me and I feel the thin, cold air. The bike idles, slow, sonorous tumble of twin 900 cc pistons.

I am at McClure Summit. High, primitive, Transylvanian in its forested darkness. The Borgo Pass of the Rocky Mountains. It crests at two miles above sea level, leaving tree line far below, and then nose-dives into a gut-wrenching trail of sidewinder cutbacks.

I look down and remember the last time I dared this pass. 1968. At night, like now.

I was twenty and this road was seldom traveled, especially in the late fall before the snows obliterated it for the winter. The surface back then was packed dirt and gravel. It had been slimy with intermittent rain, but the shortest path as the crow flies to Aspen. Just like now, I had to be somewhere soon. Then, as now, this was a place of life-scale questions.

I lift up my arms, cinch the cuff zippers, and adjust the gloves for the high-altitude cold. Clad in full Duquesne leathers, I am snug and warm. I recall what I was wearing that night: threadbare Lee

"Storm Rider" denim jacket, no helmet, just goggles and a red bandana worn bandit-style across my face to pretend to cut the wind. My ride back then was a Vincent Black Shadow. The lean wraith-lord of motorcycles, but barely a match for this treacherous road where hairpin turns corkscrew and the descent never seems to end. Just as I would hit a straightaway in the fitful, bouncing yellow of the headlamp, the road would jerk abruptly left or right, exposing a thousand feet of freefall blackness over a crumbling edge with no guardrails.

Here's the sad secret about vintage British motorcycles. The wiring harness, fuses, bulbs, and connectors were typically manufactured by the venerable firm of Lucas Electric, aka "Lucas, Prince of Darkness."

Clear as breathing in this alpine night, I remember goosing the throttle of the Vincent. Edging to sixty, and, *of course,* the lights went out.

All stories, they say, are but one. And every life, in the end, is just a story. I survived that night to live my life and, just maybe, tell this tale. In fact, I've already started it. My iPad, the writing app already christened with a fresh set of notes, rests next to my old man's journal in the saddlebags.

I snug on my Shoei full-face. The helmet's paint job matches the Harley's. The motif is an eagle crossed with a lion, all wings and talons, fancifully rendered in red and yellow on black. A narrative plays in my head. It whispers, smooth and deep as a Hollywood voice-over: *A gryphon's charge I wear upon this steed. This you shall know me by, should we meet again.*

The kind of stuff that rolls through my head. Maybe *every* biker's head. Brando and Marvin in *The Wild One,* Fonda and Hopper as Captain America and Billy in *Easy Rider,* Michael Parks in the TV series *Then Came Bronson.* Angels, Outlaws, Banditos, Saints, Crusaders, Sons of the Desert, Sons of Anarchy, name your mounted tribe.

I haven't ridden much in years, but it never leaves you.

If you don't like adrenaline, risk, Zen, speed, danger, freedom, if you don't have secret dreams, you don't ride.

I pull the visor down, click to high beam, clutch and tap the gearbox into low. The bike pulls hard at the handlebars, wheels eager.

I breathe deep and take a last full look down the pass. I can feel, somewhere out there, the edge of reality warping up. Like a gathering thunderhead, a free ride is coming, but not now.

Now is exactly as I see it: a vast darkened amphitheater with endless, shadowed rows of spruce and pine, deep and untouched. An expanse of mountains with no light, save one, alone and incongruous on a far ridge. It is a somber, yellow light, as if a lone tartar watchman has indulged a candle in some high tower of a mysterious count's keep. A lone mortal among all the night's undead.

For such surely accompany me on this overdue journey. I don't know if I'm Hamlet, or the prodigal son, or a self-centered Boomer. I do know I will look for clues. I will throw the truth bones with two dead men. The first, my murdered father.

The second, John Fitzgerald Kennedy.

I ease out the clutch and bring the bike alive. It noses down the first set of steep turns. I shift into second, picking up speed, down the zigzag mountain, into the blind curves of some unreeling truth.

At least, I think, *the next couple of days' ride—Texas—will be smooth and boring.*

CHAPTER FOURTEEN

LOUIE—3:00 A.M.

Louie pulls the chain with the gris-gris from around his neck, hangs it on a hook next to the shower. Next to a chain with a crucifix. He undoes his ponytail. He studies himself in the mirror. Jerky-lean, collage of tats across his back and shoulders. Seventy-plus feels like fifty, feels like a hundred and fifty. The HGH—tiger blood all right.

But not much longer, he muses in the hot spray and steam. *You're a comet Louie, about to leave a last hot trail.*

He closes his eyes, lets the water cleanse. He can see the long-ago priest's face even now, whispering to him. *Think about your sins, son, let the waters flow.*

Young Louie's punch came next. Hard. The priest going down, his head butting the floor, the sound like a Louisville slugger connecting full-swing with a brand-new Spalding. *Bwaak.* The man's head bouncing on the tile in accord with simple physics.

That time, Louie left the shower going.

This time he turns it off. He steps out.

He remembers it was the first time he killed. Later, as it became his journeyman's trade, came the Big One. Then the cleanups.

He dries, reaches for the hook, and carefully lifts the chain. The gris-gris hangs, swinging like a pendulum. Over the years, it has hardened into an indestructible, sweat-cured little leather bundle enmeshed around a red amulet.

He knows he could leave it off, get rid of Carlos.

Walk free this last mile. Same old debate. *Not yet.*

He slips the chain over his head.

He still owes Carlos.

Carlos still owns him.

As the Little Man said, *omertà is forever.*

CHAPTER FIFTEEN

BANNER'S BLOG— BOSSIER

Spyflow.com

My first assignment at KNOLL was gathering old information, "dark data," say before 1980.

I got promoted to analyst because of the bang-up job I did. You'd be surprised what still exists and can be vacuumed into the NSA's maw: court records, police files, parking tickets, newspapers, airline passenger lists, phone archives, public school archives, an entire five-year corpus of records, tapes, and reports of SSD, the Mexican secret police, boxes of stuff lost or hidden by the Warren Commission.

I was told to expect "blind spots"—people, events, documents that just don't show up in any database. Sometimes they were never recorded. Sometimes they were deliberately cloaked in a kind of secrecy. "Deep concealment" is the term. A special, sometimes lifelong, status reserved for imbedded spies and tradecraft journeyman with special roles and skills. A life lived in the shadows.

Anyway, you put all this together with the sea of data already held by the agency, and start to use the toolbox of search and relation algorithms. I started analyzing—semantic analysis, facial recognition software, call tracking.

I, or rather I and the programs, found one helluva clue: a set of reel-to-reel tapes from a deceased ham radio operator who was listening on various channels that November day. A freelance reporter was all over it already, and his computer spilled its guts into the NSA system.

I turned the material over to my boss.

Last month I was elevated to PRISM, the Bloomberg Ultra screen of the NSA. It provided a powerful new look among all the well-known JFK conspiracy theory connections—Oswald, Ferrie, Bannister, Ruby, Giancarlo. What surprised me was I kept getting a set of unique, high quality relationships between four persons: Carlos Marcello, the Louisiana Mafia kingpin, his lawyer, Mike Maroon, an "Unknown," and suddenly, some guy named McIntyre. Soon I had McIntyre and everyone around him vacuumed up—phone, email, Internet, his shrink's notes and voice recording of their sessions, his entire law firm's files and data, same with his wife, Mary McIntyre. In a flash, I knew him better than he knew himself. That's when I started calling him Winston, after the hapless guy in Orwell's *1984*. A man watched. A man headed for big trouble.

The "Unknown," however, still hovered in the shadows. A few fragments of data and maybes—an Angola Prison work detail reference, a Rikers Island medical file that was empty. No birth certificate, no school records, no census trail, no picture, no DL, no Selective Service registration. Nothing.

The *place*, however, that recurred in that set of relationships was the most interesting. A couple of documents I retrieved pretty much sum up what the place was and what it was like in 1963.

The first is a news story. A political reporter for the *Crescent City Pirogue*, likely no stranger to wild nights in New Orleans, had traveled north on assignment to Shreveport and visited the obscure, "little sister" town huddled on the east side of the Red River. He filed this story a mere nineteen days before the assassination of JFK:

───────────────

Sin City

When astronaut John Glenn observed lights down on Earth, he certainly saw Bossier City.

Huddled across the river from Shreveport, this little town looks by day like any other haphazard collection of gas stations, convenience stores, greasy-spoon eateries, and low-rent motels.

The town straddles Highway 80, which leads due west to Dallas, Texas. Residents here say that highway is really an electric power cord of money, and a magic carpet ride for Texans wanting a good time.

This is because when night falls, the place bursts into seedy glory: giant neon rocket ships, flowing Niagaras of glistening lights, and crazy-crystal extravaganzas. A three-mile nonstop strip of blinding, flashing, multicolored lights, endless booze, deafening music, girls, girls, and more girls. Every bar beckons brightly and shouts the singular message of the "Bossier Strip": Come Hither for Sin!

John Glenn couldn't miss it, Texans can't resist it.

─────

Now, put that imagery side by side with a "verbal history" interview recorded by the LSU Oral History Project in 1988:

You have to ask me a bunch of questions, because I don't know,
I've never done this before. So shoot away.

What is your name?

Charlie Tyner. Folks always call me funny names.

Like?

Neon Charlie.

Where are you from?

Yeah, I was born 1930. In a rice field in South Louisiana. At least
that's what my momma said. Came up to North Louisiana,
sixty, hell more than that ago. Tried once to go back. No way.
Big-time clannish down there. Like I was a Yankee, maybe
worse, from New York City. Some little motherfucker says,
what you doing down here? You know, I mean god. I drifted
back to Bossier. Ended up in the bar business.

How did that go?

Well look, I'm different. Always have been. I love flashing lights.
I changed two things and turned it all upside down. First, all
girls up front. With the customers. Bartenders, waitresses. They
don't steal so much.

Second, big, gaudy lights. They draw customers in. Like frog gig-
ging. I built a bunch of bars like that.

Gambling?

Hail yes. Out in the parish. The Sheriff, you know

So you were a big success?

Well, mostly. I invented the formula. By late fifties early sixties,
seems like the whole world knew the Bossier Strip. Not Shreveport, just the Bossier Strip. Guess I was making history. Helluva
thing for little ole me.

Did you know Carlos Marcello?

Hell, everyone on the Strip knew Mr. Marcello. Big-time when he
came to town. Up from South Louisiana.

Were you business partners?

Well, not really. I want to back up. Let me put it this way. I got
some partners and built the Countryside Motel. Named after
a place Mr. Marcello owned down in New Orleans. Anyway,
it was on the Strip, out on East Texas Street. Big bar called
The Gold Room. Done up my way. Then the partners, Mike
Maroon, from here in town, but really it was Mr. Marcello.
They'd bitch and say I've got to get my ass out of there. So
that's what I did. Maybe '59

Any other information?

I just now talked too much. That's all I'm gonna say about them.
Don't ask me no more about that.

So, people, connections and a place. I got a big corkboard and
pinned up pictures and notes, tied together with strands of colored
yarn. Red for an established connection, green for interesting, gray
for unknown. Questions like "Sin City?" "Winston's father?" And,
at the center, in all caps, "MOTIVE?" Old-time gospel, low-tech
gumshoe stuff.

Bernsmith came by, studied it, stroking his chin and humming
"Hmms."

I should've known something was up right there.

That's my data limit for now. Gotta go.

CHAPTER SIXTEEN

BUS—GHOST STOP

So much for a boring ride across Texas.

I am scared, writing this exactly as it happened over the past few hours.

I was just west of Amarillo on I-40. The far end or the far beginning of absolutely nowhere. It is afternoon. The sun slides over my shoulder, warming my back and illuminating all the prairied world in front of me. I see an oasis of cottonwood trees up ahead. Poking just above the trees is the top of a salvaged oil derrick of the kind that, in this part of the country, often signals a truck stop and diner. At the same moment, just as the thought of a burger and fries settles in, an unmarked exit lane of old asphalt looms up. A crude sign points the way and says "EAT." On impulse, careful to check my balance, I hand-brake and take the exit.

The road winds off the highway and becomes a one-lane strip of decaying blacktop heading straight for the copse of trees. I pass by a downed billboard, presumably advertising the diner up ahead. It is laid over into a wild tangle of untended mesquite brush and tumbleweeds. Ruined by years of wind and freeze and neglect. One leg of the billboard, its end shattered into a grayed claw, reaches out into the roadway. I bank around it and think, maybe this is still New Mexico, because it sure isn't up to Texas standards of road maintenance. I glance over as I pass, and in the disorder of the tumbleweeds and brush, an original US Route 66 sign, bullet-holed and rusted, stands sentinel. That's crazy. Those original signs get a thousand bucks on eBay.

I think about turning around, but the momentum of hunger and the need for a pit stop draw me into the long shadows of the first huge cottonwoods. I pass beneath their canopy and rumble into a little corner of American Roadside. I pull up to the gas station.

And stop.

The gas station is closed. Boarded up, the gas pumps yanked over on their sides. The overhead sign is a remnant of the old Sinclair logo, minus the dino's head.

I look around. This might once have been a bustling hamlet huddled around a country crossroads, full of people and vehicles. Now nothing moves. All the other buildings are similarly abandoned. The Crazy-Q Diner gawks with the blind eyes of shattered windowpanes, its door gone so that its façade makes a tormented, open-mouthed face. Sort of a flattened version of Munch's painting, *The Scream*. A trading post, once home to moccasins and other Cherokee souvenirs, is plastered with a few sheets of paint-peeled plywood, as if they bandaged over some ancient trauma. The derrick has a loose crosspiece that hangs from a cable and intermittently gives a melancholy clang. Wind chime from the outskirts of hell. I can hear the highway drone a half-mile away. Even as I listen to the whine of a lone semi, it feels like an echo from another planet.

I look up for clouds, because the light seems to be changing ever so slightly, as if diminished by a sepia filter. Color bleeding out so that cottonwood green, blue sky, faded red of the trading post, all ooze over to shades of tan.

Well, I still have to pee. I hit the kill switch, tilt my bike on its stand, and get off and walk over to a patch of weeds. The entire hamlet is overgrown with three-foot-tall prairie grass. As I stand there, between the derrick and the boarded-up gas station, I smell something low and ominous. I step toward the gas station, its every window and door boarded over, as if implacably guarding its contents. Some of the plywood looks new. The smell gets stronger. Lots stronger. It's not even a smell. It's a foul, gag-inducing stench. There are flies, hundreds, maybe thousands of them. Buzzing and relentless. Too many to be so concentrated. There has to be . . . a source. I think maybe a dog or a cow has died in the grass. I look around.

In one part of the grass are cars, scores of them, lined up side by side, facing the same direction, as if directed there over decades by a meticulous parking lot attendant. Overgrown by weeds, they are all makes and vintages. 1950s Chevrolets. Old Ford pickups. A 1960 Ford Galaxie Sunliner with its canvas roof stove-in, a once-hot orange GTO with an air scoop, a Volkswagen hippie van presenting faded flowers and peace signs. A 1990s Dodge station wagon with Indiana plates, luggage rack on top filled with untouched luggage. A minibus that says "Heaven-Sent Bible School." Then, laid on its side, nestled in the grass that pokes through its spokes, is a full-dress BMW motorcycle. The kind no one ever leaves lying around.

Suddenly the pattern is obvious. They are lined up in a rough chronology, older to newer, none with collision damage. As if over the years they'd been driven in fresh off the highway, carefully parked, and just left.

But the cars are not the source of the smell. Everything—grass, cars, clanging old derrick, flies, the brown-tinted light—is overwhelmed by the reek. This is something organic and gone to rot. I see the flies moving in and out of the eaves of the gas station.

Two mangy, slat-sided dogs appear and begin to slink and circle behind me. I see the grass moving and above it their tails, stiff and unwagging. Like jackals.

I look past the clutter of buildings, hoping to size up my exit. All the roads are barricaded. Old oil drums, cars, bare-metal mattress springs, the top of a demasted windmill, blades missing like a snaggletooth, bent over and scarecrowed. The hamlet is a closed compound.

I see one dirt road with weeds down the middle. It leads away, maybe a hundred yards, to a decrepit farmhouse, rusty, tin-roofed, and pluming curious dark smoke out of a stovepipe chimney. Odd for a Texas summer afternoon. A hailed-out, almost paintless old truck, maybe a 1953 GMC, stands ready in front of the cabin.

I hear a screen door squeak open and then whack close. On the porch stands a figure, a fat man, no hat, longish hair like moldy hay, as if self-cut once a year. He steps off the porch and walks over and gets in the truck. He sits there, obviously staring at me, a dim silhouette in the windshield.

The truck starts, coughs, stops and restarts. It idles, crouched and facing me like a beast languidly opening its grill mouth and regarding its prey. I hear gears grind under a failing clutch. Ever so slowly, it begins to roll toward me. Gravel crunches and pops under the tires. I feel frozen, just watching its inexorable approach. It creeps, like a cat, to get within charging distance. Never accelerating, just closing.

Finally it stops, maybe thirty yards away, the grill facing me, the shadowy man sitting motionless in the cab.

The door opens and he steps out. He ignores me. He walks to the back of the truck and lets down the tailgate and pulls out a shovel. It is shiny, the blade freshly sharpened.

He reaches into the pocket of his overalls and pulls out a ragged trucker's cap that looks as if it has accumulated years of sediments. He doffs it casually. It looks like a bucket on top of a haystack. The overalls are unwashed, spoiled with streaks of something dark. Beneath the suspenders he's wearing a faded red T-shirt with arching words. It looks like "Red Raiders." He has on big old rubber boots that squish and squeak.

He hefts the shovel, expertly and with deft balance. Back and forth between his hands. Like he's warming up. He demonstrates the implement like this for pointless seconds, then shoves it into the truck bed and scoops out some gravel. This he carries forward to the front of the pickup, disregarding the ground. Still looking at me, he scatters the scoopful randomly and putters it around. Pat-pat. There is no hole there. The jackal-dogs circle closer. He stops and leans on the handle and just looks at me. No hello. No wave.

Nor was there gonna be any from me. I've already made the calculation, *could I take this guy?* and decided here, alone, him with a long-handle shovel, *no way.* I back up to my bike, keeping my eyes on him. I reach a leg back and straddle the seat and my hand finds my helmet secured to the sissy bar. I strap it on. Visor up. My eyes on him. Him looking at me like I'm a piece of meat.

Suddenly, with the grace and surprising speed some fat men possess, he hefts the shovel and starts walking briskly towards me. The bike starts at a button push. Kickstand up. In gear. Clutch out. I'm moving. And so is he, running straight at me.

Now comes the horrible calculation of the chase. He changes direction, getting the angle on me.

My head dithers in the abstract as he closes the distance. The fateful geometry of life or death chases, the weather gauge between high-masted privateers, the aspect angle of Fokkers versus SPADs in blue, puffy-clouded skies over France, the attack envelope of Top Gun versus the Bandit.

I see him shift into a trot, then a scary, intent sprint. The shovel in both hands, his big jelly belly rolling, legs going faster and faster. He's definitely got the angle on me. I goose it, hell with the gravel, and lurch and correct my balance with one foot. I pass him by as the shovel swings out, missing me by inches. The whoosh fanning my face. I gun for the frontage road, spin and recover as bullets of gravel shoot back at the bastard.

I backtrack on the old asphalt road and pull up to that mysterious exit. Looking at it from this angle, there is a road sign. "Do Not Enter." I survey a quarter mile of rough grass to the east-bound side of the Interstate, and realize just what this is. A trap. The EAT sign set up sparingly, a fatal mechanism unfolding in response to some obscure and unknowable chemistry. It woos travelers—the few, the tired, the unwary—into that exit lane and down the battered one-way blacktop from which there is no exit. Like a pitcher plant or a lobster trap, it lures its victims down a path that they realize too late is inscribed with Jim Morrison's famous line: "No one gets out of here alive."

Well, I got out. I'm sure other folks did too, the frantic mud grooves through the highway shoulder grass and the busted median fence show that clear enough, like the trackway of a frightened herd. But some didn't. I start to call 911, but hesitate. Hassle. Cops. I've got this nagging feeling of being digitally tracked. Little hiccups in my iPad. Recently a suspicious app showed up unannounced. Something about crowdfunding, but clearly one that I didn't order. I deleted it, but who knows anymore? Maybe it is all my imagination. I throttle up and the bike growls and fishtails, following those other tracks across half the interstate and through a rift in the fence, astounded drivers honking, to the safety of the eastbound lanes. I go a few miles, get bars back on the phone, then think better. I pull over and make the 911 call. All I have is intuition, but I describe the signless exit and weird . . . uh, *hamlet* and crazy farmer in detail. I can tell the operator thinks I'm nuts. "Let me get this down in my notes," she says. She sounds like my shrink. "Just go look," I finally say, then add, apropos of nothing except that raunchy smell, "Something's rotten in Denmark." I hang up.

A few hours later I am through the red-cut canyons around Amarillo and back in the flat country. Vectoring southeast on Highway 287. Adrenaline like a stiff wind to my back, pushing me out here before I can settle down. The borderlands between real and surreal are there, this road traversing them without signage.

I realize I'm tired as hell. The bike and the wind are beating me to a pulp. I need to stop and rest and regroup.

I see a town up ahead and pick a neon motel sign: HOVERING ROCK.

CHAPTER SEVENTEEN

BANNER—DECISION

Here's what convinced me that I was neck-deep in the shit. The ham radio hound that had some interesting tapes from November 22, 1963? The guy had passed on, but a reporter was on the story. Then the reporter, the tapes, the story, fell into a black hole. Actually, the reporter, by all measures a seemingly happy guy, jumped off a sixth-story balcony of the Dallas Hilton. Why he was there, no one knew.

So I'd put the crosshairs on him, and a couple of weeks later he's offed under definitely unnatural circumstances. His computer and notes, the original tapes, all gone.

I knew, deep down, that my employer, especially Double-Dis, knew what was going on. I was feeding victims to a monster.

Worse yet, I could feel the TCC, like a giant constrictor, coiling and encircling me, its jaws unloosening, its dead predator eyes fixed on me as its white mouth gaped wide to envelope and slide me into its gut. I would be part of it forever.

I feigned the flu, took sick leave, got drunk with a BFF. She and I talked in analogies. Her advice: trust your gut.

I packed on Sunday and started driving. Miami by Tuesday. On this boat by Thursday.

I kept thinking: *If I make this up as I go, they won't be able to out-guess me.*

Hell, they probably know my every step before I do.

CHAPTER EIGHTEEN

BUS—
HOVERING ROCK

I pull into the parking lot of the Hovering Rock Inn. The place is squat and U-shaped, a sundowner motor court built in the 1930s before commerce passed it by. The office is at one end. The rest consists of little units that have seen better days. The Bates Motel without meticulous Norman to keep it up.

The doors have dents, scratches, off-tint paint jobs. One droops open, held by a single saggy hinge. The parking lot is a mixture of potholed asphalt and sandbars of gravel. One unit looks tenanted for the long term. A hail-battered Ram pickup sits in front of a door propped open for air. A kitchen chair waits under a bank of windows covered with aluminum foil. Two mud-caked dirt bikes loiter against the wall in a nest of old oil cans and rusty sprocket chains that coil ominously like patient snakes.

I pass the units by and park. I open the door to the office and something above me rings like a tarnished tinker bell. The room smells deeply of marijuana.

A skinny, unshaven man in a dirty wifebeater holds something behind his back and peers around the door. Behind him is a TV playing a cable channel with dusky, naked gladiators fraternizing with dusky, naked noblewomen. A real woman, less noble and coifed in hair rollers, eases past the man and up to the counter.

The couple is probably in their mid-forties. They are sun-fried a deep brown. Too much UV has hard-cured their faces and necks into rhino hide. I can't help but stare. Deep fissures frame the woman's mouth as she says, "You're lucky we're still taking guests."

"Yes ma'am. Appreciate that. Can I check out late tomorrow?"

Her eyes narrow, then relent. We both know this dump never fills up. She hands me a pen and registration pad, the rate, forty bucks, circled in red.

"Where ya travelin' from?"

I look up. "Colorado. Junction City."

"Damon, listen here. He's from over by the river junction, Colorado."

I'm surprised. "You know it?"

"Oh yes, we go up to the Grand Mesa every year. A sun health gathering."

"I see."

I mentally eye a bizarre gathering of unbeautiful nudists, all slathered with mosquito repellant, then force my way back to the moment. We exchange pleasantries. Her name is June. I pay in cash. That low-grade paranoia that itches me suggests that I avoid credit cards, turn off the location app on my electronics. I get ready to go.

"Where you headed?"

"Dallas, then Louisiana."

"That's a lot of Texas to get across." She's checking my road leathers.

"Yes, ma'am." I look at a news clipping displayed crookedly beneath the counter glass. Picture of a rock, maybe the size of a Volkswagen, incongruously suspended ten feet in the air. It is surrounded by a post and crossbeam fence for viewing. It looks to be midday. Deep shadows are pooled on the manicured grass beneath. Looking up at it is a goofy-looking tourist dad in shorts and flip flops with his two kids. They just stare. I think about the EAT back up the road, whether they were heading toward it.

I see that next to it is a picture that shows the rock on the ground, having fallen and knocked down part of the fence. The heading says, matter-of-factly, "Hovering Rock Falls."

"That really true?" I nod at the pictures.

"Fell down twenty years ago. Never rose back up. My folks owned the tourist attraction. Lots of tourists then. It's all a-failed now. Can see what's left out back if you want." She pauses. "Free."

I grin as my mind conjures up an array of off-beat rural tourist attractions—some of which I've actually seen—places that make you purse your mouth and dip your chin and sound a long *hmmm*. Places like Mister Ed's Elephant Museum, Gravity Hill (put your car in neutral and ghost children pull it uphill), Carhenge, the Creation Evidence Museum (spearpoints in giant amphibians, overlapping human and dino tracks fossilized together), Devil's Rope Museum (all things barbwire), and the Texas Prison Museum (ten bucks extra, you git to sit on Old Sparky).

I can't help myself. "But that's the news? That it *fell*?"

"I hear ya. Folks want to hear the little news. They don't question the big story, even if it's a B-I-G L-I-E." She leaves the implication of the last point hanging in the air. "Oh well," she whooshes and hands me the metal key on a chain with a die-cut image of *the* rock attached. "AC should be working. Give it a while after you turn it on."

"Thank you. Last two questions. You have a fax?"

"Number's on the receipt. $2.50 a page. What's the other one?"

"Where do I get a drink?"

She points out the door and signals left with her thumb. "Next door. Hover Bar."

I lock my bike, thinking about her "Big Lie" jewel of wisdom. The Thousand Year Reich, The Missing Gap in the Nixon tapes, The Damaged IRS Hard Drive, and, of course, the Lone Nut Assassin, come to mind. I start to walk over to the bar, then divert to go around back. A small field, couple of yard cars, banks of chicken coops and rabbit hutches, and there it is. A tumbled down fence and the famous Hovering Rock, fallen to the ground, its impossibility now returned to roadside ruined glory, weeds along its edges, a fence rail poking from beneath.

Unlike this forlorn rock, however, I can still get higher than a kite.

I turn around, head straight for the bar, and walk through the open door to country jukebox sounds and beer smells. The place is big enough to have a bandstand but short on patrons. Starting with shots and beer chasers, I think about my old man, eternal patron of so many bars. I decide to help this joint make up for a slow night.

I pull out my cell phone. *Time to check in.* The home phone rings to the end of its string, then surrenders to voicemail. No one at home. Same with her cell.

I order another beer. The place has arrays of neon signs that shine randomly, so that after a while my shot glass and beer mug give off gauzy, intemperate sheens of blue, then red, then yellow.

I ponder whether to get really plastered. *You've earned it,* comes the voice. The metrics of drunkenness pass by for consideration. I jettison the folksy measures, *Drunker than Cooter Brown*, and opt for a journey measured on The Writer's Scale, Level 1 being the everyman's buzz. A level that fails to distinguish a serious writer from every other journeyman, be they plumber, lawyer, or hack. The upper reaches of The Writer's Scale, however, are uniquely conducive to old-style, tough-guy writing. As heroin used to be to jazz. As psychedelics have been to . . . well, not much. Hunter Thompson maybe.

But . . . back to The Scale, yes. Soaring in quantum jumps, the levels ascend: Two (say, Dorothy Parker), Three (Tennessee Williams, Faulkner, McCarthy), on and on.

I order another shot and beer back. I study anew the colors in my shot glass. Almost hypnotic. I begin to bar-dream.

Pretty soon, there he is. My old man, in uniform, leaning against his squad car, shifting his lean, wire-tension frame. He is smoking, tapping his cigarette, telling me about being a cop out on the highway at night. *Last cop before the Utah line.* He throws out phrases: *Bank robbers. Fleeing west. One-car roadblock.* And then the one that really sticks with me: *No backup.*

The scene morphs to just that: him standing beside his squad car banked sideways across the white line on Highway 50 out in the Colorado desert near Utah. Red light blinking strong and steady. Three in the morning checkpoint. The raw excavation that eventually would become Interstate 70 a quarter mile to the south.

The on-off view of his face lit up with the red light, hand on his holstered pistol, trigger guard unsnapped, looking deeply into the night to see whatever might be coming. You could read his thoughts. *No back-up.* Then he looks right at me and . . . I can't hear him, but he mouths the words: *Find my killer.*

I disturb the spell by taking a drink. I gulp, head in hands, a single tear, distilled from undisclosed decades of frustration, falls and ripples the drink aura. He is about to tell me more, perhaps a name, when the view helicopters up and away until his squad car is small and blinking, a tiny firefly in the empty desert night. The lights of a car approach from the east, pistoning out cones of yellow from the high beams. The car stops at the roadblock. After a moment, silent muzzle flashes, tiny sparks, shooting both ways. Then it stops. The strange car slowly backs up, turns around, heads back the way it came. Unhurried. Not fleeing anywhere. The lone red light on the squad car flashes on and off, slower and slower, like a fading heartbeat, or a dying star in an otherwise starless night.

"What you lookin' for in there, cowboy?" I look up. The lady smiles. She is one stool over and late-night-bar-scene good-looking. A regular looking for something irregular.

I peer once again into the amber scrying pool of my drink. "Don't know. Maybe those *were* the droids I was looking for."

"You're not the only one."

"Yeah?"

"Couple of others, like you. In here the other night. Said some old man wearing a hoodie put a spell on them."

"Yeah, spells?"

She nods at the door. "Lots of that out there."

With that, I wipe my hands on my face, clearing the bleariness, not trying to hide my wedding ring. I look her over again. "From around here?" I ask, giving a *round-here* nod.

"Always, seems."

"You know a weird little ghost town couple of hours back up by the state line, just off the interstate? Old oil derrick sticking up."

She eyes me, weighing my description, thinking of her answer. "I'd have to see it."

"You ever see the Rock?" I nod towards the back of the motel. "I mean, hovering . . . up?"

She smiles, ready for any double entendre. "Yeah, as a little girl. Saw it myself. Stayed right . . . *up*." Her smile lingers as her hand caresses her Lone Star longneck.

I could do this. Who'd know? More than that, who'd care? Now that's the real question. I pull out my phone, set it on the bar, stare at Mary's number. She didn't call back.

"One other question."

"Sure, honey."

"You make it with me if I wear a tinfoil hat?"

"Now that's a pickup line."

"It's not a pickup line, just curiosity. Buy you another?"

Without waiting for the answer, I nod to the barkeep, leave a ten to cover her drink, and say goodnight.

A few moments later, I lie alone on the creaky bed and think. Something is out there, wheels are turning, forces stand across a path as yet unseen. Ghosts? Haints? Hay-headed fugitives from slasher flicks? Or real people with real agendas?

I have three names linked to whatever happened in Bossier City: Marcello, Maroon—both dead for sure—and this mystery guy, Louie. Is he still around, and what kind of dude would he be?

CHAPTER NINETEEN

BUS—REFLECTIONS AT 3:00 A.M.

I wake up in a cold sweat at three a.m. Who else in the world, perhaps someone I might be connected with, haunts this hour?

This is the time my old man always talked about: when women and children sleep the sleep of the dead, and those who hear the distant tom-tom must stare at their reflection in a bitter pool.

For me the pool is convulsed, boiling up things no longer content to swim the solemn depths. It's Shakespearean. It's me, considering an exquisite vengeance. I silently rehearse Hamlet's lines *. . . the very witching time of night . . . churchyards yawn, and hell itself breathes out contagion.* And the perfect summary:

Now could I drink hot blood.

I sit up, drenched in sweat, heart double-pistoning like an adrenaline-fed supercharger. I'll never be right until I set things right. As in ferreting out the truth. And dishing out paybacks. If there's anyone left to settle up with.

Even as my breathing slows, I feel the twinge, that out-of-body, "the-world-is-a-paper-thin-façade" quiver. The mental equivalent of what people describe as the portending visual aura before a migraine, or the unease of animals before an earthquake.

I exhale a whoosh and try to settle down. I dig in my saddlebags. I open the old man's journal, this portal where his echoes resonate into me. I read:

```
    I am no longer a young GI, killing a tank at the
Kasserine Pass, no, nor could I methodically make a
long shot kill or close for combat as at San Pietro-
-were I now to cross the Volturno--I would fall
out of the assault craft. I am no longer a young
sergeant of infantry leading a patrol up the slopes
of Cassino, I am far past the time of covering
withdrawal for the team for Venafro. And yet, as
it had for the men of Spain, an envelope had been
placed in my box, no one knows from whence it came,
a simple buff, unstamped envelope, bearing in the
upper right corner the plain black words "Tel Aviv."
    This is music of a prior day, to exemplify, moving
across the square toward the fountain at Venafro,
rifle at guard, walking hard, not soft as a cat,
but challenging. This is what makes your pulse beat
quicker, your breath come shorter and the adrenalin
course throughout when moving to a gun call. This
is personal--man to man--the instinct that makes a
winner or a killer, or the lack of it a coward.
```

I lean back on the pillow, hands behind my head, and get real. Own up to myself. I got it easy. I may or may not be a coward, but this late in the game, I'll never have to be a killer. It's all just fantasy and BS.

I fall into a cascade of troubled sleep.

CHAPTER TWENTY

BANNER'S BLOG— THE RED CHAIR

SPYFLOW.COM

A warning: if you clicked on this site you triggered a recognition algorithm in the NSA's XKeyscore system. If you also show interest in the anonymity protections of TOR—the layers of encryption provided by a worldwide network of volunteer computers—you will definitely earn more points. Eventually, you will merit personalized scrutiny.

In any case, now that you're here, I will share a secret story that should make it worthwhile.

Edwin Snow, 32, has a four-day beard, his backpack hanging on his lean frame. He gets off a train on the Moscow Metro's green line. He surfaces and walks a deliberately erratic path for a half hour before entering the Metropol Hotel. He lingers in the lobby, goes to the bathroom, sits again in the lobby, then takes the elevator to the eighth floor.

He has been studied every step of the way. KGB, CIA, NSA, MI6, Mossad, even me . . .

He is the most watched, most wanted man in the world.

He exits the elevator, walks down the drab hallway that hosts an irreducible smell of tobacco and vodka. He stops at one door, squares his shoulders, knocks, enters. Inside are a journalist and a photographer, doing a spread for a popular US magazine. The meeting is "secret." As in baloney. ES is an exotic, one-of-a-kind bug being surveilled by a dozen or more organizations.

Of course, he knows it, and, except for his personal security, could care less. He is important. He enjoys it. The photographer persuades him to work with certain props, notably an American flag. They get the money shot.

I won't go into what he said. You can read it for yourself in the forthcoming issue of the magazine.

What I can tell you is a little story about how ES got there. Something he told only me, just before he crossed the line of no return and flew to Singapore.

"Banner," he said, "I'm forever a loyal American, but I can't stomach the 'keep my job' mentality of this place. We are on the brink of an abyss of government spying. Worse than Senator Church and Senator Tower discovered in the 1970s. If we go over, we may never get out."

At this point at the infamous Wiretapper's Ball in 2011, we were drunk. We commiserated.

He goes on. "Here's what triggered it for me. In 1975 Senator Tower had a special chair, a huge, overstuffed, red leather thing that sat in a corner of a semiprivate enclave next to the bar in the Jefferson Hotel across Lafayette Park from the White House. He did a lot of business from that chair. The CIA bugged the chair. I listened to recordings they made. This was the cochairman of the Senate special committee that was investigating our government's spying on its own citizens, and they're spying on him! Tower sat in that very chair and talked with his staff, with other senators, about the bridge to tyranny being built by the CIA."

ES let it stay right there, his mind already sweeping toward decisions that would remake his life.

If you think his story is a bit unsettling, I can offer a counter-punch. Something to make the NSA squirm. As they fear, there is a "second leaker." In fact, there are several. Not counting me.

I would say, compared to those people, I should be small potatoes. Except and unless someone really cares about who killed JFK.

As ES said, "The smoking gun they care about will be the political death of important people."

CHAPTER TWENTY-ONE

BUS—INTERLUDE

Morning. In a stream of dawn light I open the door, pull back the curtains, and sit on the bed. I call home. No answer. Maybe she's at the gym. I try her cell, leave a dispirited voicemail and a text flat as a pancake. My head hurts just enough to let me know that the mental squall has dissipated. What I have here is an All-American hangover, Level 2 or 3. Far below the Level 10, Full-Hemingway, I'd toyed with at the bar. Just enough to galvanize action, sharpen the mind. Which is good because I've got some sleuthing to do.

I'm starving. Across the highway sits an open Texas Freeze that offers its own unique breakfast surprise sandwich. I sit outside at a warped and ruined plastic table that is its own work of art, a statement about rain and sun, freezing and unrelenting heat. I take a picture of it. As for the sandwich, I try it, delicately, like a man might try fried grasshoppers for the first time.

I'm thinking about Marcello, the man my old man apparently sucked up to, feared, ran from. What kind of man was he?

Somewhere around here a digital Good Samaritan has set up free Wi-Fi. I grab the bandwidth and troll the deep sea of the Internet. I pause, thinking how someone in this dried-up, one-stoplight

Texas town might be eavesdropping. Hell, no one in the world knows where I am, much less cares. I resume and it's good fishing. I find the full skinny on Carlos Marcello.

He was born in Tunisia in 1910. Sicilian by heritage. His family moves to New Orleans the next year. By the 1940s, he is the undisputed Mafia kingpin of Louisiana, Mississippi, and all of Texas that matters, namely Dallas and Houston. Interestingly, he is the single most independent Mafia boss in the country, needing no permission from anyone within organized crime to conduct his business. He can do whatever, kill whomever he wants. In fact, no other Mafioso can set foot on his turf without his permission.

By 1960, the articles say, he controls a billion-dollar empire. Just about everything in Louisiana: docks, judges, governors, cops, gambling, drugs, prostitution, extortion, graft—and hell, probably even floods, hurricanes, and tornadoes, not to mention boll weevils and sweet potato rust.

The clincher for me is an old news photo of the man coming out of a federal courthouse. He is glaring over a cigar. He looks pissed and powerful, the kind of person, you ask: *Who would EVER fuck with this guy?*

So what's that got to do with my old man? I scan his journal for a while, letting the sun heal me. I find a couple of pages typed on the stationary of the Adolphus Hotel in Dallas, apparently after he left the Captain Shreve in early '64. He was the classic itinerant manager, a role that in another era might earn him a nickname like "Chainsaw"—as in go in, hack, cut, rip, kick ass, take names, fire people, and generally scare hell out of the staff until they shape up. Here's how he described it:

```
I had the creeps being back in Dallas. Too soon.
Too many shadows of too many goombahs and Secret
Service types tailing me, hanging around the lobby.
Watching.
```

But I stayed and did the job.

Now, the work here is over, the job done, the challenge conquered, and I sit in my suite, work weary, depressed; gone the glow of a job to do, gone the obstructions and obstructers placed deliberately-gone the driftwood and the people who were hangers on.

I look around. My briefcase is closed, left are only a jug, a bucket of ice, a bulging finalized file. I have only to turn it in and this operation is phased out . . .

Everything is following the unusual pattern, the employees, new and old, are probably in the midst of a celebration of my leaving. And there would be no farewell for me for this little moment of triumph that I was paid for, sent for, and it was only a job well done, done quickly and decisively. It was over.

Building a final drink, I call the airport to arrange limo service, notify the front office of departure time, and taking my drink I wander out to the pool, sit in the sun and bat the breeze with a couple of girls in the pool and again feel the letdown from the job, the leaving. Would it be ever this, to go from place to place, be called here and there, to hack and cut and tear down only to build again--or would the time come when the white line would be just a word, just a road?

I call room service, send a boy for another jug, ice, a full setup. What the hell, I might as well get my ass plastered, and to hell what the goddamn employees think.

I flip through the finalized file. This part is simple, it is done and in a short while I can go-go

onto the white line, to another town, to new places
and to new people.

Or maybe not. Someday soon, I will see an exit.
Get away from the feeling of being shadowed, from
the godawful burden of knowing too much, of having
done too much. The problem is that you can't do it
this way. You don't, ever, just say goodbye to the
Little Man. You have to pretend you are taking that
new job, staying in touch.

Then cut and run.

I sit at the table, eat my mystery sandwich, and think about my
old man's instinct to go for the road. Looking up, I study the highway. In the clean, sunlit air it glistens, radiant and happy. It leads
straight out of town, disappearing in a beckoning curve.

I am becoming fixated on the white line. As if by following it,
somewhere out there, elusive as the wind, is the It. The Thing that
gnaws at some men. Now, it has me firmly in its mouth.

I reload my saddlebags and head out, duly beckoned.

CHAPTER TWENTY-TWO

BANNER'S BLOG— SPY TOUR

Spyflow.com

The Wiretapper's Ball—a trade show façade that is the gathering of the tribe of surveillance geeks. Where governments, cyber technology, organized crime, a few terrorists' fronts, and all social media meet to make sure they are up to speed. This time it's in DC.

After the event, Edwin and I, along with our IGT friend, drive up to Atlantic City. We check out the casinos, the neighborhoods a few blocks away, which probably looked devastated even before Hurricane Sandy. Then we go to Tuckerton, New Jersey. You wouldn't know it, but this prosaic little village has been home to two of the world's biggest communication facilities.

In 1912, right next to Tuckerton, the Germans quietly built the world's second tallest structure. The first was the Eiffel Tower. This one was an immense radio tower. Its signals could reach Europe. Embarrassingly, the US government was oblivious as to who owned the tower until after the start of World War I. One German message sent from the tower said, oddly and simply, "Get Lucy." Shortly thereafter, German submarines sank the *Lusitania*. The tower's remnants, massive concrete blocks that held the guy-wires, survive to this day. We scrambled around them, children among giants' toys. Then we did a tour lite of the other mega communications facility.

Just offshore from Tuckerton, the sea swarms with cables that, like a hundred-armed squid, coil and intertwine together to a common landing, a nondescript brownish, windowless building less than a mile inland and reaching deep underground. Here is one of, perhaps *the* largest, data collection points on Earth. This is snoop-central for the NSA's entire digital surveillance system.

The feds hope they won't be caught with their data-pants down a second time.

CHAPTER TWENTY-THREE

BUS—THE NOW

We all know we are products of genes and environment.

Equally important, I hold, is that we are thrust into the world with momentum, headed down a particular, if unknown, path. Call it fate, circumstance, heritage, family history. It affects who you are and, if you listen, can tell you a lot about yourself. I'm thinking these thoughts as Highway 287 smooths out and I pass a simple road sign that points north and says "Burkburnett." I've known all along such a sign would be out here somewhere, and I've known the little cabinet of family lore that name would unlock. Oral history told and retold until it feels like an old epic movie. Mix Hollywood fables—John Wayne in *Red River*, James Dean in *Giant*, maybe Daniel Day-Lewis in *There Will Be Blood*, and you get a feel for it.

Even closer is Faulkner's famous text from *Intruder in the Dust* about Pickett's Charge at the Battle of Gettysburg. It's about how fourteen-year-old boys in the South can always conjure up that exact moment on a July afternoon in 1863: the hills outside a little shoe-manufacturing town in Pennsylvania. Brigades are poised, lined along a rail fence. Rifles and big guns laid ready. Furled flags loosened in their covers, eager to sweep and flow. The final order has not been issued, the lines and drums and yells and smoke and booms and wavering flags and blood and death have not yet begun, and maybe never will. NOW hangs in the air, like the Hovering Rock.

Cut for a moment from Faulkner to the McIntyre family history. Circa 1840s, a Virginian by a different name gets in serious enough trouble that he lights out for the Republic of Texas and eventually disappears into Mexico. A few years later, he returns with money and the made-up name of McIntyre. He settles near Burkburnett, steals land from Comanches and Mexican settlers, and rawhides together a cattle ranch. His son and heir is John McIntyre. He was not a slave owner. He was, however, a believer in what today seems odd, but was then real and less than thirty-years fresh from the Alamo—Texas rights. He decides, as they said in his day, to see the elephant. He enlists with the renowned Texas Brigade under General John Bell Hood. It is the only Texas unit to serve under Robert E. Lee in the Army of Northern Virginia. Over the years, he sees hard action at Antietam and the Seven Days Battle.

Forward to July 2, 1863. His regiment, the 5th Texas, comprised of barely four hundred men under the nurturing command of Colonel "Aunt Polly" Robertson, has double-timed for fifteen hours in a dusty column of ten thousand to be placed in the order of battle. It is two o'clock in the afternoon.

They have thirty minutes to rest. Their rally spot is still there, a little wall of rock a hundred feet back in the woods, opening in front of them to a field beyond which rises an anonymous jumble of massive rocks that, in an hour's time, will be bloodied and inscribed in history: Devil's Den, Slaughter Pen, Valley of Death, Bloody Run, blending to Little Round Top on their right flank. Sister regiments from Arkansas and Louisiana are coming up and organizing beside them. It is hot. Cannons boom in the distance. The time is near.

As Faulkner noted, it could be now, or the horrible event might never happen, might not come to pass.

The fourteen-year-old boy inside me relates to this, imagining the minute details, the lightness of body after depositing bedroll and knapsack to the rear, looking up to see a sunbeam casting down through a swaying cobweb of diamonds in the branches above, a yellow butterfly dancing between butternut hats, a green dragonfly bravely sallying into the field, feeling the shudder of tension and fear running shoulder to shoulder through the ranks. Men relieving themselves, men preparing.

After that hushed-breath moment, NOW happens.

A cannonade erupts, as if heaven is reversed and the ground itself is giving forth thunder and lightning.

On a signal, brigade by brigade, the men step forward by the thousands, hastily dress their lines, check their musket loads, and advance into the field. They progress into the open in long, orderly lines of march. They progress to double time. A shrill, warbling yell ripples up and down their ranks. They address a rattling volley of shot at their enemy. In a moment all is smoke and dust and fear and anger. Death wings the air, canister and shot come like low-voiced banshees, .50-caliber minié balls drone by like huge wasps. Whiz and the thud of impact. The raggedy butternut line advances straight into the Yankee position and chastises them severely. In turn they are punished. The line of battle falters and drifts off, to places now of equal renown: the Wheatfield, the Peach Orchard. It is in the latter, in a fog of acrid smoke, that one such lead wasp cuts the air and thuds and John McIntyre falls, the ball imbedded in his lung, his mouth bubbling out hot, red blood.

Somehow, he lives. By evening, the fields are being cleared of the wounded. Surgeons, red-drenched and standing amid the sweet, coppery smell of a working slaughterhouse, curse and cut and probe without chloroform in a haze of screams. They find and pull out John's bullet.

Now begins the journey. Stretchers. Lurching hospital wagons. Endless night-day click-clack of a southbound railcar. A week later, a hot humid dawn heralds the crossing of the Red River by ferry at Shreve's Landing. He can smell the river, now low and braiding around sandbars. A jolting buckboard wagon trip follows. North across the Texas plains to Burkburnett. There he lies on a bed on the shaded front porch of his family's ranch house. Damning the heat and the Yankees and fading. His last words, muttered and prophetic: "Don't sell the ranch."

But of course they did. Reconstruction came like a biblical storm and took everything. They kept the family name, false though it may be, got foreclosed, moved away, and the last bits of family wealth dissipated in the wind.

My parents, when they came along, were still Texas dirt-poor, still lamenting the loss.

None of this matters, except I spent the core of my life trying to break that pattern, to at least metaphorically get that fabled ranch back.

End of the movie, except for this ironic epilogue. I pass a complex of shiny new gas wells fracking the Haynesville Shale. Descendants of the oil boom that in the 1920s, long after the McIntyres' departure, marched off northward from Kilgore to become a forest of wooden derricks festooning the view from that rawhided ranch front porch.

I sense Fort Worth and Dallas up ahead. I am approaching the place where all this family mystery—right up to the mob connections, the events in Dallas and the things I saw, the flight, the shootout in the Colorado desert—seems to cross tracks with history.

CHAPTER TWENTY-FOUR

BUS—THE ORACLE OF DEALEY

The night road is empty. Above me, a star-sprent heaven glistens, its brilliant ornaments conjuring the image of a jewel thief with torn pockets traipsing by our corner of the universe. No doubt embarked on his own white-line journey. If him, then so are we all.

The pistons below me rumble the deep and happy sound of smooth riding. My speedometer pegs eighty-five, cruising the night too fast for cops to catch up. The air is dense with deep country smells, moisture from irrigation wheel lines, growing alfalfa, porch trellis jasmine, manure, skunk.

A distant, lone headlight appears in my rear view. In a moment it is close. I glance back and it is like an oncoming, yellow-eyed locomotive. It roars up beside me. It is another bike, its growl so deep it makes my Harley sound like a timid kitten.

In the brief moment that it is next to me, I see that it is big, scaled larger than life. It is not just dull black. It is almost opaque. As is its rider. He is huge. Sheathed in metal and leather, his battered helmet sports a stubby antenna. The shape is unmistakable. For just a moment, he turns and his eye slits regard me. I am sharing the highway with a night-riding Boba Fett.

Boba slows and we jointly ponder this improbable meeting. Here then, is a fellow bounty hunter, paladin of the night journey, each of us tethered as common satellites to some singular star. But which of those myriad jewels control us, and whichever it may be, does it care what cycles at the far, infinite string of its powers?

Then he, it, the apparition, is gone. A red taillight diminishing in the night, perhaps going airborne. Watching that point of red accelerate away into a final wink and nothingness, feeling the cool, inky breath of the evening air flow into the deepest recesses of my lungs, I discover the vast, inexpressible *aloneness* of this ride. Just me and whatever's out there.

Wherever this is leading, I'm in it.

Lord, just gimme some keys to these questions.

■

I make it to Fort Worth by two in the morning. Eating a fast-food burger, I lay back on my bike, feet up on a picnic table. I doze and then, by the gray neon glare, read another entry from my old man's journal:

```
It is dusk when I pull off onto a long neglected
shell road, drive down an alley of live oaks. A
burnt and lonely ruin greets me, wrought iron and
a slave-built veranda constructed high above the
ground, smoky white columns reaching from southern
earth toward southern air, and I am alone--for this
is Belle Helene and lies just off the river road.
I build a fire, sit leaning back against a column.
I mix a drink, feel like the last man on Earth,
am content for the night moves around me and it is
moonrise. The river road comes alive, the hum of a
high-powered car, purposeful and knowing, this is no
jalopy pick up or white trash heap, I sip my drink,
sit up--and from the river road, headlights turn
```

in, it is as ordered: Texas car, a white '61 Chevy,
4-door Impala, and suddenly the past is present.

Enough. I'm fading. I get up, go inside the diner and order hot
coffee along with a couple of Mega Monster energy drinks. I start
pouring it all down, readying for the road and googling JFK websites for the hell of it. I find something that stops me short. I read
and can almost hear the voice of Lee Bowers, the rail yard tower
operator who, on that fateful day in 1963, was looking down at
the backside of the fence above the grassy knoll. He testified to the
Warren Commission:

> "Just a few minutes after this car left at 12:20 p.m. another car
> pulled in. This car was a 1961 Chevrolet, Impala, 4-door, I am not
> sure that this was a 4-door . . . color white and dirty up to the
> windows. This car also had a "Goldwater for '64" sticker. This car
> was driven by a white male about 25 to 35 years old with long
> blond hair. He stayed in the area longer than the others . . . He left
> this area about 12:25 p.m. About 8 or 10 minutes after he left I
> heard at least 3 shots very close together. . . .
>
> "At the time of the shooting . . . there was a flash of light or
> . . . there was something which occurred which caught my eye in
> this immediate area on the embankment . . . [T]here was some
> unusual occurrence—a flash of light or smoke or something which
> caused me to feel something out of the ordinary had occurred
> there."

Lee Bowers died in an unexplained single-car accident in 1970.
Same year, same unexplained status as my father.

I surf the net through endless fan pages about the Beach Boys to
learn more about the legendary Chevrolet 409 engine. It was the
subject of their 1962 hit "409" and an option for the '61 Impala.

I put the pad aside, gulp the last Monster, and breathe deep. I dig back through the journal, flipping pages till I pick up the rest of my old man's story. He is again waiting for delivery of a certain car in South Louisiana:

They, men like me, were wheeler-dealers, con men and racket boys; they were the "white liners," they had cars that were different, wore clothes that were different, did not then and do not now categorize readily or pigeonhole with the accepted norms of social behavior. Somehow they equated tangibles with intangibles, and reality with fantasy. They had a phrase, so often used "on the nights the ghosts walk, then we must needs harvest the crops sown of yesteryear," and they were bugged and moving constantly, seeking to find what it was that was out there, out in the land of the ghost and the realm in which they moved, for truly there are things out there.

For now, this night, I am clean and sober. But the need remains--remains in the form of expensive tweed jackets, splitting the take from booze, from girls, from delivering glassines of H, paying bets on horses, numbers and football, and a shared contentment in mixing a drink in the bell room, usually 7 and 7 with a dash of lemon, the folding green laying in obscene piles and the vice cops biting their nails and I both like and respect those cats. It was maybe a game of cops and robbers, but to all concerned, it was a challenge. Give the cops a little, send them favors and, most of all, stay tight with the Little Man. He wants me to moonlight

running the Bossier Town & Country, I do it. Kick
ass, take names, bite my tongue and say yessir to
Maroon.

   Now I'm in south Louisiana where they told me to
be. The car, white but grayish in the moonlight,
stops. A weird duck, bald, total alopecia, gets out.
He has a message from Marcello, another task.

   We switch cars. I drive the Chevy street legal
but souped-up--to East Dallas that same night. All
night.

No way! I think. I search around. The entry is undated. How
many white '61 Impalas were out there anyway? I tell myself the
clues are still half-assed. As we say in the legal profession, *show me
the fucking proof.* All I really know is I'm about to resume driving
the night, reverse-engineering the flight path taken by my old man.
Stay cool. Stay on plan.

   I get back on I-20 and in a half hour take a random downtown
exit in Dallas. It doesn't matter which one, because, with the unerr-
ing instinct of a returning salmon, I get to my destination in five
minutes.

   I park along Dealey Plaza, at the corner of Houston and Elm. I
shut off the bike, let silence fill the vacuum, and just take it all in.

   The world here is asleep, the downtown empty. The scale in
real life is smaller, much smaller, than in the imagination or in any
movie. A pallid glow from the street lights floats over everything,
giving the landmarks a luminous gray tone. The hulking box of the
Dallas School Book Depository glowers over the corner, its windows a matrix of blank eyes. Even the infamous sixth floor corner
suite is impassive, unyielding of information. The other landmarks
are right where they are supposed to be. The Live Oak Trees lim-
iting a shooter's vision from that window. The acute slow turn
onto Elm. The Pedestal on which Abraham Zapruder held his 8mm

camera that would capture the world's most-viewed amateur film. The Grassy Knoll and the Wooden Fence. I am sure the fence has been replaced several times, what with souvenir hunters and all. Beyond the fence, the railroad yards are gone, along with the control tower from which, I now know, Lee Bowers watched a white 1961 Chevy Impala, muddy to the windows, prowl the lot and park near the fence corner less than ten minutes before JFK bought the farm. I look across to the triple overpass under which the fleeing motorcade sped, leading to Parkland Hospital where JFK died, where two days later Lee Harvey Oswald died, and, fifteen years earlier I was born.

Like pieces on a board game. My old man might be one of them. If so, a pawn. Surely, just a pawn.

I stand there, atop the knoll, helmet in hand, surveying the scene. I blow out a breath and let my instincts flow across the scene. There's nothing left here. Only a conspiracist's watering hole upon which a thousand amateur experts, like buffalos in heat, have stomped and over-stomped, trampling any signs into oblivion. I fancy that if any ghosts yet linger, my antennas will detect them. All is quiet. Distant honks and a far off siren warble, but nothing here.

I start to go when I hear an electrical whirr and erratic scuffs on a sidewalk, all of which herald a figure emerging from shadows between the streetlights on Elm. A man wearing a cowboy hat is driving a motorized wheelchair that is towing a grocery cart with a gimp wheel. He maneuvers to a spot below the Zapruder Pedestal. He stops and checks out my ride before starting to unpack the cart. Quicker than a ball-and-cup scam, he sets up a sling chair and folding table. Upon this he fusses, placing his wares.

I go down the knoll and approach him. Below his hat brim I see a type A face, all focus. A guy that might put a timer on the sunrise. He sees me and nods amiably, like he's a baker and I'm the first customer of the day. It's fucking four in the morning.

He looks at me. "Like your ride, man. Milwaukee or York?"

"York factory-custom, 'cept for the added paint."

"Nice, I got flames on mine. Twenty-four volts. Go eight miles per hour."

"What's baking?" I ask as I check his ride and scan his wares: books, DVDs, T-shirts, postcards, fridge magnets, pins, and bumper stickers.

"The Truth," he says, solemn as an oracle.

"Then I'm buying." I pick up one of his books titled *Closer Than You Think*. It bears a cover with a noose encircling a smiling JFK. I flip it over, check the author's photo. It's him, maybe twenty years ago.

He's bustling, meticulously arranging things in final order as he talks. "City wants to run me off, get rid of me. They already tried before the gold anniversary. The street vendor ordinance has a grandfather clause. So, I set up here every day, before the tin hats even get up. Squat on my little piece of the First Amendment. They're afraid, you see. Afraid of the Truth."

There it is, the Believer's Intonation.

I nod sympathetically, still looking at his book. It says "Best Seller." I piece it together. He's an aged conspiracist who once wrote a book that did so-so, probably a blip on the lists. I can identify with that. Now he can't let it go. A Boomer, all right, still caught up in that JFK watershed moment. Ditto.

He's studying me now, checking out my helmet and leathers. "What're you here for, Easy Rider?"

"Searching for an old trail."

"A man once went looking for America, eh? Don't be so vague."

"OK, since you know all this stuff." I gesture at his stock in trade. I can tell I'm about ready to blurt out something over-the-top. "My family was involved with Carlos Marcello." He raises his eyebrows, nods, encouraging me to continue. "My . . . father . . . worked for him," I say. "He took off in early 1964, like he was running. He was murdered five years later."

"Ah, case never solved I bet. You got that look."

I stay quiet. We are like mannequins let loose for the night.

He leans back in his sling chair, cracks his knuckles, gets his oracle game face on. "You came to the right place. I can tell you some things you probably don't know." He gestures, inviting me to sit on the sacred turf of the Grassy Knoll. I oblige, resting my butt on my helmet. He harrumphs. I'm looking up at him, listening like a schoolkid. "It starts in 1961. There is a convergence between the Kennedys and organized crime. Their one goal: get rid of Castro. Remove the Red Menace ninety miles from our shores, *and* reopen Cuba to gambling and Mafia control. After the disaster at the Bay of Pigs, all that disappears. The Kennedys turn inward; they wage war on organized crime."

The guy chuckles in a hoarse whisper. "Now, seeing as Papa Joe Kennedy made his money bootlegging with organized criminals, this strikes some in the Mob as ingratitude."

He lets that jewel sparkle for a moment. "So here's the point. No Mafia person was more in the Kennedys' crosshairs, or held more personal animosity toward them, than Carlos Marcello. And that's saying something. More than Trafficante, Hoffa, Giancana. Here's the kicker: after Bobby Kennedy harassed him in Senate hearings, Marcello is subjected, at what he believes is a direct order from the White House, to a surprise arrest and deportation. What we would today call "rendition." No notice, no warrant, no hearing, no due process. Just a high-speed, light-blinking, siren-wailing ride to the airport in New Orleans. They put him on a plane and dump him in Guatemala. The next two months, probably the worst in Marcello's life, stamp upon him an indelible hatred for the Kennedys.

"Members of his family fly to Guatemala City, accompanied by Mike Maroon, his personal attorney and confidante."

I note the name. The Shreveport lawyer again. Pieces are clicking together.

"A month later, arrangements have been made to fly the entire group back to the United States. Then, at the airport, right in front of his family, Marcello is denied boarding. Worse yet, he and Maroon are transported by force to an army camp in El Salvador.

"Now the real ordeal begins. They are informed they are to be taken to Honduras. Six hours into a miserable drive on bad roads in a small, decrepit bus, they are abandoned roadside. The middle of nowhere. Two fat, urban, out-of-shape, middle-aged men in city clothes. They walk. Up mountains. Down mountains. Through jungles.

"Three days later they stagger into a remote airstrip and talk a pilot into flying them to Tegucigalpa. Exhausted, dirty, bruised, and mosquito-bitten, they check into a hotel. They sleep for two days. Now it is personal, damn personal."

The guy lights what I hope is his first cigarette of the day, plumes out a breath, resumes.

"After slipping back into the United States, Marcello resumes his presence at his headquarters, the Countryside Motel in Metairie, outside New Orleans."

"The Kennedys continue to pursue him. On the day of the assassination, Marcello is in a courtroom in New Orleans being acquitted on more federal immigration charges." He chuckles, "Talk about an alibi."

I can see Marcello, a man pushed to a *me or them* strategy. I pair that with a lesson I'd learned long ago: when you force a man to the back of an alley and he turns, watch out. His instincts become crystal clear.

I ask, "You know New Orleans, Metairie, down there?"

"It's all as picked over as here. No clues left."

"I'm going over to Shreveport, Bossier."

"You may be onto something, sonny. No one's ever poked around there."

I feel the dawn coming, the grackles in the trees getting restless. I stand up. He thumbs his book to the table of contents, points at a chapter entitled "Witness Eliminations: Lee Bowers Rubbed

Out—Senator Boggs's Plane Disappears—Dorothy Kilgallen's Last, Lost Chapter." He holds the book up and shakes his head. "The odds for all these people, witnesses, dying off like they have, is staggering. One in a trillion. Something, somebody is out there. Maybe still out there."

"You're not afraid?"

He laughs. "Me? Hell no, I've slipped over into the crackpot zone. Just another whiney voice, all of us together drowning out the Truth."

It is, of course, customary to reward an oracle with a token of thanks. I buy his book. I don't need to ask for the autograph. He automatically opens the cover, clicks his pen with a flourish, and signs away. He clearly relishes the moment. I see he's addressed it to "Captain America." He slides a glossy brochure in as a free bookmark and hands the book to me. I see the words at the top of the brochure:

Final Evidence: The Mexico Files

I turn the brochure toward him. "What's that about?"

"Nine days from now there's an event right here. On the knoll, ten a.m. Big show, as they say. Tent, press, speakers. We're going to unveil something new. I'll be speaking there. You should come." I think about that, smile at him, say nothing. A helmet raised in salute and I'm almost gone. No telling where nine days might lead.

As I straddle the Harley, I look back. He waves, raises his voice, "Remember, Easy Rider, there are still keys to the Truth! Keep looking!"

I will. For me, whatever happened back then, the place to look now is crystal clear. Three hours due east. To Bossier City and whatever ghosts of my old man and Carlos Marcello still lurk there.

CHAPTER TWENTY-FIVE

BUS—POINTS EAST

At my age, trying to go through a trunk of old family pictures is almost impossible. You just bog down with sentiment. East Texas is like that trunk.

I discipline myself to make only one more stop before I get to Bossier.

Not counting a nap at a roadside rest area, which I remember from my mom's flight west. Plastic tablecloth on the picnic table, bologna sandwiches. She was always trying.

At three in the afternoon I pull into Longview, Texas. Growing up, we had lived there for several years. I find Johnny Colino's. "Serving Cajun Seafood to East Texas for Seventy Years." The kind of place—the special *grown-up* place—a kid never forgets. I go in, sit at the underlit bar and eat shucked oysters and étouffée and chase it down with a frosted mega stein of beer. Only one, 'cause I am still making the last hour or so into Louisiana. The barkeep doesn't really know much of the history of the place, but tells me that Johnny Junior had left it all to his daughter, Gracie. She isn't here. No, he doesn't know much else, but I might like to look at some pictures on the wall in the back.

I take my beer, start on one side, and get a pictorial lesson of the intertwined history of Longview and Colino's. The first wall has sepia-toned images. I stare back in time at a frenzied orgy of thirsty oil rigs. Old cars, old signs, a flashbulb shot of the inside of Colino's with dressed-up post–World War II adults at white-clothed tables. Everyone smoking. I move along the gallery to a series of annual shots of the staff. All black folks in the kitchen and all white folks in the dining room. By 1953, they were taking the picture of everyone together. A nice touch. 1957, '58. I stop at 1959 and peer into the photo. Past the frame, past the glass, *into it*.

There, on the left side, dressed like all the other waitresses in a dark, navy-themed uniform, hair done in an *up* "poodle" style, hands clasped in front, a hopeful smile on her face—is my mom.

If the picture were colorized, the hair would be red, the lipstick orange-red, the look, Lucille Ball.

She'd worked here for one year before my old man got the job at the Captain Shreve Hotel and we loaded up once again and trekked over to Bossier City. She looks out at this lost world, her eyes measured by the loss of her first husband, my brother's dad, in the war. A working mother with three little kids. There it is. Hope. The blind, foolish thing I inherited. She always had it, even in that last year when she also wore a waitress uniform at the lunch counter at Woolworth's Five and Dime in Junction City and kept telling herself that the lump in her breast couldn't be cancer.

That gets me pretty misty, so, earlier than I'd planned, I call Gene Wray, my brother. He's still in Bossier. He picks up.

"Boliver Shagnasty."

"Fuck you," I tell him.

"Eat shit, little brother, what's up?"

"On my way to see you."

"Same old story."

"No. Really, I'm past Dallas, in Longview."

"Hail no!"

We exchange more insults about who should've gone to see whom over the years.

"Been, what, five years since we met at the Dallas game?"

"Yeah, your Cowboys *still* stink."

"Bring back Aikman and Smith, maybe go back to Bob Hayes."

"He wouldn't be the world's fastest human anymore."

"OK, things change. We change. Wuz up, anyway?" He senses my pause. "And don't bullshit. I can still tell."

I hem and haw. Worse, I bullshit. I end up with, "So, I got on my bike and just headed out, pretty sure I'd go this direction."

"Listen to you. You're afraid of this place. You gotta be chasing something. Or something's gotta be chasing you. Think of this: Mom would want you to fess up—especially to me."

That pretty much cracks the dam. My thoughts just spill out in disarray. The fling as special prosecutor, the old man's journal, even my aloof shrink that peers over her specs and studies me like some exotic jungle bug preserved on a pin. I mention Mary, as if the situation is merely annoying, like a dirty side-mirror on this hot rod of troubles. I can't keep it in order, and he knows I am *still* holding something back.

"Bus, get on over here. I'm just damn glad to see you. I figured you were still some kind of warrior philosopher, talking big, afraid to leave your little realm."

Suddenly, completely, he *is* my big brother, the one who could get me to do or say *anything*, no matter how secret or stupid. Ride my bicycle blindfolded. Eat bugs.

"OK. I got this . . . question, deep down, about our old man . . ."

"You mean *your* old man."

"OK, anyway it's also about what happened in '63. JFK gets murdered. Mom picks up me and Sis and leaves. Dean skips. I think he, Dean, had something to do with the JFK thing. There was this white Chevy . . ."

"Hell, there were thousands of white Chevys. All over. Look, I always suspected he ran cars. But just errands. Don't get ahead of yourself."

I keep going, getting breathless, "This stuff he wrote. About hanging around, working with the Mob. I think he was running when he came to Junction City. There's more. The time you came to get me out at Loggy Bayou? At the cabin? I never told you everything. There was this box. I stole it from a Mafia guy's car. Well, from a Mafia guy's *kid's* car. Well, a stolen Mafia . . . never mind. That box, all these loose ends, they've been eating at me, right at the edge, all these years." I am tripping over words now, so I stop.

A long moment before he speaks. "Look, now that we're talking about it I know something about this, maybe more than you think. He wasn't my real old man, but I had to live under the same roof as you and I was older and picked up on things. Besides, you're talking to a retired history teacher. And . . ."

"The old man got *murdered* for Christ's sake!"

"Brother, slow down. *Another* midlife crisis? You used that chit. Besides . . . it's too late for *anything* midlife for you. Your Hamlet moment is fifty years late."

"What d'you mean?"

"Suddenly, you get a hunger for resolution, maybe vengeance? Now shut up and listen . . ."

I put the phone closer to my ear.

"I was playing lots of gigs that year, band leader, out on the Strip. A lot at the Countryside. The Gold Room. Marcello's HQ in North Louisiana. Same name as his place in New Orleans. Anyway, I met him, the Little Man, several times. I saw and heard a lot. Enough to know to keep my mouth shut."

"You think there's something to all this?"

"Before you twist your panties, just get over here. I can add someone else to the conversation."

"Like who?"

"Guy I worked with, Caddo Bill. Got along great with Marcello. Played keyboard. Still laces up his rock & roll shoes. Strange guy, sort of a JFK buff. He'll know more of the pieces. You get here tonight?"

"Quicker than that. Past Natchez Wheels. Into Shreveport. Over the river. There's Bossier."

"You won't recognize most of it. Big casinos now. Lots of movie production going on. Definitely cleaned up from when we grew up. Anyway, we'll eat crawdads and drink beer. Caddo gets down on this all-you-can-eat place on Wednesday nights."

"On my way."

We hang up. I climb on the bike and head out, my mind whirring on top of those restless pistons.

■

Riding pillion with me through the rest of East Texas is a memory long neglected. Tenanted in some mental ghetto, never visited by the waking. Now it comes alive. It is probably a few days after Kennedy's assassination. The world may be in shock, but some things can't be stopped. Especially Deep South football.

Dimly at first, I hear the voices, the sounds, smell the locker-room stench of sweat and tape and dirty socks. The lights are coming up, as if some central control board in my mind is amping itself up, adjusting dials, the video editor humming, the exterior red "Show Is On" light illuminated.

And suddenly I'm there.

Ninth grade. We just lost our final game, 24-7, to our scourge, our nemesis, the archrival, green-jerseyed demons at TO Rusheon Junior High School. Three thousand people showing up to watch fifteen-year-olds play. That's Louisiana football.

We squat in the locker room that smells like a hot sauce of mildew, piss, analgesic, and rank teenager BO. We are defeated, bruised, and disconsolate. Our coach, Melvin Landry, a brutal giant, is stalking among us. He is berating and livid, fixing each of us with his searing stare of supreme disappointment. Our heads hang down, lost in the pall of the utterly vanquished. His outsized anger steals the show, making our feelings about the ass-kicking we just got seem trivial.

His voice booms. "Last year I had a team that hit like high school! Pop-pop-pop-pop!" His fist pounding his open hand in quick emphasis for each pop. "This year . . . strictly junior high."

That's it. The condemnation burned in my mind forever. *Strictly junior high*.

Being a second-string smart-ass, I start to raise my hand to point out that the starters on last year's team, especially the front line, had all flunked one, two, or, in one case and amazingly for the ninth grade, three grades. No wonder they hit like high school kids. They *were* high school kids. This year we had only one flunky, a devil-may-care, ducktailed JD hard-ass named Mike Sarto, our best player.

Fortunately, I keep my mouth shut and just let the acid of those three words burn in. Football is done, and no one can stop our next move: we're gonna party.

Within the hour five of us are showered and waiting in the Greenacres Junior High parking lot for the ride. We all have driver's licenses, we just lost the North Louisiana Junior High Football Championship, and we know we can score multiple quarts of beer at the drive-up window of Carmine's Liquor Store. The world is open and sizzling, even for losers.

Just then, a car we'd never seen, a muddy white '61 Chevy Impala, careens into the parking lot, tires squealing, and slides to a sideways stop in front of us. The driver, lit cigarette cornered in his mouth, revs up the car's supercharged mill and smiles. Mike Sarto, right on time. The radio is maxed out, the volume on the brink of shattering the custom speakers. We walk up, awed, just as the Beach Boys harmonize on cue, "She's real fine, my 409."

We pile in and head to Carmine's.

By eleven, it is raining and we are drunker than, yes, Cooter Brown. We are cruising the bleary neon river of the Bossier Strip. Mike runs a flagrant red, still bragging how he's stolen this car from his old man's car lot. "They had it sitting in the garage, covered over with a tarp, the keys in the ignition." He showboats through another red. "Anyway what was I supposed to do? I took it!"

We answer, call and response, with adolescent guffaws and tough talk—until a crimson light stabs into the car's interior. On-off, on-off. This sets off a pitiful round of "Shit! Fuck! Don't look back!" and "Oh, man!" For just a moment, Mike gooses the car, as if daring the cops to a high-speed chase. Then the siren whoops, they hit us with a withering spotlight, and we pull over.

Everyone fidgets to inconspicuously ease various quart bottles—Jax, Miller, Schlitz—between their feet. The cop car doors slam shut in unison, sounding mad. You can feel their fury as they approach, gravel crunching under their boots. Almost like Coach Landry.

Flashlights beam us, throwing strange silhouettes on the rain-fogged windows. Hard taps on the glass, windows rolling down.

"Give me your license, smart-ass," was all the cop says to Mike. We are cooked and we know it. I can imagine my imminent fate: my juvenile probation status coming up. Being sent to the infamous "Louisiana Technical Institute," LTI for short, the Angola Prison for long-term juvenile detention. My mom crushed and terrified, pleading with me to straighten up. My old man unbuckling his belt, the leather strap hissing free to become an awful biting snake.

The cop studies Mike's license, then uses his flashlight to inspect each of us. Five squinting, juvenile misdemeanants, one of them a drunk, light-running, reckless-driving wiseass.

The flashlight cuts back to the license. You can sense the cops communicating, invisible to us, over the top of the car. Then the cop looks back in and asks, "Mike, you Pauli Sarto's kid?" Mike, subdued now, says, "Yessir." The "step outside" and frisks and cuffs are coming next.

But it doesn't happen. The cop says, "You boys take it easy," hands Mike his license, and walks back to the squad car.

For the second time that night, something is burned into my kid-brain. Mike's old man is definitely *somebody*, and the cops fear him. All the dots connect in a duh sort of way, and I understand what real power is. Paul Sarto is Mafia. Mike is his son. He is untouchable. Now that's power, something a white trash kid like me, already on probation for petty shoplifting, could only imagine. I wonder for a moment if that kind of power still exists in Bossier. Maybe buried, maybe mutated. Probably just dissipated long ago, like smoke in the wind.

My mind toggles back and forth between the here and then. I spot a billboard up ahead advertising Natchez Wheels. A big mechanical cowboy waving his arm out of the window of a high-balling truck.

Prior to this very moment, the closest I've been to Bossier in over fifty years was here, this sprawling truck stop, located just east of the state line.

That was in 1969.

I'd arrived on a cold, drizzly winter night. Two days earlier I'd been hitchhiking across eastern Colorado and got caught out in the open by a sudden, killer snowstorm that dogpiled across the Rockies and scoured the plains. Snowdrifts obscured the road as I stood there, middle of nowhere, alone in a whiteout, slowly freezing. Out of the fog came big headlights and I heard the rig's Jake brake blat out staccato coughs.

The truck and trailer rumbled by, kicking up snow swirls, slowing, hanging on by fingernails to the icy road. It stopped a couple of hundred yards down the road, emergency lights flashing red, beckoning me once again to take a road unknown. Another toss of the life-dice that is hitchhiking across the USA.

As I ran up, backpack jangling, the driver was hanging off the back of the trailer, its doors open. He tossed an apple to me, chomped another in his mouth, and jumped down and sealed up the trailer. He looked at me. "Get on in or freeze to death out here. Suit yourself. Hauling apples to Miami. Help me drive and you got a ride."

My destination, New York City, suddenly seemed like it could wait—a long time. I looked into the gathering death shroud that was this storm, and said, "If you can teach me, I'm all for it." He gave a nod toward the cab and I climbed into the passenger side.

It turned out the driver was a killer. Literally. Offed a man in Tulsa and served his time. He never learned to read. Drove by instinct. I helped him with the road signs.

"What's that say?" he'd ask, pointing at a road sign.

"Weigh station," I'd say.

So that's how I last arrived at famous Natchez Wheels, flying on pep pills, driving a 10,000-pound load, downshifting through twelve gears, double arming the big, unruly steering wheel of that White's Western Star, Jake brake complaining like a mean dog bark, rolling down I-20.

Fate intervened and I never got to Bossier. The driver, with his frayed baseball cap and six-day beard, breathed in coffee cup steam and said, "If you're still on, we're cutting south to avoid the weigh station up ahead."

So that time I called up my bro, said I was close but no cigar, and kept on driving. OJT style, down through Louisiana to New Orleans, Mobile, the Redneck Riviera, the Sunshine Highway, orange grove perfume *(God, what a sweet gift after that High Plains snowstorm!)*, and, finally, the aqua-tones and palms of Miami.

Today fate flip-flops and keeps me on track to Bossier City. I pull into Natchez Wheels, take a pit stop, grab a coffee, and observe the acres of parked rigs, the big sign with the waving cowboy trucker. A police van is parked next to a couple of semis cordoned off with fluttering strands of yellow tape.

Ominous, but not remotely my concern. All I gotta do is cover these last few miles.

CHAPTER TWENTY-SIX

BANNER'S BLOG— THE GRIST

Spyflow.com

Apparently, I will have to negotiate for my life. My lawyer says my asylum application is being "held up." I can't risk direct contacts because my former employer will use it as signal intelligence, SIGINT, to track me.

But here's the key: the dispatch that becomes this blog is as untraceable as it gets. Beyond TOR, beyond CALPHA. The technology that insures my invisibility is one the agency already knows and fears—the beta from a private company: IGT.

I'm talking to you, the NSA, here: you can't find me because of it. You don't have it. Even if you did, the quantum field that guards the Glass Box tells me if I'm being eavesdropped.

So here's my bid in our blind man's parley: we cease fire. You stop looking for me and I'll limit my revelations. I'll hold back on disclosing what I know and suspect about "Little Oz," that man behind the curtain on the KNOLL project. The man (or men) who doesn't want the truth to get out. What happens as other people find the missing pieces is somebody else's problem.

I'll even lay off of Double-Dis.

In the meantime, here's my message for the rest of the world.

I can still access Total Information Awareness. That is digital information measured not in petaflops, or even exaflops, but in Yoda-flops, if you will.

What that means is far beyond metadata. It is nothing less than each and every one of you. The grist is every bit of data you have, are now, and will ever generate. Every second, every image, every email, tweet, utterance, doctor visit, drug prescription, parking ticket, school exam, book or magazine read, website clicked. Your computer and smartphone cameras, whether you think they are on or not, are alive and watching you. Now multiply that by everything anyone else says, sees, writes, and utters about you.

This grist is milled by algorithms so sophisticated and vast that the product is as fine as cake flour, and then baked by artificial intelligence that can intuit and reconstruct you better than your closest friends, your children, your lovers or your spouse.

Maybe, quite possibly, better than you.

Your sense of self may be frail, forgetful, fallible. Their sense of you does not sleep. Your hates, your fears, your most intimate and private thoughts. Your love notes, whispers, cries, laughter, dreams, lovers.

All at my workstation.

That, my friends, is very close to where we are. It is where we already are for several million Americans. The only limitation is the relentless expansion of computing capacity in places like the TCC.

The TCC is an anonymous facility in San Antonio. It is a converted SONY chip factory retrofitted with an inner skin of copper. It sits on fifty acres, encompasses 470,000 square feet, and is next to Lackland AFB on the west side of the Alamo City (1 Sony Drive, NW Loop 410 and Military Drive, if you want to check Google Maps). The halls go so far in a straight line that "parallel" and "vanishing point" are meaningless. A hint at why it's there: Texas has an independent, highly reliable power grid and one of the cheapest large-scale electricity rates in the country. You can sense the hum of racing electrons and air-conditioning, and if you put it all together it would be a deafening roar, a Niagara Falls of information being sucked up by the giant digital vacuum that is the TCC and similar facilities in Utah, Maryland, and Oregon.

They can keep absolute tabs on anyone.

PART THREE

BOSSIER

"It is manliness. It is blood. It is forever."

–Alonzo R. Sarducci, *The Omertà Code*

"'Tis an unweeded garden, that grows to seed . . ."

–William Shakespeare, *Hamlet*, act 1, scene 2

CHAPTER TWENTY-SEVEN

BUS—FRAGMENTS

I am at the top of Texas Avenue in Shreveport, looking down at the Red River and, on the other side, Bossier City. I motor past rows of empty retail storefronts, the hub of commerce long since drained away to suburbs and big-box stores and the Internet. My vision plays with memories, sensing the desolation of proprietorships now long gone: Stan's Record Store, Lorantz Army-Navy Surplus, the Captain Shreve Hotel.

It feels like a city sleeping lazily on a riverbank, its toe tied to a limp fishing line, sometimes getting a bite, sometimes waking up, but mainly whiling away the decades.

Of course, a city that seldom changes makes for great movie sets for a local film industry that has reached takeoff speed.

I see a new sign on the side of a red brick warehouse built a hundred-plus years ago. It shows the iconic lunar boot print of Neil Armstrong, with a little, three-toed alien footprint overlaid on it, along with the stenciled words: "Surreal is Real."

Maybe a message there for me.

I reach what used to be called the Old Bridge, the Huey P. Long Bridge, that spans the Red River and enters into the completely different, netherworld of Bossier.

I trundle onto the bridge, smell the deep river smell, look over for the bateaux on the river side of the levee, where once squalid shacks had competed with the river at flood stage and alligators resided in mudholes beneath the flimsy porches.

It is all gone. The sullen Red is now dammed into a placid, green lake, the bateaux shantytown stripped clean and replaced with shiny high-rise hotels hovering next to faux riverboat casinos. A Disneyfied shopping experience of outlet stores is anchored next to a big-box Bass Pro Shop.

I slow down to get my bearings. Forgotten instincts set in. I somehow find Barksdale Boulevard and the road to my brother's place.

A few things have survived. I spot the ugly cinder block edifice that had been the infamous Davis Movie Theater, where once dwelled a fiendish, demonic collection of poor white and poor black kids on Saturday afternoons. Where once quailed a besieged theater manager, standing up on stage, stuttering and vainly pleading, imploring the kids to come under control. It was, of course, futile. At the start of the movie, the black kids, segregated up in the balcony, the "peanut gallery," threw all their popcorn, candy boxes, whatever they had down on the white kids. Pretty soon everyone is screaming, chanting "We want the show!" laughing derisively at the forlorn manager, as cherry bombs are flushed down the commodes and the sewage pipes are blown right out of the bathroom walls, gooky water spraying everywhere. Then the finale, a rain of movie theater debris hurled at the manager, a smoke bomb chucked up front, and everyone stampeding for the exits. So what if we missed the second matinee showing of *Rodan*, this was pure kid-crazy fun.

Now the Davis is boarded up, its marquee dangling on broken cables, the ticket booth ramshackle, trash accumulated in the plywood-covered entrances. Surrounded by a perimeter of chain-link fence topped with razor wire. *Pretty heavy security for an old cinderblock clunker,* I think.

Suddenly, I recognize the street to my brother's place. It leads into a subdivision huddled beneath a towering grove of pecan trees planted just after the Civil War. Time has diminished the houses and exploded the understory landscaping into house-hiding growth. I slow-mo down the block.

And there is his house. And there he is, standing at the door.

■

Eventually, like after an hour or so, I quit staring at his ridiculous, oversize, gray-flecked and dyed-brown Fu Manchu.

I settle in with the discovery, the renewed fascination that here is a chunk of flesh and blood relations, kin, right in front of me. We talk like crazy, whos and whats and what-happeneds and remember-thats. He shows me his place, the creaky, boxy three-bedroom ranch built in the baby boom of the 1950s. Over the years he's added on. Now his place is overbuilt for the neighborhood, with a three-car garage, great room with fireplace, bedecked as a mead hall. A pool swallows the backyard.

As for the neighborhood, the subdivision originally targeted white enlisted men and their families from Barksdale Air Force Base. Now it is gentrified with diverse neighbors, black, Asian, Latino, gay, and the signs of a suburb in transition—random home remodels, portable swimming pools, trampolines out front, a few yard cars, and decades of Deep South overgrowth that obscures whole sides of houses, save the chaired porches, and the willows that droop heavily onto the roofs.

As we talk, I see who my brother has become in my long absence. He's retired from teaching history in the Parish public schools. He has two aged Toyota pickup trucks. "Yeller" is of a faded, hand-painted color roughly fitting the name. "Scar" fits the other: black with bashed-up sides and no tailgate. I meet his dog, Trusty; some of his many cats, most of whom clearly regard me as an annoyance, if not outright trouble; his free-form garden, a miniature Versailles of tinkling fountains and carp pond. A few odd projects, started with the zeal of flea-market bargains, that have slowed but would never be declared failures. At the far back, well hidden, is the kind of shop every good redneck dude has, built from the finds of yard sales and the throwaway pile at unfenced construction sites. No building permit, ever.

As I unload my saddlebag in one of his bedrooms, I realize I am embarrassed—not by him, but for myself. I've been gone so long, indulged so many years of half-ass excuses, holed myself up in my little town, and let my brother grow older apart from me.

I can hear our mom imploring, "He's your only brother, so quit going after him with that hammer!" Needless to say, our daily fights growing up had been house-wrecking legends. Enough broken furniture and shattered dishware, even an occasional blood splatter, to put a John Wayne bar fight to shame.

I lost every one of those fights, except the last. On my fourteenth birthday, I bloodied his nose. He looked quizzically at the blood in his hand, then at me, and retired from the lil brother fight game.

I look at him now as he rattles on about the rain gutters getting full of leaves again, skunks getting under the house, and I see a guy who is contentedly himself, just himself, for all he is and isn't.

That simple truth slices my existential legs out from under me. I know, clear and heavy as a biblical revelation, that next to him, I am an artful fake. Worse yet, a *lawyer*. Deep inside, I have no idea who I am, even to the point of denying the question as at all relevant. Like the bluff, well, of a lawyer.

Until now.

And even now, the blather of, cut-and-run excuses of, "Gee, gotta go," is locked inside me in mortal combat with the blunt realization that I can learn a lot here.

Maybe even about myself.

We are in the backyard. He stops talking and raises his hands, showing off the evening. A gauzy curtain of southern night is descending. Smells so rich you could slice them. The nosey tang of newly mowed grass, chicken frying in an open screen-doored kitchen, whiffs of drifting barbeque smoke, and the deep bass aroma of moist, living earth. Nearby, a cicada begins playing its tireless, one-string harp and a few bats and swallows flit in the near-dark sky as Venus glistens in its vigil through the pecan branches. In the hedges, the first fireflies are winking, starting their paranormal light-show cadence—alight all at once, then dark, then the syncopated flashing that is a flawless yet unfathomable tongue.

An hour later, full dark, we make plans for tomorrow: breakfast and the nostalgia tour of Bossier. We'll use Yeller and drink lots of beer along the way.

After a quiet moment, he says, "You remember Bruce?"

"How could I forget?"

"I saw him."

I must have had some kind of stun-gunned look. He continues, "Last week. He hangs out near the Kickapoo Corner."

Another picture postcard from the past floats in my mind.

"He's alive? Here?"

"Yeah, he panhandles and pushes a grocery cart with bags and all kinds of crap."

"As in homeless? As in, we might be able to find him?"

"You got it."

This changes everything. Bruce Dumas was right there with me that night, with Sarto, the cops, the car, the box. One more span to nail down on this burning bridge.

It occurs to me, how am I going to explain all this to Mary?

CHAPTER TWENTY-EIGHT

BUS—THE TOUR

I don't. I dillydally, get ready for bed, then finally grab my cell and call her. I'm surprised. She answers. We, or at least I, talk. I tell her the easy parts, but not what I'm feeling inside. I somehow imagine she knows. What I don't imagine are her long silences. A quiet as deep as the unfathomable distance between stars hurtling toward different ends of the universe.

I do my best denial gig and shrug it off. I get to sleep around eleven, eager to see tomorrow.

At eight o'clock the next morning my brother and I are parked in a strip mall parking lot, drinking coffee from styro cups, eating fried dough.

A bag of Southern Maid Donuts sits between us. Still a bodacious indulgence. At the first bite, we can't help mimicking an old TV commercial, each of us intoning sotto voce, "Hot! Hot! Hot! Southern Maid Donuts!"

We chomp and slurp and look at the sparse traffic along Texas Avenue. A desultory flow, like the old Red River in late summer. It is sunny, with a few cumulus clouds, like grand ships billowing across a calm, blue sea. The promise of the moment is that it is about to get bright-hot and muggy. The fresh asphalt around us is already slow-cooking, giving off that poignant, petro-product smell.

We are here because this is the location of the old Kickapoo Restaurant, once an anchorage for twenty-four-hour breakfasts along the Bossier Strip. The restaurant is gone, wiped from the face of the earth.

"You think he'll be here this early?"

"No, I saw him in the afternoon. We'll hang for a moment and then circle back."

Gene points, his hand holding a styro cup and half a donut. He talks with the other half of the donut in his mouth. "Up there [chomp], by the old Huey Long Bridge, there's still a couple of the [chomp] places from the Strip. Used to be seventy or so. Now maybe a half-dozen joints even standing. Most of those [chew] are closed or changed to other businesses. Up there was the Amber Inn . . ."

"Also known as the Stagger Out?" I say.

"Yeah, hah. And right across the street here," he points, his hand again doing triple duty, "used to be Fuqua's Cycles, the badass biker shop, where the uniform of the day, every day, was duck-tails, pegged chinos, engineer boots, and cigarette packs rolled up in the sleeves of black T-shirts. Wild One, with real people instead of Brando and Marvin."

I stare, building up the image in my mind. "And, little brother, up there and off to the left a bit, was the Davis Theater. Ring a bell?"

His words flip the switch again. I see and hear, like a loop tape in Technicolor and hi-fi audio, the cherry bombs thudding in the restroom pipes, toilets exploding like Old Faithful, walls cracking and spraying liquid. Me and Bruce among a multitude of other fiendish kids wreaking havoc and discovering the insane power of the mob.

"How could I forget? I drove by yesterday."

"Well, here's the weird thing. Rumor is it's all preserved inside."

"Whattaya mean?"

"Charlie Tyner, Neon Charlie, the guy who pretty much invented the Strip, a local legend, he cleaned it up and restored it on the inside. Back in the late '70s. Then he sealed it. Tight. Now his estate is still wrangling and the place sits entombed, behind ten-foot, barbwire-topped fence."

I'm speechless.

"So, you ready for the grand tour?"

I scrunch up the empty donut sack and offhandedly chuck it toward a distant trash can. Three-pointer. I nod. "Let's roll."

We cruise a few blocks, turn off Texas and over to Shed Road. Gene slides into tour-guide monologue.

"This road ran for thirty miles, all the way out to Benton. The whole thing covered by a shed roof. So they could haul the cotton up to the gin without it getting wet in the rain."

I nod. Useful history factoid.

"The first commercial cotton gin in the United States?" I give him the Indulgent Tourist Eyebrow Lift.

"Right here in Bossier. 1843." I withhold the eyebrow.

He comes to a hard stop at an unguarded railroad crossing, the railbed cut through a thick stand of trees. Lousy visibility. He looks both ways, then goes through.

"Since when're you a school bus?"

"Never know, little brother. Southern Pacific has the right of way. They don't slow and they don't stop—for nothing. People been killed right here before. Ever since NAFTA these trains come highballin' through town at all times. The only regular one is at night, the one the locals call the 9:11."

"Some number."

"Yeah, unlucky as hell. Wanna see where we used to live?"

More turns, areas vaguely familiar by feel as much as by sight. We end up in Plantation Park, the rundown rows of apartments that we grew up in. Where the old man would go on benders and play out encores of the dreamy death dance with the three SS soldiers. Where we grew up on the white-knuckle side of falling all the way into the chasm of being, indisputably and finally, poor white trash.

The apartments have been remodeled, with new paint, but it doesn't help.

"Let's get out of here," I say. Soon we escape that dark cloud and ease into light traffic on Texas Avenue. I feel better.

We pass an auto body repair and sales lot that looks like it has given up the ghost, except for a shiny black Beemer 700-something sitting by the side door. The sign says "Sarto's Sales and Repair." I think, *that name, gotta be.*

My tour guide breaks the reverie. We're on the Strip now. "If I put my mind back," he says, "I bet I played in half, maybe thirty or so, of the old clubs along here." We make a leisurely cruise, him pointing out the paved-over, rebuilt, or ruined shells of that sinfully glorious empire. The grand emporiums of vice, most of which I recall from marveling at the extravaganzas of their lights as a kid, are virtually erased: Kim's (parking lot), The Twilight (dry cleaners), the Sho-Bar (boarded up), The Carousel, The Merry-Go-Around, The Skyway Club, the Fountain (all gone). And the Kismet (apparently now operating the front room as "Mickey's Billiards").

"Hey, look at that!" I follow his eyes to a miserable little motel huddled behind a Denny's. "It's the old Allighta Motel. Also called the Allnighta."

"So?" I said, looking at the hailed-out cars and lawn chairs propped against open doors to substitute for air-conditioning. Slutty city cousin to the Hovering Rock Inn.

"So, *that* is where Elvis stayed. Before he made it big. Before his breakout on the Louisiana Hayride. Hail yes, little brother. There's more history around here than a Quaker graveyard."

"Like?"

"Seein' as I taught Louisiana history for a dozen years, here's some more local gems. Martin Luther King gave his first 'I Have a

Dream' speech in Shreveport." He looks over at me to register my awe, or at least another raised eyebrow. This time I oblige.

"Here's another: the last capital of the dying Confederacy was in Shreveport, along with the last rebel army, E. Kirby Smith's Army of the Trans-Mississippi. They fooled the Yankee gunboats with fake cannons guarding the river. Called it Fort Humbug." His voice registers the accumulated weight of touristy factoids. "Like I said, the first commercial cotton gin in the US was in Bossier Parish. Captain Shreve opened up the Red River by blasting out a miles-long logjam called The Raft. Shreveport was once a close second to both Nashville and Memphis as a music recording center. Now this area is becoming a big movie center. It covers pretty well for Santa Monica, Washington, DC, just about anywhere. And, of course, there's this hallowed ground we're treading, the Bossier Strip."

"OK, handy tips, but they won't help me bake a cake, change a tire, or find out what the hell happened to us. You and me. So, back to the Big Question. Did Dean really meet Elvis?"

He laughs. "Sure, I knew about that. When he ran the Captain Shreve. The King showed up. Dean got him into some clubs on the strip. '62 maybe? Incognito, like the El was dressed down and wearing a flatcap and shades. Marcello met him, treated him like royalty. My friend, the guy you're gonna meet, knows all about it. He was playing there that night, at the Gold Room."

We travel another mile. Where the Strip once glittered, there are new mega-churches with parking lots measured in acres, big-box stores, medical equipment suppliers. I note a sparkling, New Age–looking Harley dealer.

"Kind of nuevo-bleak out here."

"The sin got washed away. What's left gathered down by the river. The riverboat casinos. Even there, it's antiseptic. Out here is peaceful suburbia. The last stop is coming up, there, on the left!"

I see a decayed late fifties Modern–style motel, a boxy, board-ed-up structure attached. A single car sits in the lonely parking lot.

The rusted sign, barely hanging on to its pole, says "Countryside Motel."

We pull into the lot to give some company to the one car. Then we just sit there for a while.

"This is it?" I say. "Marcello's place? Where Dean worked?"

"Yeah, wouldn't know it now. Our old man moonlighted at the front desk, kicking ass to make the place hum. Who knows what else. Maybe Marcello's family still owns this dump. In its day it was lit up Disney scale." A touch of nostalgia inflects his voice. "The *Fabulous* Gold Room."

I look up at the sky, swan's belly clouds rolling in, portending a long, slow rain. "I'm gonna come back later and check in here, just for the hell of it."

"Suit yourself. Let's finish and ease back to the Kickapoo. See if your friend shows. I bet he panhandles every afternoon near the Pick-N-Save."

Rain blips the windshield. I think about Bruce, the miracle of his being here.

■

Way back then, Bruce Dumas had two stunning aspects. The first was that he was a natural athlete, already tagged by coaches, even Landry, as a future all-state fullback. He had game, and was supremely confident about it.

The second, highly unlikely aspect, was that we were best friends. I was his opposite: gangly, skinny, cerebral, shy, a couple of years from getting my own growth.

Whatever wan light I possessed just added to his glow. Maybe we'd end up with me as his wingman, Spock to his Captain Kirk, Tonto to his Lone Ranger, Robin to his Batman. Right now I was pretty much just a goofy sidekick. As friends, however, we shared a secret passion, a luminous belief that we were inexorably headed to some great destiny, some golden moment of ruling that would sprout from the hot Southern nights and our fevered adolescent awakening in Bossier City. The portents were there. Football immortality awaiting him. Me? Miraculously, I'd just gotten a date with the Barksdale Commander's daughter, a future Miss Teenage America finalist. So hope there too.

That time was so perfect. Just like fireflies. And in two weeks it all blew to hell.

A week after my sudden abduction to Junction City, with no more goodbyes to anybody than a departing Fuller Brush salesman, a similar fate befell him.

He was an Air Force brat, and if that means anything, it means moving. Sometimes abruptly. His dad had served at Barksdale a long time, but he was in intelligence, and whatever went on, the gears clicked and orders came, and they were gone to Palo Alto, California, in a week. Some hotshot project hidden in an obscure research building tucked away in an arroyo in the foothills around Stanford.

Any other kid would've thought California, yeah! And felt he'd gone to heaven. It didn't work out that way for Bruce. Maybe he was too arrogant, maybe his trace of Louisiana accent made him a bit of a joke. However it happened, football, the defining thing in his life, busted out. Coach's favorites, whatever, he never got past second string. Meanwhile those same teammates back in Bossier *did* get a state championship, *made* all-state, *got* glory. Glory that was his destiny and of which he was robbed.

The firefly lost its light.

In time, he found another luminous glow. It's all chemicals, right? So why not just tune in, turn on, and light up your mind? As for reality, drop out.

So he became—in sync with legions who saw Timothy Leary as a guru—a full-on psychedelic doper. Nothing was too strong, nothing he wouldn't try. Of course, he had a favorite, oh yes, and on one mighty occasion I was to become intimately acquainted with it.

Fast forward a couple of years. We've hooked up with big plans for me coming out to that warm California sun. I quit my miserable gas station job in Junction City, get on my first motorcycle, a ridiculous little Yamaha 250 cc two-cycle rice rocket. It's an early, cold June. To avoid the rain and freezing wind, I ride the draft of huge eighteen-wheelers going eighty miles an hour through the night. I'm trailing three or four feet behind the rear bumper where they can't see me. If they even touch the brakes, I'm dead meat. I let their draft suck me in, pull me deadly close in a shelter of warm, whirling air. Like hugging the vortex of a highballing cyclone. Insane, but it works.

I make it to the Sierras and the bike throws a timing chain and dies.

Two hitchhiking days later, I'm there: San Francisco. June, 1967. Summer of Love. Foggy morning with a seeping cold confirming Mark Twain's remark about June in San Francisco being the coldest winter he ever spent. Smells of docks and fish and wharfside ocean. Corner of Haight and Ashbury. Ground zero for the psychedelic revolution. I'm standing where Bruce said to meet, next to Glucken's Grocery, and he comes up and I don't recognize him. He has long black hair, unwashed curls, sandals, a full beard. Sort of Jesus-like. Except Jesus didn't wear opaque wire-frame shades and a paisley headband.

"Look, man," I remember him saying, sort of slow and guru-like. "I'm up *here* . . . and you're down *there*." His hands, one above his head, one below his waist, demonstrate the ladder rungs of our disparity, especially the sorry, pedestrian, unexpanded state of my lowly, straight consciousness. "We gotta get you up *here*. With me." His low hand rockets up to the other.

In hindsight, I believe the thought actually crossed my mind that this could be incredibly stupid. That he's a doper and I'm a roper, if you know what I mean. The instinctual warning evaporated as we moved into the crowd.

"Stay close, I'll tell you what to do," he says. The place is jammed, young people sitting down, laying down, selling beads and flowers on the street. The air redolent: burning hemp, patchouli, BO. The whispered sales pitch of "Lids, grass, hash. Lids, grass, hash" refrains every few feet. This is a river of easy drugs.

Bruce puts a hand on my shoulder, eyes a wary couple of hippies that look like serious purveyors. He says, "Gimme your money. Stay here, you're straight." He says it like it's a profound disability. "You'll freak 'em out." I shell out my little wad. He goes over. They talk. I overhear words like "tabs or caps?" They look around, furtive hands passing. Bruce checks his palm.

He scores six caps of industrial-strength, pure, authentic Owsley Blue Dot lysergic acid diethylamide. The Good Housekeeper's Seal of Approval, the Underwriter's Laboratory-certified Gold Standard of acid. Each single capsule guaranteed to blow your mind. The creator, Owsley, was already a legend. The tale tells of a fugitive chemist with mobile lab facilities. He had just made the FBI's Ten Most Wanted list.

We promptly drop three caps each. I figure out later that this is like letting your sanity do high trapeze without a net.

I am never the same again.

So that's how I got these flashbacks, these little replays of that cosmically strange trip. To remind me, I guess, but of exactly what I'm uncertain. To ensure that I never forget that Alice-world, alien-abduction, feeling? To know forever the sheer sensation of drowning in the translucent, bottomless waters of some fall-down heaven?

To tell the truth, where I went and how long it took is a maze, parts of which I'm still too scared to remember. It was a Trip of Trips.

But here's where it ended: a rock concert, night, music by Country Joe and the Fish, light show by Diogenes Lantern Works. A dense, sweating, throbbing crowd. Guest cameo by Grace Slick, working through the throng with her Stratocaster held aloft like the torch of rock 'n' roll truth.

All this is seen through my eyes that had somehow perfectly evolved into fish-eye lenses. One hundred eighty-degree vision. People were big luminescent aura-blobs, like bubbles in a lava lamp.

By this time, I'm coming down, mellowing and groovin', feeling hyper observant, occasionally drifting up to the ceiling to get a bird's-eye view of myself.

Suddenly I am on the floor. Big moon face in front of me. Mustache, no-eyes mirror shades, mean acne scars (which I ponder for quite a while, the pits being sort of lunar in their depth and concentration). The face is talking, framed by a white riot helmet with an upturned visor.

It dawns on me. *Cop.* I raise my hands in passive, friendly, cooperative supplication. He cramps one wrist in a control grip, rolls me over, and cuffs me. I can hear the tumblers clank, as deep and echoing as dungeon gates.

"Quit yelling!" he yells.

I ask, in what seems my quietest, least aggressive voice, "Who's yelling?"

He whacks me with his baton and now I'm definitely back, awake, sober, and hurting like hell. Blood oozes and then cuts a rivulet down my face.

I think I see what's happening. Maybe even why I was (maybe) yelling. A commotion in the crowd, people giving a hard time to the riot cops, cries of "Pig! Let him go!" Then the crowd parts, torn by hard-ass cops in riot gear, followed by a bunch of guys in white coats. They are hospital orderlies, bustling through like a conga line. Six of them are carrying horizontally a long, human-size white pupae. It is wriggling and squirming. They are struggling to control it. Then I see it's not really a giant wriggling insect. It is Bruce in a full straightjacket, only his head protruding, vicious and screaming with flying globs of spittle.

"I AM AN AMERICAN! You cannot do this to me! I AM AN AMERICAN!"

They go right by me. His eyes catch mine. I'm powerless. At this point, I'm kneeling. I rotate my cuffed hands to the side and show him and plead and cry for someone, something to save us. Time has stopped. Just the echoes of his screams, howls like those of a caged animal. Nothing is going to save us. Not now. They carry him away. He has gone *there*. All the way this time.

The last I ever see of Bruce is his feet doing futile little kicks where they stick out of the white cocoon. That singular image will stay with me forever. My best friend going over to the far side of the river of reality, enshrouded in white, ferried by insane-asylum orderlies.

Months later he writes from the California State Mental Hospital at Piedmont. Someone had cut out portions of the letter. He is doing better. He no longer thinks he is a new species. He isn't the New Psychedelic Man. Then comes the killer part. "Why didn't you save me?"

I write back.

I never hear from him again.

Fifty-some years later, I am back in our old 'hood of Bossier City. My brother and I are hanging at the once-famous Kickapoo Corner. We are looking for Bruce, hoping he's on a daily schedule.

We stand around, drifting over to an awning to avoid occasional raindrops.

This goes on for a half hour, when around the far corner of the mall emerges a figure trundling a grocery cart. A couple of the wheels are sticking, like the Dealey Oracle's rig. He forces the cart onto its path, pushing the beast from the side.

The figure gets closer, and somehow I recognize him. A quirk in the shoulders, an attitude of the head. He has scraggly, gray hair that tries to flow back to a ponytail, but is so thin on top that it becomes a sad, bedraggled halo. He is stooped and he shuffles and mutters.

I walk up to him but he pays no attention to me. He stinks, fetid, as if the plastic bags on his cart carry something foul. I touch his shoulder. "Bruce?" He looks up through strands of loose hair that stick to his bulbous, alkie's nose. The eyes go from annoyance to what I'm sure is a glimmer of recognition. *Hello, my old friend*, I start to say. We are finally gonna connect, meet and shake hands on that burning bridge.

He stares at me for a long moment, and says, "What the fuck you want?"

I admit that's not what I expected. Shock? Surprise? Maybe even an "Oh my . . . God!" of pleasant recognition. But this?

I clutch at the chance he's confused, doesn't recognize me. "Bruce, it's me. Bus. Your old buddy? Remember? Football, Coach Landry?" I whisper a last stamp of authenticity. "The Country Joe Concert?"

He levels a stare at me with eyes that tell me he knows exactly what he is about to say. Like he's been waiting a long time to say it. If he can remember it.

I stop.

He fumbles in the wild assemblage of plastic bags tied to his cart. They look like giant, dirty fungi. He is mumbling now, like the insane homeless person I'd secretly prefer at this point. Addled. A kind of modern Ben Gunn long marooned on the Treasure Island of his seafaring consciousness.

He triumphantly holds up one of the bags, unties it, reaches in, and thrusts a crumpled bit of cloth in the air. I know what it is. It's the red athletic letter—a boxy "G"—we all wore in that last game. A pitiful little memento, artifact of a life long ago gone off the rails. "See this!" He shakes it in front of my face, and asks once more, "Why didn't you save me?"

I feel myself getting frustrated, losing this moment. "I couldn't! I was cuffed! I didn't abandon you!"

His eyes are once again rheumy, evasive as minnows. I reach out and tap his shoulder. He shudders, sweeps my hand away and finger-stabs my chest. The minnows are gone, replaced by wolf eyes. "You were there. You, you and my parents. You left me to rot in the puzzle palace. Wanna know the diagnosis, the bottom line? 'He went too far.' What kind of quack says that? I finally got sent to a halfway house. Thanks to Reagan. I just walked away and . . . nobody gave a shit! Nobody ever gives a shit!"

This is going south fast. Gene pulls me back, but I blurt out a final question. "Where are you living, sleeping?"

He ponders that, dubious about whether to answer, then says, flat and simple, "The Davis." He turns to manage his plastic bags, dismissing me.

We leave him standing there, raindrops dripping off his nose, dithering like Ben Gunn once again.

CHAPTER TWENTY-NINE

BANNER'S BLOG— DRZ

SPYFLOW.COM

They are still trying to hack me, find me. So, no truce. I'll keep on blogging. Today I want to talk about missing information.

For the NSA, it's harder to destroy data than to collect it. The whole edifice is based on absolute acquisition—each, all, every, whenever, wherever, forever. Loss of data is bad. Destruction of data is a sin. Deresolution, *derez,* DRZ, is biblical, Tron-level heresy.

The only reason to *derez* data—find it and dissolve it into nothingness without any recoverable trace, without *remanence*—is to hide something. Or somebody. Maybe for "deep concealment." Maybe for reasons forever unknown. The office favorite was a guy named "Owsley," a 1960s drug manufacturer who was on the FBI's Most Wanted list. Aside from a bad picture, there was no record of him. No date or place of birth, hair, eye color, driver's license, fingerprints, etc. Nothing. A ghost, and he stayed that way, finally becoming a kind of cult hero, surviving as a footnote to the Grateful Dead, or as a character in obscure books like *Mirkwood.* More on that later.

Older data destruction techniques such as file deletion, over-writing, degaussing, local-pulse, media destruction, are quaint and ineffectual. Even data "in the cloud" exists at some, usually mani-fold, points in time and space. These may shift, but you have to find and trash the data everywhere it exists. The NSA's current system, DRZ, is based on tagging the data and encrypting it, then destroy-ing the keys to the encryption. Essentially casting it into the void.

After I compiled and isolated certain data, namely the Bell South phone records of eleven calls made by Carlos Marcello's lawyer, Mike Maroon, to Lee Harvey Oswald, David Ferrie, and Jack Ruby, along with a flurry of calls from the Captain Shreve Hotel, Room 949, and Room 218 in the Countryside Motel in Bossier City, Louisiana, all on November 20-23, 1963, they directed me to DRZ all the information, everywhere it existed. I did. Except for one place: my own files. That's when I started making the plans that led me to here. Of course, here could be anywhere. Maybe even a house across the street from the TCC in San Antonio.

OK, NSA, how's that for a taunt?

CHAPTER THIRTY

BUS—MUDBUGS

I'm shaken, still sorting through the encounter with Bruce when we arrive at Mudbugs. Gene and I sit in Yeller. What is now a light drizzle plays a jazz riff on its roof.

"Let it go, little brother, he's . . . confused."

"I can't just let this go. Where the hell does he even sleep?"

"He said where. Maybe the Davis. Come on."

We get out and lumber through a potholed parking lot with dappled pools reflecting red-and-blue neon. They make goo-goo eyes at us. The rain disregards my collar and sends a rivulet down my neck. An outdoor sign buzzes a beautifully simple message: "Crawdads. Cold Beer."

That sounds damn good to me.

The place is open-air and tin-roofed, giving off a languid pattern of rainy splats and thunks that mingle with clinking mugs and the steady whomp-whomp of a circular fan imbedded in a swamp cooler on the wall. Behind the bar is a huge copper pot, big enough to boil a man. Pulleys and chains lift the lid and basket. Up comes the lid, a cloud of succulent steam erupts into a hot, moist sea-spicy smell. The basket, holding thousands of red-armored crawfish, is hoisted up. You lift your nose, just to savor the air. We sit at the bar and the waitress—raven hair, green eyes and freckles, a Cajun version of Daisy Mae—flashes an inquiring smile. We don't need to say a thing. Just nod. She gets a big scoop and puts it in the basket and spills a pile of boiled crawfish on an extra-large pizza tin. She ferries this over, followed by mugs of cold beer.

Silently, we set to, just as big hands clasp our backs. "Gotcha, Teach!"

Gene jumps, then looks around. "Chief, son-of-a-bitch! You still got that talent for sneaking up."

The man standing there is impressive. Not too tall, but built like a bull. Black hair nicely cropped, dark brown eyes, a squared-off face with high cheeks and a big noble nose that Caesar would envy. Maybe a cousin to Iron Eyes Cody or Wes Studi.

"Careful, White-Eyes," the man whose name is Caddo says, "I lift what little hair you got." He looks at me. I got none. "This guy, he can't be your brother. No hair. Looks too smart."

We shake hands, my fingers feel like they are being squeezed by a rock. They talk shop, catching up on which band guys from the old days are alive, who has the most bum-luck story. Drugs, diabetes, narcolepsy, car wrecks, divorce. And, always, broke. No money and lots of broken dreams. The usual calamities for musicians.

I look at them and I see survivors. My brother always had his day job, shoveling American history to ninth graders. Caddo is more of a question, but he's clearly doing his thing, whatever that is. Pinkie ring with nice rocks, fresh haircut, designer polo shirt that would command a hundred easy at Nordstrom's. A little odd because it is long-sleeved. All in all, not bad for a semiretired musician.

Gene gives a plug about my pro bono legal work for tribes. He brags that my firm sponsors an annual powwow near a traditional "Council Tree" in Colorado. The Ute tribe got run off in 1880, but the sacred tree stayed. A massive, two-hundred-year-old cottonwood still greening up every spring. He lets on about another tale: me versus the city fathers. Caddo jumps in, asks a lot of questions about the tree. I wrap up with: "The tree's now on a half-acre nature preserve. Tribal members still drive their pickups there, do their ceremonies, collect any fallen tree limbs, and carry them back to the rez. Sacred stuff."

He is thinking, and says just two words, "Yeah, sacred."

I follow up, "What's your Tribal Nations heritage?"

"Well, as Gene here knows, I'm not Caddoan. Just one of those handles you get. Caddo Bill, Chief, Two Hatchets, hell, even Tonto. No problem by me, 'cause I always adapt. I make folks . . . comfortable. Played on the Strip long before black musicians got in."

We're rolling along now, shucking crawdad tails, dippin' five-alarm Louisiana hot sauce, and washing it all down. Gene gives Daisy Mae a signal. More of everything.

"So, to answer your question, mostly Kickapoo. Too many syllables for a nickname. You ever hear of them?"

I think of the parking lot we were at this morning. The long-vanished diner. The image on the sign, a clichéd chief in profile with full warbonnet regalia. I nod.

"We, my clan anyway, never signed a peace treaty. Just kept moving—a hundred years, two thousand miles. Pennsylvania, Minnesota, Ohio, Missouri, Kansas, Texas—where we whupped up on the Confederates at Dove Creek. Then, finally . . ." he stops to drink and clean up his hands with a toilette wipe, "finally deep into Mexico. Some as far as Zacatecas. Our name means 'wanderer.'"

I see him in a new light. His people always distinct even as they were mixing in with different cultures. I imagine them using a veil of assimilation as a tool to survive, to keep and hide their inner identity. "You ever visit your people?"

He looks up, casual, swallows some beer.

"Naw, not much. They don't recognize us, our family, as real tribal members. Old records shit." He lets that sit. It feels way too abrupt so he continues. "I sometimes visit the rez. Oklahoma." He nods toward what I guess is northwest.

Gene finishes a crawdad, sucks the head, and joins in. "Caddo's part medicine man, maybe witch doctor. Anyway, he knows the spells."

I can't tell if they are pulling my leg.

"Yeah?"

Caddo lowers his voice, registering for credibility. "My grandfather was a shaman. For real. Taught me. Sometimes we did it for white guys, for money. They don't believe it, but we do. Sometimes that's enough. If the white man buys it, it can also go away. If we decide so." He's looking at me with a witch doctor grin that lacks only pointy, filed teeth. He's sizing up my reaction.

"So what's *it*?"

"Spells, magic, good luck, hoodoo. Protection. Keeping secrets safe."

I nod, go with it, ask the big question. "OK, so you still believe in your medicine?"

He keeps the grin, reaches for his shirt front and systematically undoes a half-dozen buttons. He pulls his shirt open, subdued, Superman-style. I see an indecipherable swarm of tattoos and something else. On each side of his chest is a scar, maybe two inches long, deep. I know what they are. They are rare. "The Sun Dance," I say. "It's illegal, the old way." I look at my brother, hold up my hands, fingers curved like eagle claws. "Pierced." I say that with respect.

Gene is looking, slow on the uptake. I help him out. "Think of the old movie, *A Man Called Horse*, Richard Harris. Guy gets raised up by ropes attached to his chest muscles by eagle claws. They finally tear out, you get those scars."

Caddo says, "That answer your question Kemosabe? About believing?"

This moment quiets things way down. The shirt front gets

buttoned up, the witch doctor grin goes away, we eat and drink. The conversation drifts back to music.

"Yeah," Gene is saying. "Caddo and I played all the clubs on the Strip. He's one hell of a bass man. We laid down the rails for all kinds of music for a couple of decades."

Seems like the time is good as any, so I get to the point. "Gene tells me you knew Carlos Marcello."

"The Little Man? Hell yes. We, your brother and I, had the house band at the Gold Room for two years straight. Marcello came up from south Louisiana pretty regular. To get away from the FBI down there, I'd guess, and oversee his gold mine on the Bossier Strip. He liked to chum it up with the band, buy us drinks, all that. Talked to me a bunch, saying 'we're related, 'cause Sicilians were wanderers too.' Nice guy. Loved cigars. One thing, though. Once you're part of his organization, you never leave. And you don't cross him, ever."

"Like the Kennedys did?" Now I'm coming across pushy, but I stick with it.

He looks at me like this might finally be a line-crossing question. "Yeah, maybe. You writing a book?" He eyes Gene, looking for an OK. Gene gives it.

I'm answering. "No, just trying to piece some things together."

Caddo weighs this for a moment. "Well, he had lots of . . . different visitors at the club and the Countryside next door. Suits, politicians, military brass, Cubans, lots of Mafiosos. Plus all their entourage."

"Maroon?"

"Oh yeah, Mike. The lawyer. Marcello's front. Ran the club, always pretending to be a big shot when the boss was away."

"How about . . . oh, Lee Harvey Oswald?"

He looks at Gene, does an uh-huh nod, and manufactures a knowing smile at me. "I knew it! You're a conspiracy nut! No worries. I go to the JFK-conspiracy convention in Dallas every year.

Gonna be *huge* this year! I keep up on who's figuring out what. Look, let me give you a piece of advice: all the clues, whatever, are long gone by now. Like they say, someone would've talked. Whaddya care?"

"I'm working on some personal questions."

"Like what?"

"My old man was . . . involved."

He looks at Gene. "The desk clerk guy? Your stepdad?"

Gene winces. "Hardly."

Caddo looks back at me. "All I know is Maroon was always bitching about him. Errand boy for Marcello, then he scrammed out somewhere. End of that story. Anyway, I'll give you a Marcello story." He takes a dramatic pause, then says, "Elvis."

He lets another beat pass. He takes a deep breath, ready to roll with this little jewel. "One night these goons come into the club and clear out the patrons, leave the band and all the girls. In the back door, dressed like a nobody off the street, walks The El. Marcello knows he's coming, treats him like royalty. King to King. Then there are a bunch of pops and flashes and I see a newspaper guy with a camera, somehow got in. I thought they were gonna kill him. Some night, yessir, huh Gene?"

"I've heard the story enough I think I was there. But I wasn't. I was laid up, maybe flu or something. Missed a week of gigs."

It isn't lost on me that Caddo hasn't answered the question about Oswald. Then I get surprised.

"Anyway, I'm 'bout done. You wanna know about Marcello? Most people don't know. Or they even say he was never involved with Bossier. The Chamber of Commerce and the big casinos want to paint a pretty picture of this town. Old history, like the Mob, even the Strip, is, well, unsavory."

"Caddo, I still would like to know. Any thoughts?"

"I don't know anything about that. But there is one guy, ex-Mafia family, gone legit. Entertainment promoter, investor, all that.

Big talker, 'cept he can back it up. Some of the old-timers in his entourage might know something." He pauses, looks around, "You oughta meet him. Mike Sarto."

I can tell from how Gene and Caddo look at me that my jaw just dropped. "Hell," I say. "I know, knew the guy."

"Well, pick up this tab and I can set up a meeting. I'm sure he'd like to see you." He looks at Gene. "Chow down *ami*. I'm gonna make a phone call." He looks over to Daisy Mae, who is watching us closely, "*Melette, plus biere, s'il plait.*"

The guy's got more hidden sides than a deck of one-eyed jacks.

CHAPTER THIRTY-ONE

BANNER'S BLOG— THE IGT GUY

SPYFLOW.COM

I mentioned IGT earlier. Here's what it is and how it happened. You got to understand that the NSA is a hall of mirrors. I start spying on people (within my mission at KNOLL, of course), the agency spies on me spying on those people, I spy on them spying on me spying, on and on. You get it.

Anyway, the letters stand for I-Gig-Tam. That's Inupiat for "secret berry patch," an important piece of proprietary information if you're an Eskimo living on a subsistence diet. Anyway, as I said before, I met the guy who developed it. Goes by "Richard." He was at the Wiretapper's Ball, where a lot of those unaccounted for black ops' billions get spent. Edwin and I sat at a table with him. He's a geek's geek, a retro-nerd lacking only the pocket protector and slide rule holder on his belt. Yes, he had tape on his glasses. He didn't have a booth, and his business card was a translucent piece of plastic. No writing. Only an imbedded chip.

But his technology was interesting: a suite of vicious anti-spy tools.

First, he said, was the Komodo Dragon. Someone hacks you—Russian, Chinese, Korean, whatever—they unknowingly get infected. The virus stays with the hacker. It progressively spreads. The relentless Komodo Dragon follows the hacker's trail, doubles back and picks it up elsewhere on the net if necessary, and keeps working until the hack is sick and dying. The Dragon finishes it off.

The whole scheme is currently illegal, and likely to hurt some innocent bystanders. To that he said, "As General Grant observed, war is hell."

Second, IGT has an encryption system that is better than TOR. All but unbreakable, and even if broken into, it has a quantum detector to alert for intrusions. If Heisenberg is right, you can't fool a photon into believing that you're not looking at it.

The guy said that NSA demanded that he imbed a "back door" for their access. He refused.

Last I heard, he got harassed with a surprise audit from the IRS and driven into bankruptcy. He sold out and went off the grid, to some remote place in Colorado called Sinbad Valley. IGT holds some patents. The NSA is trying to steal his technology.

Meanwhile, he's an unofficial fugitive from the NSA. There are lots of them. Some don't even know that the truck has hit them. Anyway, the IGT guy, they broke him.

The stock and patents ended up in the hands of a small-town lawyer in Colorado. Like Dorothy, like Bilbo, the lawyer is a small person who happened to fall into a bigger story.

The Glass Box got me into every digital file in that lawyer's office, the attorney-client privilege being immaterial to my search.

So far, I've got to admire the guy. He's Mulder to my Scully. He sees the connection and believes first. He'll jump in feet first. Leaving me as the skeptic.

He thinks he's checking out his father's history, some old relationships in Bossier City. Someone should warn the poor bastard he's swimming in a lagoon full of sharks.

CHAPTER THIRTY-TWO

BUS—MEETING SARTO

At eight the next morning, Caddo leaves me a text. The meeting with Sarto is on.

At ten, the air is clear and muggy, heating up like an empty radiator. Alone in Gene's truck Scar, I pull up to an unmarked side entrance to the sprawling horse racetrack known as Bayou Downs. I'm looking forward to this. Get some info, catch some nostalgia, a secret part of me wanting to size up Mike Sarto, maybe climb a rung on that adolescent pecking order.

The Downs is a track of regional renown that mints money as a racino. The ponies are kept on pretty much for legal show, so to speak. The real action is in the army of slots I glimpse as I pass by the main entrance.

Buses coming from a 200-mile radius are already unloading the day gamblers. Retirees, rest home patrons, bored housewives, jobless types with enough dough to play the cheap slots and do the buffets.

I walk up to the side door, look at the people, think maybe they're doing a movie today. Three middle-aged goombahs are loitering outside the door. Gassed back hair, big shades, jogging suits.

One suit is brown, one blue. The third is an atrocious purple with white piping down the legs and sleeves. Tones befitting a dying bird.

I must be expected—because, first thing as I walk up, they come along each side, spin me around, and frisk me. They bend me over. Invasive fingers check behind my scrotum. An unexpected penetration up my wazoo. I flinch and get shoved. Guy in the dead-bird purple suit. Asshole, so to speak.

Purple Suit extends an arm, gesturing for me to go forward. He finishes with another mild shove to my back. "Top floor. He's waiting." I turn to look at his smirk, then go forward. I'm thinking the guy's way too old-school when I hear him say, just loud enough, "Fuckin' lawyer," to my back. I decide not to counter with my own pleasantries. Suddenly, I'm not feeling too optimistic about rung-climbing.

Through the door is a little lobby, an air-conditioned oasis with an open elevator. I go in, push the up button, and feel the ride. The door opens to a tasteful sign that says "Turf Club." Behind the sign is an expanse of white linen on empty tables. I look around for some version of the Mike Sarto I remember—sitting in the driver's seat, cutting an attitude somewhere between snot-nosed and arrogant, hair with a duck's ass, in a car that two traffic cops know is dirty in every respect. Mud all over, Texas plates, no registration—which means stolen—driver intoxicated and driving reckless. Just ran a pair of reds. You don't walk from that.

But, as I've recounted, Mike did.

I scan around. Actually, I gawk. Near as I can tell, there is only one guy in the place. He's at a far, far table, a hard, black silhouette against an immense bank of sunbright windows overlooking the clubhouse turn.

The silhouette studies me as I take the long, beggarly walk. When I get near, my eyes still adjusting, the figure stands and makes a grand gesture of open arms. Big hug time. I step to the side, so

I can see him. Yeah, it's Mike. Still with those killer good looks. Still those jarring blue eyes. His hair is full and dark, gray in a few decorous spiffs. He smiles with white teeth and calmly buttons his night-blue suit coat. Cut to fit. Italian. Five grand, rock bottom, even in a recession. He should've gone to fat by now, like how I remember his old man, but he is liposuction trim. Six buttons on the suit coat, middle-top buttoned, the others laying easy on a flat belly. White shirt and gray tie to finish the look. Man on his game. Some guys just got it forever.

"Bus!" He does the magnanimous, big-smile, open-arms thing again, gestures to a chair. Bling flashes on his cufflinks.

"Sit down. Get you something to drink. Eat?" A waiter appears as if from thin air. To stay in the spirit, I order a Moretti, the beer with someone's nice Italian uncle on the label, guy wearing a green hat. Sarto looks me over. "Long, long time. I'm having trouble remembering how you looked back then."

"No reason to. I was second, hell, third string."

"Yeah, that's right. The smartass. We had a good time, good jokes. I liked you. But, man, you were *skinny*. You got your growth somewhere. Shame you moved away. Funny thing about that team, Coach Landry kind of put his brand on us. We never wanted to lose again. The rest of us, we all stayed together and went on to the new school, Flightline High. Brand new. Won state as seniors. Kicked ass. Our scrawny backfield, you remember, Bertrand and Hebert, ended up the state's leading rusher and scorer. Touchdown twins. Those assholes from TO Rusheon that kicked our asses all went to old Bossier High. Never went anywhere. We beat 'em every year."

I am a sucker for listening to this stuff. "Yeah, but you know what we were?"

"Yeah, Bus, *strictly . . . junior . . . high.*"

We laugh and I look at him and I realize what a slob I am. Neither one of us needs to say anything, it's that evident. He is wearing his plumage. I might as well be wearing a wifebeater and Carhartt overalls, maybe unpacked from a paper sack in the stinky lavatory at the back of a Greyhound bus. Come to think of it, I'm not wearing much better.

OK, I think, *my shirt has a collar.*

He knows what I know. "Don't look at the suit, Bus. You were always smart, but you were also a white trash gawker."

Just like that, I'm falling into that junior high pecking order. Alphas, betas, zetas. I've learned a few things since, one being to shut up and listen. I nod and sample Signor Moretti's brew.

"Whatever happened to your buddy, Bruce, the fullback? He could've been all-state too. He moved away that year too."

"He moved to Cal." I pause for a moment. Out of respect for Bruce sitting homeless not ten miles from here, I lie. "We lost track."

The waiter brings me a fresh beer, just in case. Mike's amber drink, no doubt a rare single malt, waits untouched.

We talk awhile, which amounts to him talking and me deflecting with polite comments and questions. He alludes to his promotion business, gets his mouth rolling. I start to see where he changed. From JD to Divo. As I ponder the transformation, he stops and finally takes a sip. "No shit, Bus, I'm glad you're here. Actually, I pulled up the info on you."

I find this gearshift troubling, but go with it. "Oh? How?"

"Google, Facebook, LinkedIn, Martindale-Hubbell. You're not hard to find. You've done OK compared to the goofballs we hung out with."

I doubt this is just a compliment.

"You're a lawyer, figured out your own money game. I like that. That Leaks 2.0 thing, that's a tough break."

I must've stiffened.

"Don't tense up. I'm not stalking you. Hear me out." He leans forward, his hands in prayerful repose. He solemnly spreads them on the table. I know damn well he's been stalking me. He is about to make a point.

He stops at the sound of a chair scraping somewhere, as of some-body getting up. Boot heels clacking slow and steady. I glance back and see a tallish figure, maybe my age, a hick, coming out from a far corner of the room. He's heading our way, deftly winding through tables and chairs. Boot heels signaling a hard man's walk.

I turn around for a fuller view. Despite the noisy boots, the guy is moving with a silky, dangerous smoothness. The boots look damn expensive. Not so the rest. He's wearing a brown T-shirt with "FUQUA CYCLES" emblazoned on big gold wings. Dragon tats coil on his arms. He wears a busted-down baseball cap. Thin gray ponytail out the back. And something that stops me cold.

Beneath the brim are eyes that aren't eyes. To call them black holes would be a cosmic understatement. They are power-siphons from the Land of Naught.

I hear a distant finger snap. I look back at Sarto as he raises an impatient hand, shoots a mean index finger at the man, then gives an open palm. The man stops, just a hint of insolence in his atti-tude. Sarto juts a thumb hard to the side. Just like that, the man pivots to leave. The clacks recede until the kitchen door whooshes open and closed.

My neck hairs won't go back down.

"Who's your cowboy?" I ask.

"Him? Just a harmless old guy we keep around the ranch. Totally harmless."

Somehow, I don't believe a word of that. I decide to get into this conversation. "So, Mike, what're you *really* doing these days?"

He stares at me, gauging something. "I was gonna tell ya. What ya think, gambling? All that shit, extortion, protection, numbers, girls, dope? It's over. My old man's stuff. He ran all that in north Louisiana for a person of . . . mutual interest."

This is getting direct pretty fast. Fine with me. However he knows my shit, he's got me tagged. I go with it. "Yeah," I say. "The Little Man."

"Don't let him catch you saying that."

"The guy's dead."

"Never count a man like that out."

I look at him and scrunch my face like he's daft. "Anyway," he says, "my old man never made nothin' in terms of real money. So I changed. I started with the promotion business. The trick is getting the engagements. There's a knack."

"I bet. So, Mike, getting to it. It's been a long time. Every conceivable statute of limitations has run. No eyewitnesses around. It's just stuff for the history books now."

"You're getting ready to ask me something."

"Yeah."

"So ask."

"Your father worked for Marcello. Did he, Marcello, do Kennedy? Who else am I gonna ask?"

"So you're asking me about my old man?"

"Yes, and mine. Mine worked off and on for Marcello. Something went on. Remember that car you had, after the TO Rusheon game?"

An echo of something whispers across his face. Back then the cops would've called Pauli Sarto right after they stopped us. I imagine Pauli, in his own wifebeater shirt, slapping the hell out of his kid for joyriding in that car. Like my old man, a generational thing. I see my own father's belt coming off, snapping angrily through the last belt loop, the awful command, *Drop your pants, grab your fucking ankles!* The belt doubled in half, the arm rising . . .

"So . . ."

"Huh?"

"So you wanna write a history book?"

"Maybe. What I really want . . . I just wanna know."

"I read about your last try at a book. *Hollywood Reporter*, the Tolkien thing. What's the name?"

"*Mirkwood*."

"Yeah, lots of controversy. Amazon best seller list. Briefly. Couple of awards. How's the movie deal coming?"

The guy has me pegged. "They're pitching it as a TV series. *DaVinci Code* meets *Game of Thrones*. You know, *We love your book, we change it all.*"

I sense it's deal time. "You angling for a signed copy? I got a better idea. Let's us actually do a book. A tell-all story, Mike."

He looks like his mind is gazing through binoculars, seeing a world far beyond his usual range. He starts to talk with a different tone, like a guy for whom sincerity is an untested, alien thing. Trying it out. "Tell you the truth—and you let on to anyone I'll kill you—I'm not too proud of what went on in my family. Lotsa rough stuff and, like I said, no . . . *wealth*. Nothing to show but bodies dumped in the sloughs. You showed up at a good time, Bus. I'm thinking of making changes. I been thinking big. You know Silk Road?"

"Yeah, they got busted."

He drifts away, musing to himself, then comes back, "I don't need those guys out front. They're expensive. They're dumb asses. I need IT guys, a CTO. I should outsource my little muscle group, farm it to the Rosinis in Dallas. No decent vice left around here anyway. Grass is essentially legal. Hard drugs are tied up with the Mexicans. I'm gonna let them all go."

I wait a polite moment. "Mike, you gonna tell me what really came down?"

"I got one better. Lots better. You own a company owns some patents, right?"

I didn't see this coming.

"You give me the stock, those patents of yours. Connect me with the guy that invented it. Then I'll tell you something you *really* wanna know."

The guy doesn't beat around. I hesitate, wondering what else he knows about me. Maybe some dirt on me and Mary. Who knows?

"You carry a gun, Bus?"

Another non sequitur, just to keep me off balance. "Yeah, I got a concealed license. I'm sure you know that."

He waves one hand. "I don't believe in licenses. Too much red tape."

"You, Mike? You one of those antigun people?"

He gives me that here-comes-a-story look. "So, you know I'm Italian?"

"I won't hold that against you."

He leans toward me. "Fuck you, I'm gonna tell you something. It's important, so listen. My dad, he had a wise Italian grandpa. My dad's six, eight years old. His nonno is dying, calls him to his bedside. He pulls him close, whispers, 'Pauli, I wanna you listen-a me. I wanna you take-a my chrome-plated .38 revolver so you will always 'member me.' My dad's a wimp as a kid. Wants to be a baker. Imagine that. Anyway, he whines, 'But Nonno, I don't like guns. How about you give me your Panerai watch instead?'"

"'You listen-a me, boy. Somma day you gonna runna da business, you gonna have a beautiful wife, lotsa money, a big-a home, and maybe a couple of bambinos.'"

"'Yes, Nonno, but . . .'"

"'Listen. . . . Somma day you gonna come-a home and maybe find you wife inna bed with another man. Whatta you gonna do then? Pointa you watch and say "times-a up"?'"

He gives a big jokester grin. "That-sa true story."

I give a treacly smile as a substitute for the hickster knee slap he's expecting.

"Since we're talking things Italian, Bus, you wanna know where my family's from? Sure you do."

"No idea."

"A little white-washed mountain village named after a saint."

He's playing with me again. He pauses. I take a long, nonchalant pull on the Moretti.

"Called San Pietro."

A wash of beer comes out my nose. This guy's seriously fucking with my head. I fumble, wipe my nose on my sleeve. Po' white trash style. He has all the advantage now.

"Back to what you *really* wanna know. I'm gonna tell you." He waits. "I'm gonna tell you who murdered your father."

I'm frozen.

"Say something, Bus. Breathe."

I blow out a breath, look around, eyes feeling like big, rolling marbles. I detect the cogs of mighty gears of doubt, of vengeance, all meshing together. I see myself inflicting old-time gospel, blunt-instrument, pipe-whacking trauma. On *somebody*.

"Don't get ahead of things, my trailer park friend. Bring the stock and patent assignments tomorrow, fully executed. The contact info for this Richard guy. I tell you everything then."

"OK," I stammer, then I try to gain some rhetorical ground. "Who's the assignee? Sarto Olive Oil Imports?"

"Don't get smart. Leave them blank."

He stands. No handshake. No paisano hug. Conversation over.

I walk out, bewildered. As always, he's the alpha, I'm the zeta. No matter, I'll grit my teeth and play this out.

So I buy a six-pack of something called Cajun Red and check in to the Countryside Motel.

CHAPTER THIRTY-THREE

BUS—KEYS

The motel room, the whole place, is dull, bland, rundown, smells like decades of tobacco smoke. The mattress feels like lying on top of your aged, spindly grandma. I pop a lukewarm Cajun Red from the laboring fridge, sit on the bed, get into a pensive mood.

Surprise, anger, they flow together like curls of smoke from a revived watch fire. I have huddled by these embers before, thrown the bones by their reddish glow, hoped to see pieces of the truth.

In front of me is a pile of keys. The metal key for this room, my tubular Harley key and fob, Gene's chain with truck ignition keys somewhere among its two-dozen mysterious choices. Atop this pile is the key and cut-metal image from the Hovering Rock. I just found it in my saddlebag. I'll send it back, but for now they all seem to be saying something.

San Pietro. Saint Peter. The Keeper of the Keys.

Important keys are all around me. Some invisible. Some encrypted in a cipher I can't begin to comprehend.

Each bespeaks a lock. Each lock a secret. Each secret a risk.

I open the old man's journal, flipping pages, speed-reading. I scan for words from the free-verse text of his mind. *Flight, white line*, *dreams*, then *36th* and *keys*. I slow down. I backtrack and read the entire passage:

    I am alone, scared. Ramey and the rest flattened
    by the church wall. I peer at Saint Peter through
    a blast hole in the nave. The apostle is on a
    surviving fresco, kneeling, bearing unbearable
    sadness. His hands lift upward, holding the keys.
    Whatever the Popes and padres say, this Texas boy
    knows the meaning.
    Saint Peter is saying, please Lord, don't give
    me these terrible keys. I know not what locks, what
    divine secrets they govern. Give me not powers to
    bind and to loosen in heaven and earth.
    A lot of my buddies have already been loosened
    out there. Starting ten yards from the line of
    departure. Still men, in uniforms, some fashioned
    into grotesque poses, all bearing the drab T on the
    blue, flint arrowhead of the 36th Texas.
    An hour ago, a real priest peeked in, maybe saw
    me, then hurried away. Now I hear the boots, the
    shove at the sanctuary door. They enter, glance
    about, lift some wreckage. After a bit, they joke,
    they smoke, rest their rifles in the corner and
    peer out a broken window. Waffen-SS. Tipped off by
    someone.
    Sooner or later, they will find me. No prisoners
    here. Whatever is going to happen, it is NOW.
    Bayonet in hand, I rise, step between them and their
    rifles.
    Nineteen years later I get a note from a guy
    named Pauli Sarto. One of Marcello's. We sit in the
    Sternwheeler Bar at the Captain Shreve, I savor the

edge and jolt of the seven and seven, order a beer
back. We talk the shit and Pauli asks me about the
war. I avoid it, but the guy likes to talk. He's got
ancestors from a little Italian town. Father the
mayor, uncle a priest.

I shift to the beer, and ask Pauli where?

Campania. North of Naples. Little village. San
Pietro Infine.

Fucking A, I think. In my mind I hear a gun call,
assemble on an empty drill field, alone, listen to
the bark of a roll call of dead men. No answers.

Pauli won't stop, the Little Man wants you to do
something.

I know that means an order. He says the Man wants
a car, fast, stolen, Texas plates, clean, VIN tag
pulled. Delivered in two days.

I'm a pimp disguised as a hotel manager. Provide
petty vices to the guests, discrete and smooth,
broads, Mary Jane, horse. Mostly broads. I also get
cars. What the hell?

What the Little Man wants he gets.

What he wants me to do, I do.

I put away the journal. I need a break. I try calling home again,
then again. A slow burn getting hotter with each unanswered phone
call. She's always punctual to a fault—email, voicemail, texts, letters, everything. All timely answered.

I let it ring and ring and roll over. Redial and same thing again.
I retrieve the voicemails, see what's in there. The box is full. I listen
and clear them one by one. She's let them go for days. Of course,
half of them are from me. They start as long-form reports on my
what and where, steadily disintegrate to my being noticeably ticked
off, transition to a few acceptable-level curses, then, the last one, a

moment's silence followed by a very politically-incorrect expletive. It is mouthed as I stab the call dead on my cell phone.

Something's wrong.

I start to call around, maybe get Rick Van Pelt to check on her, but decide to wait. Let denial come to full flower before it dies. I send an email to Tooey. I need answers to a few questions about those patent assignment forms. I ponder how to get ahold of Richard. Through the slot canyon and somewhere in that isolated valley. A half-dozen hidden outlaw cabins and dugouts. As off-the-grid as it gets.

Finishing off the last beer, I pull out the Oracle of Dealey's book, lie in bed, and lean back on the skimpy pillows. I flip pages, scan a section on Congressman Hale Boggs, Warren Commission dissenting member who savaged J. Edgar Hoover and, the next year, went missing on an Alaska flight that disappeared without a trace. I muse on Alaska, glaciers, open water, twin-engine Cessnas that seldom fail, vast mountains, swift weather, maybe some other factor. Maybe someone.

The last of the Cajun Reds puts me to sleep.

■

"So, how'd it go with Michelangelo Sarto, white man?" Caddo extends his big hand and slides into the booth. We are at a place called Catfish Landing, indulging another of Caddo's gastronomic fetishes. I'm sure tomorrow will bring slab bacon and grits smothered with leavins gravy.

Gene arrives, skips the fish, orders well scotch. Something called the Lonely Piper. I sneak a sip. I understand the name.

I start the conversation slow, being careful. "Sarto's the same guy I knew."

"And?"

"Well, it feels like a deal with the devil, you know? Once you start, you're in with both feet." I was being too cryptic. After all,

Caddo set up the meeting. I look at him and maybe he doesn't care. He's going after catfish tails like they were going extinct. "I got two questions."

"Shoot, man." Caddo picks a bone from his teeth.

"Who's Sarto's hillbilly, the guard dog?"

Caddo blows out a reluctant breath, looks around, looks at me, leans in so he can talk quiet. "Look, don't fuck with that guy. He's got his rotors backwards. I hear he's getting worse. Back in the day, he was part of Marcello's entourage. Not Italian, much less Sicilian, but they, he and Marcello, had a thing. Guy's loyal to a fault. Think Dobermans, Rottweilers. Only one master, ever. He's *not* the proverbial harmless old guy. Now, we gonna eat or just jawbone? Oh yeah, your second question."

"I'll get to that. You just reminded me."

"Yeah?"

"You said there aren't any clues left?"

"That's right. The ashes of that campfire grew cold long ago my friend. If there ever was a conspiracy, someone would've talked. And, even if that's wrong, there's no one left to talk now."

"Well, here's a maybe. Been percolating in me a long time. A buddy of mine, back when I lived here, we stole a box of stuff from Mike Sarto's car. A few days after Kennedy got it. A car his old man had hidden inside a shop. We went joyriding. What happened is a long story, but later Mike went to take a pee. Being a burgeoning kleptomaniac—I was already on probation and one collar away from LTI—I looked around, popped the trunk, and inside was a rifle with a scope. A .270 I'd guess today, and a box. On top of the box was a billfold with a couple of hundred in it. We took the money, left the rifle, threw the wallet away, and hid the box in some bushes. Mike never looked in the trunk, never knew squat till his old man chewed his ass out the next day, maybe slapped him up the side of the head. Maybe a lot more. Later that night though, my buddy Bruce and I retrieved the box, took it out to my brother's cabin. Out on Loggy Bayou. Stupid kid stuff. Then Bruce's car died." I let all this percolate for a moment. "Want to know the connection?"

Caddo is chewing on a mouthful, all ears just the same. He offers, "Fascinating."

A bit condescending, but I keep talking. "The car that was described by Lee Bowers, the dispatcher for the railroad who was in the tower just behind the fence at the grassy knoll? It was the same make and model as the one we went joyriding in, muddied up big time, with Texas plates. The car came into the yard and parked next to the fence. Guys with what looked like radios. They got out and then, when all the commotion got going, they jumped back in and careened out of there."

"OK, spare me the Oliver Stone movie. No one else ever saw or talked about that car, right?"

I shrug. "Yeah, so?"

"I'm going to let you in on something even better. I told you they have a big convention, sort of a JFK-Con, every November in Dallas. I go every year. I know everyone there, everything that's going on. Last year a guy bragged he did a FOIA request and eventually got to look at boxes of declassified records from the Defense Department. Want to know what he supposedly found?"

Gene puts down his drink, does a drumroll with the silverware. I shrug, raise my eyebrows.

"Seems they routinely did U-2 training overflights from Barksdale to LA and back. Every day. Two weeks at a time. There were spy-plane photos of Dallas, Dealey, that very hour. Want to know what showed up?"

The drumroll stops.

"Supposedly, a late-model, white Chevy was sitting right there, behind the fence that overlooks the grassy knoll. Can't read the plates from photos from that era, so maybe it's still a dead-end. That's my info."

"Where's the guy, the photos now?"

"No one knows, said he was gonna write a book. He never came back, sorta disappeared."

I look troubled, which doesn't get better as he asks the next question.

"Where's your famous box now?"

Now I pull out an irritating little fish bone. "I don't know. Maybe still out there. Still wedged in a cubbyhole behind some paneling."

Gene jumps in. "Locked turn-off from Road 640 to Loggy Bayou. Gate's been locked for years. My ex-wife's old man's property. Some kind of Napoleonic Code land dispute. The meander of the bayou shifted over the years."

Caddo keeps his eyes on me. "You goin' out there to find the box, Masked Man?"

"Yeah, maybe tomorrow. First, I gotta get back to Mike about something. In the meantime, I got a suggestion for you idle guys."

"Send Tonto to town, eh? Get him beat up."

I smile, lower my voice to a Clayton Moore deadpan. "Stay clear of the saloon, my faithful Indian companion, and the general store . . . and the livery stable . . . and, well, just hang around on the street. In fact, just listen. Don't talk."

"Fuck you, Kemosabe. You have sickness in head, cannot fix with medicine. Now, what's your suggestion?"

"It's about that little-known Elvis sighting at the Gold Room. Whatever happened to *those* pictures?"

■

After the catfish and slaw overdose, my brother drives me back toward his place. I fill him in on the weirdness from Sarto. The San Pietro thing. The deal Sarto is dangling in front of me. That and taking a look for the box at the cabin should piece it together enough for me. Then go . . . to the police? Rick? FBI? Richard Belzer? Jesse Ventura? Crime Network? Nobody? I decide to defer that worry.

"So how do I actually get out to Loggy Bayou?"

"Ask me later," he says. "I got the combination for the gate, key for the door. I'll draw you a map. You'll need it."

Gene turns into his place, seesaws over the curb, and parks on the lawn. From this angle, I can see the grass is worn through in two lanes. The yard has hosted its share of cars. He says, "Wait here," goes in, and returns with a black ballistic cloth bag.

"Hope that's for money," I say.

"Somethin' better, but first let's check your pulse. This is all moving pretty fast. You trust Sarto? You gonna do his deal?"

"Trust him? No. The guy's got some agenda. He has me cased. Probably even knows I hate mayonnaise."

"Everyone knows that."

"OK, but anyway, yes I'll do the deal. I'll go back with papers in hand. I'll give him just about anything to find that guy."

"Careful what you ask for, little brother."

"So let me ask *you*, you trust Caddo?"

"Pretty much, but . . ."

I narrow my eyes.

"For all our time working together, I always had, still have the feeling he's got another side."

"Like he said, he adapts to survive. You think he's really Kick-apoo?"

"How would I know? How would he know? His momma told him? Life stories got handed down, changed around. Pretty soon it's all made-up."

"So what's in the mysterious bag?"

"You want to keep poking around this town, have weird conversations with third-generation Mafia guys? Poke at stuff that's been long buried?"

He unzips the bag. He pulls out a gun. "Glock, 9 milli auto. Cleaned, oiled, full magazine. Your little friend. Keep it close. Lemme show you how it works." He does. I pretty much know already, and follow with a Hollywood-cool work of the action, then put it back in the bag.

I ask him, "You think this is necessary?"

"You got something off the bubble about guns?"

"No, in fact you wanna hear a story? This wimpy little Italian kid is talking to his wise grandfather . . ."

CHAPTER THIRTY-FOUR

BANNER—DEATH CHESS

Spyflow.com

I'm playing life-and-death chess. Blind. I can see my pieces on the board, but not my opponent's. Make that last part plural. This is a multidimensional board.

There are still things that the Glass Box, in fact all the digital surveillance and SIGINT and eavesdropping in the world, won't show. Our innermost secrets, our hearts, our spells. And, if you believe in such, our magic. Maybe also very good assassins, both human and drone.

My hosts are making their own moves. I'm now a pawn in my own chess game. Spycraft is partly commerce. To avoid being traded off, my hosts need to see I'm a high-value chess piece, a queen of information. I show them some moves, some capability, but not all. That's the tribute I pay for this fragile asylum.

So I may get traded, and that's probably the end. I'm stuck on this chessboard and everybody's got a move.

In the meantime, I've got this guilt to fix. I'm going to do what I can—deal, reveal, intervene—for one particular pawn I helped create, even if reaching out to him gives me away.

Winston, Bus, stupid Mulder, I'm going to call and you damn well better answer.

CHAPTER THIRTY-FIVE

BUS—THE DEAL

I am late getting to Louisiana Downs. Traffic, this being race day.

This time Mike's goombahs are all business. They are wearing ill-fitting business suits. Purple Pants is attired in a Penney's off-the-rack gray with overdone pinstripes. He goes easy on the pat down, avoids my nuts, and escorts me up to the Turf Club. Nice looking waitress. She escorts me to a private room with windows overlooking the crowd.

A box of open-air seats lies just outside the room. Mike is there, gazing out at the pageantry. The heat is pure Louisiana midsummer. Ninety degrees by ninety percent. He's wearing an off-white linen suit. He looks cool as a tropical breeze. As usual, I'm underdressed in a short-sleeve shirt and jeans. I'm sweating a river.

I sit down next to him. The waitress, unasked, brings me a Peroni. Close enough.

He smiles, shrugs, starts talking. "Nice crowd. Means a couple hundred grand in receipts. Gotta love that human instinct for gambling. You a risk-taker, Bus?"

"I've got enough demons. I'm too scared to gamble."

He's still looking at the infield. "Baloney. I think you wanna take that long-shot, chips-all-in bet." He gazes to the infield, then turns to me.

I feel a rivulet cascade from my left pit down my side. I hear the stadium crowd getting loud. The betting windows are open, the announcer is announcing, the thoroughbreds on parade. And the money flows. Time to play all my chips. "So, I'm here. Let's do the deal."

He won't start without an advantage point, and he gets right to it.

"You know, Bus, we talked about our old men. I think down deep, you're a lot like your old man. Most sons of drunks are. I hear he was smart, too smart. Always trying to beat the odds. So, he never went anywhere, except the white line and on to his next errands list." He pauses. "In the end, he was a dumb-ass."

I swallow hard, but it doesn't work. I blurt, "Fuck you, Mike. And the sorry horse you rode in on. That's an Out-West saying in case you don't know. Along the same lines, fuck your old man too. He was a crook and a lackey for Marcello."

Maybe that touched a spot. He cuts back.

"He was made. That's plenty."

"Plenty of what? Sucking up? Lying? Dirty secrets? Now, let's cool down and get this deal done."

He gets philosophical. "That's what all this is about, huh? We're always trying to escape those shadows. Our old men. But we can't run fast enough. Life won't let us."

I pull out an envelope, put it on the drink tray in front of us. "In there are assignments of my interests in I-Gig-Tam. My associate, Enrique Escamilla, will put any other details together for you. Now, the name you got and how to find him. And as much else as you know."

"And your guy? The IGT man?"

"I'm working on that. He's not a phone guy anymore, and he's pretty soured on the Internet, even social media. I'll follow up."

He ponders that, picks up the envelope, opens it, and flips through the forms. Signature, notary, all there. The dumb-ass won't figure out what's missing till later. When his lawyers pore over it.

"OK for now," he says, "I know a few things. For starters, I can tell you this: you never got past your poor white trash ancestry. Yes, your old man, I heard how he ended. Went down shooting, boots on, all that. You gonna beat that in your life? He was a drunk and a pimp and an errand boy, but at least he had a moment."

"You gonna layer on insults till I leave, or we gonna come to a deal? Besides, he had lots of *moments*. He was a war hero."

"Ah, yes, San Pietro. The Sartos' ancestral home. In a way that makes us related. Six degrees of separation, all that. My grandfather was the mayor. Like your old man with Marcello, he had to, *cooperate*, as they say. He worked with the SS to root out partisans, the Resistance. Helped the Krauts plan how to take the US Fifth Army apart, bleed them for trying to take his town. Five times they tried, five times they got their asses kicked."

"Let's you and I cut the hostilities, Mike. Before you keep that envelope and before I connect you with my mystery guy, Mr. IGT, I want you to tell me the whole story. The JFK-Marcello thing. All of this had to do with Marcello, didn't it?"

"Everything around here had to do with Marcello."

"Well, if it was that way, then, just to test this out, someone would've talked. If it *was* a conspiracy."

He looks me straight in the eyes, to underscore that he knows that I know that I'm talking about something bigger. It reminds me that, maybe back in '60, '61, when whatever conspiracy there was started to gel, you didn't really have to *say* a thing. That old lesson again: back-of-the-alley clarity. It holds across the board, from debt restructuring to murder. The Kennedys had pushed a lot of men, prominent, powerful men, down that alley to that brick wall. Marcello was among them. I'm still thinking and Mike starts talking.

"I can tell you this. Carlos didn't work with crowds—never more than a handful of people. That's all you need. Then you clean up any messy leftovers."

"Such as?"

"Old weeds. New weeds. Your old man was an old weed. After he ran, he should've stayed hidden, kept a low profile. But he didn't. He started poking around. That's his mistake. Now, to *the* mystery man. His job, all these years, is to trim weeds. Over time, kind of a long list really. David Ferrie, Bowers, more as they crop up. Lots really."

"All those others?"

"Who knows? Maybe someone else is also out there, cleaning up too. He just takes care of the Marcello household."

"OK, so maybe Senator Boggs?"

"Hale? The Warren Commission guy that didn't buy into the single-bullet theory?"

"You think he shouldn't have said that J. Edgar lied to the Warren Commission?"

"Well, small planes in Alaska. They go missing all the time. Who knows what happened?"

"Your guy's that good?"

"He's not my guy."

"So whose is he?"

"You wouldn't believe it if I told you."

"Try me."

"The Little Man."

"He's dead."

Here we go again.

"Yeah."

I ponder this as, well, a dead end. A mental image creeps up—a furtive mechanic bent into an open cowl of a twin-engine Cessna, the snowcapped Chugach Mountains above Anchorage in the background. I am about to move on when Mike interjects, "By the way, you know who drove Boggs to the airplane, to that lost flight that morning?"

"No."

"Bill Clinton."

I'm stunned.

"He was a congressional aide. History's a funny thing, huh? Never know what coincidence will bring."

I'm lost on this topic, so I change it.

"What's the big deal for you about IGT?"

"Well, let's say I got plans. You know all this NSA spying and snooping bullshit?"

I nod.

"You think they're just looking for terrorists? They *mark* you just for looking at certain websites, for being a Tea Party dude, a Republican big bucks, a Chechen, for sure an A-Rab. So on that list is this innocent, trying-to-go-straight, son of a Mafia guy. Like the early Michael Corleone."

"You're full of some delusional bullshit."

"I don't want those guys in my drawers."

"Maybe they already are."

We pause, each taking a turn at our drinks. I break the moment. "So, what's a secret worth anyway?"

"You're missing the point."

"Such as?"

"Sounds corny, but it's about your word. It's really more, it's who you give your word *to*."

A fleeting thought of Mary. "Don't give me Sam Peckinpah lines."

"No, I'm serious, it's a lot more. Like Jesus, Allah, Buddha, voo-doo, your mom. All that." He looks straight at me, finger pointing at my chest. "No one crosses Carlos. *Not. Ever.*"

"Well, you're telling me a secret, and you're getting what you want."

"In this case it won't matter."

"Why?"

"Bus, you're a new weed."

"I could take that as a threat."

He raises his eyebrows, leans his head back, shrugs and sips his drink. His attitude says, *No sweat on me.*

"Up your ass, Mike. The deal requires you give me a name."

"You've seen him already."

That makes the guess easier. And it's not purple pants. "Your cowboy boots hillbilly?"

"His name is Louie Diamond, and he's easy to find."

"Why?"

"'Cause he's already looking for you."

Below us, the crowd is roaring. The horses are thundering past, three abreast in the lead, a likely photo finish. Sarto pockets the envelope in his suit coat, dismissing me and watching the ponies. The jockeys stand in their saddles, gearing down their mounts.

As I leave, I'm already looking over my shoulder. I pass the wise-ass smirk of Purple Pants, knowing I'm safe with him. I look at my cell phone. Like the roll of the bones, up come two text messages. The first is from my brother:

Meet us at the Caddo Parish Archives. Now.

The second is more urgent:

Call me. We have to talk.

It's from Mary.

CHAPTER THIRTY-SIX

BANNER—
YOUTUBE VIDEO

Hello. This is Banner McCoy. Ex-NSA. Fugitive spy. My blogsite, spyflow.com, got bricked. Don't ask. I've decided to show you the real me. And to speak directly.

The odds against my survival keep going up, so you should read what I wrote before on spyflow.

For now, I'm gonna share something special, something to knock your socks off.

I've only got a little time. Either the agency will find me, or I'll get traded off. Also, this video may get pulled down before it streams. So here's the update.

My project at NSA, code-named KNOLL, is a corruption. It aims to hide the truth about the murder of JFK.

There is a guy named Louie. He's almost invisible. I tried to track him, but got nowhere until the Glass Box got a feel for his movements. And I got a bit more intrusive. After all, after snooping on the presidents and prime ministers of our allies, and hacking into the computers of the Congressional Oversight Committee, what's left?

Louie, I discovered, is a fallen-away choir boy. He may no longer partake of the flesh and blood of Communion, but he digs confession. Every few weeks, different parishes.

Saint Peter's Catholic Church is in Bossier Parish, Louisiana. It protects itself against claims of various interpersonal improprieties. It has a motion-activated recording system in several areas, including the south transept, in which the confessional booth is located.

Once in their system, and with some processing, I get this. The video is blurry, but the audio is a jewel.

You will first hear the priest. He sounds young, earnest, humble in his role as God's instrument on a late Thursday evening. Perhaps like Saint Peter himself, trembling as he holds the terrible keys. His voice sounds like a teenager next to Louie's whisky-scraped old saw of a voice.

They are both in the shadowed confines of the confessional, separated, I imagine, by less than a foot and a flimsy bit of wallpapered plywood. The little latticed window slides open and each can hear, smell, sense, the other. They share a hushed, almost physical intimacy. There with Jesus. Empowered to hear and to forgive. The priest begins, followed by Louie, the Penitent.

"Are you prepared for the Sacrament of Penance, my son?"

"Bless me father, for I have sinned. My last confession was a month ago."

"Did you since take the name of God in vain? Did you sin by calumny or detraction of others?"

"Worse."

"Did you view pornography?"

"No."

"Unclean hands? Have you abused yourself?"

"Well, some, a lot, but that's not the point."

"Do you remember and honor the Sabbath, take Communion?"

"Father, I don't make it to regular church. I don't like crowds, drinking the blood of Christ. It's sorta medieval, sharing the village cup and all. But I do go to confession every so often. I got sin, and I know it. I need, I love confessing. So much I keep confessing the same sins."

"Why? Do you doubt the Lord's forgiveness?"

"Yeah, I think I must. On these ones, yeah. So I keep trying. I'm going to get specific now: more than ever before. 'Cause time is short."

"Of what sins do you accuse yourself, my son?"

"Of the Laws of Moses, the Big Ten, I'm batting pretty good. Only one is really bad, and one is really good."

"Yes."

"Now, first, you gotta know something. If after I tell you, you think about blabbing, I'll come back and tear through this place, your congregation, like a bobcat in a chicken coop. You can leave now if you want, Father, I wouldn't think bad of you. Wouldn't think of you as an apostate, an imposter . . . You still wanna hear?"

"Y . . . yes. Speak from your heart."

"Ok, here it is. You know JFK?"

"Of course . . ."

"A fellow Catholic."

"Yes."

"I shot him. I killed him . . ."

There is a long silence. "To lie at this moment would be a sin."

"And I killed about twenty others. I didn't know hardly any of them, but they knew too much."

"You speak too casually of breaking the Fifth Commandment. Have you remorse?"

"Some, but I got a makeup."

"A what?"

"The Fourth, I get credit back, maybe for that."

"Honoring thy father and mother?"

"I got no idea about my real ones, but I got an adopted father of sorts. He saved me. He still tells me what needs to be done."

"And you do it?"

"That's what honor's about. You give your word."

"My son, I worry that you are lying to yourself and to God. Would you like me to call someone for you, the police?"

"What happened to the forgiveness part? I ain't fucking lying, Father. Hell, I gotta go."

That's the end. You can see him leaving, hear the echo of the confessional door banging, the sound of bootheels clacking away on the tile floor.

I'm sure this YouTube video of me will also get pulled right away, buried by the NSA. Then they'll start to analyze it, looking for clues. Sniffing for my whereabouts.

CHAPTER THIRTY-SEVEN

BUS—ARCHIVES

My call to Mary's cell ends with me leaving another voice message. Par. I'll try later.

I go looking for Gene and Caddo.

Like many American cities, Shreveport used to support two competing newspapers. One for the morning, the other relegated to the afternoon. The two-paper business model succumbed long before the digital revolution began to erase all print newspapers. The *Shreveport Gazette*, the afternoon rag and the weak sister in the market, folded in 1991. With it went eighty-nine years of continuous coverage of the first draft of North Louisiana history, much of it staunchly segregationist. Being a proud, family-owned, and brutal competitor to the end, it gave the surviving newspaper nothing. The *Gazette*'s entire repository of news, clippings, records, and photos were gifted to the Caddo Parish Archive Repository.

The Repository is an old municipal power plant gutted down to the beams and cement floor and fitted with climate control and blackout windows. I am guided to a document review room by a nice, gray-haired lady docent. Gene and Caddo are huddled in a cubicle surrounded by banker boxes. The room is stuffy and airless, but Gene is smiling like a Cheshire cat. As soon as she leaves, he holds up a manila folder, browned along the top edge like it has been in a tight file drawer for decades.

"Little brother, you know those high-falootin' auctions they hold in Hollywood, celebrity artifact stuff?"

"Yeah, it's called Julien's. Lots of dead celebrity stuff."

He's slowly waving the folder in front of me, like a hypnotist. "You got it: James Dean's cigarette lighter, Whitney's costume jewelry, Elvis's comb. Some of it of dubious provenance."

Caddo jumps in. "And pix?"

"Sure, but these days you at least gotta have the original negatives for authentication."

Gene holds the file open for a peek. "Wanna look?"

In the file is a glassine envelope with 35mm negatives and a short stack of 5" x 7" black-and-white prints. They are face down and I turn the first one over.

There are only so many moments when fate, luck, *joss*, really go your way. If life is a craps game, I just rolled an unlikely series of naturals. Right now those bones are coming up seven and eleven and telling me everything. I hear Caddo talking.

"These were never published. Somebody put the kibash on printing a picture of Marcello. Elvis or no."

The first is a solid, newsworthy shot. Grainy, perfectly consistent with Kodak Tri-X film used by photo journalists back then. The image shows several men seated at a cocktail table overburdened with drinks. One of them is Marcello. He is looking at the camera, surprised, trademark cigar in hand. Next to him is, yes, The El. Obvious even though he's wearing a flat cap and shades. He is laughing, looking to the side. Beside him are the nice legs of a waitress. The arms of two men show up on either side.

In the next picture, the camera has shifted right. Marcello is still there, pointing at the camera, his mouth a big angry "O." Elvis is gone, his chair empty, and what could be the back of his pants exiting the top of the frame. At Marcello's other side, trying to raise a hand to block the camera view—it's uncanny to see—a dead ringer for Lee Harvey Oswald. That's because it *is* Lee Harvey Oswald.

Pulling away, his weird face in profile, is someone who has the strongest resume in the Cavalcade of Weirdos that orbit the JFK murder. I'm recalling the chapter in the Dealey Oracle's book. The guy is wearing a bad wig on top of a narrow face with glued-on eyebrows. Defrocked priest, gay, rabidly anticommunist—this is 1960s New Orleans, remember. And to the point: Civil Air Patrol instructor to, and known acquaintance of, Oswald. Personal pilot for Marcello. The guy is David Ferrie, who mysteriously died right after New Orleans DA Jim Garrison revealed his reopening of the JFK case and leaked Ferrie as a person of interest. You could spin the rest of the conspiracy lots of directions, but this, this blunt black-and-white 5" x 7", is enough.

The rest of the picture shows another guy way back, maybe Maroon, and a single arm reaching into the frame. The arm has a long, encircling tat, maybe a lizard, that slithers out from a short-sleeve shirt. Similar to my brief view of Louie's arms, but different, thicker maybe.

The third and fourth images tell the end of the story. Both are without flash. One shows a double door with a promotional sign to one side saying "The Famous Gold Room." The last image is blurry. The photographer is about to get intimately acquainted with the gravel in the parking lot.

Gene Wray is holding a note: "This was taped to the index for the box. It says: Files of Devin Carlyle, assignment pool photographer, missing without notice in December, 1963."

Caddo asks, "So, counselor you're the hotshot here. What's all this mean?"

I hesitate, musing on the legalities. Inside the courtroom, the law says we got nothing. "Fifty-year-old pix from a defunct company and MIA photographer, with no way to establish an evidentiary foundation. Probably not even a business records exception for the hearsay rule. Not to mention the inevitable claims of Photoshop fakery."

Their look—telling me I'm being obsessively obtuse—gooses me to change gears. "Of course, this isn't a courtroom. What we really have here is lightning in a bottle. Jet fuel for the press. Vindication for the conspiracists. The world will eat this up and ask for seconds. More important to me, this is at the Gold Room. It confirms what I've been afraid of. About Marcello and our . . . my old man."

Caddo is right with me. "Look, these are priceless. Who would've ever guessed they were here? We can't leave them now. Let's pack up, return all this in good order, make note of exactly where in the boxes this came from, and . . ." He starts to slip the file under his long-sleeve shirt. A blue tattoo, a piece of something, appears before the shirt covers it.

Gene Wray grabs the envelope. "Not getting your sweating belly on this! I'll just carry it out."

I am still staring awkwardly at Caddo's shirt. I check my watch. I think of Mary, wince. "Brother, you guys take them. We'll put it all together later. Let me keep your truck and draw me that map to Loggy Bayou. I'm going to finish this up. See if memories are real. Then go home. Right away."

"Just like that? You gonna see Bruce, check out the Davis?"

I shrug, intent on my wrap-up.

■

His map takes me into country I don't remember, out past a place called Red Chute, past the last gas stations, down a one-lane, farm-to-market road, deep into bayou country. I stop at a gate.

I'm looking at the gate, notice cell phone coverage is drifting in and out, when I get a call. The caller ID says "Unknown." It buzzes, buzzes again. One more and it will flip to voicemail.

I accept it. I hold the phone to my ear without saying anything. The line sounds distant, scratchy.

A lady's voice—unfamiliar, young, some variant of East Texas or North Louisiana. She starts without any hello. "Bus, listen to me. You are in way over your head. Don't trust anyone."

"S'cuse me?" For just a second, I think it is a setup by one of the guys from the Flashbackers Club, pranking me.

"Bus, people are watching you, waiting to see if you find . . . what you're looking for. You're close."

"Whah . . .?"

"You called Mary the b-word on her voicemail yesterday. Before that, you told Amalie about the broken mirror, where you see things in the shards."

I can't even grunt a sound to respond to this.

"They will find a way to get you. They . . ."

Click. The line goes dead. Someone, something cut it off.

I look at the phone, then jump as a loud BLATT! shakes me. A Dodge Power Wagon has come up fast and roared around me, honking and leaving a dense cloud of dust. I make out a couple of four-wheelers rocking against their tie-downs in the bed.

I look at the road, I look at the map, I look at the locked iron gate that guards the road to the cabin. Gene has scribbled the combination to the lock: 1963.

Thunder sounds to the northwest, distant but unmistakable on the darkening horizon.

PART FOUR
WINDSHIFT

"I am but mad north-north-west. When the wind is southerly,
I know a hawk from a handsaw."

–William Shakespeare, *Hamlet*, act 2, scene 2

"Data, data, data . . . I can't make bricks without clay."

–Sherlock Holmes, *The Adventure of the Copper Beeches*

CHAPTER THIRTY-EIGHT

BUS—LOGGY BAYOU

The law disfavors memory. As I deal the cards of justice with judges and juries, and across settlement tables, recollection isn't just fallible, it is plastic and self-serving. There is also a corollary: worlds revisited are diminished from their memory. Current reality is usually smaller, grayer, dingier.

I am about to test these principles. After locking the gate behind me, I maneuver the pickup until the logging road succumbs to overgrowth. The air is dense and muggy. I park and shoulder a small backpack in which jostle the Glock and a rig axe—a mean cross between a hand axe and a framing hammer that I took from Gene's toolbox. I start walking, alternatively thinking about the bizarre phone call, probably a mean jab from Mary via one of her vampy, cougar friends, and this moment, this brink of *finding*.

A half-mile and I am pouring sweat. My heart is pounding. The pines loom up lofty and straight, like a cache of giant's spears, perfect for harvest. Perfect for tree rustlers. The trunks intermittently sway and creak. A quickening breeze plays melancholy, tuneless notes among them.

I round a curve in the track, and there it stands. Like nothing I remember. Deserted, hailed-out, paintless, draped in Spanish moss. Tin roof sheeting gone in places. The whole structure leaning dangerously. If a building can be a character straight out of central casting, this one is. I look at it and see a dozen "cabin-in-the-woods" movies. Perfect trap for one of my flashback sequences.

I step gingerly on the porch. An unholy, prolonged squeal echoes along the warped boards. I freeze, crouched and wary, an intruder in a devil's lair. I imagine something furtive watching me through slats, from inside the cabin. My eyes cut every direction, searching for the inevitable demonic signs, maybe Wiccan omens. The only clues are piles of torn wire screens and bits of raccoon and mouse crap.

I listen for a moment, then blow out a breath. Something tells me to slow down and take stock. I turn and sit on the porch, letting the sweat cool, trying to piece together where all this is going. What I'm doing here, the dead certain feeling of the middle falling away back home. The enigmatic caller a few moments ago. Even the blunt question, more practical than cosmic, of *what exactly is real here*. The breeze sighs and whispers the only answer: yes, a serious storm is coming.

I indulge this reverie for a half hour, perhaps more, when I hear a distant four-wheeler, out there somewhere, crunching in low gear through the goose brush. Maybe headed this way. Maybe going off to some duck blind. Maybe timber rustlers. Gene said no one should be out on this peninsula of land bounded on three sides by an oxbow of dark water rich with gar and snapping turtles and spiked with long dead trees.

I check the time and verify it with my eyes. The light is on its slant. Bars of yellow and shade angle through the trees. I got maybe a half hour to get this done. I scrounge in the backpack and get up, rig axe in one hand, Glock stuck in my pants. I ease the screen door open. Gene's key reluctantly unlocks the old Slaymaker on its hasp. I push open the front door. The hinges complain until the door wedges against warped floorboards. Enough room to squeeze in. The interior is suspended in dusty time. Motes flit and waltz above a gauzy dance floor in the angled window light. Tables, chairs, woodstove, kitchen hutch are all cobwebbed but orderly.

Exactly, I think, a false façade for that lurking demonic presence. Something disturbing—perhaps a note, a wall marking, a sound from beneath a locked door in the floor—will undoubtedly appear. Talisman to the Bad Thing that must reside here.

I won't be waiting around to say hello. I pull and check the pistol, lay it on the table, and proceed down a short hall to a closed door. I remember that a bedroom clung like a barnacle to the back of the cabin. I push open the door with the rig axe.

The bedroom is there, but it is in shambles. A back door is partially open, as if pried that way by some long-ago wind. Debris and weather have entered here. A screen door is the lone sentinel at guard. I scooch an empty bedspring and frame away from one wall and begin to rip into the Sheetrock with the alternating business sides of the axe. In a moment, I'm absorbed with the havoc of hacking and pulling and dust. From somewhere, some Atlanta CDC person starts whispering in my ear. *Hantavirus . . . facemasks.*

No matter. I am into this now. I move to the next wall, rip out a big slab of loose, rotted covering. I repeat this, on and on to the next section. It's all mayhem but no discovery. I've somehow misremembered, maybe imagined, all this. I give a roundhouse swing into an intact section, twist the blade, and pull out a three-foot chunk of wallboard. I stop. Anticlimactic as hell, it's there. I put the axe to the side, reach in, and wrestle the box out from between the studs, setting it down like a treasure chest. I sit on the floor and carefully open the top flaps. My breathing is heavy with excitement and exertion.

I cease breathing.

A four-wheeler is idling out front.

In a moment, the porch board squeals, the screen door opens. The wooden door, bottom-sagged, scrapes the floor like grimy buckteeth.

I hear bootheels. Clack. Stop. Clack. I huddle in this back room, the wallboards torn out, the moldy box beside me. I stare at the rig axe. Too far away. I visualize the boots exactly, as if from the perspective of a cockroach. Cut-heeled. Exotic leather. Damn exotic, maybe Coelacanth skin. Clear as a church bell, I know who it is. Those boots are worn by the man who murdered my father.

The boots wait. Cautious now.

Any thought of vengeance is fleeting. It's also way too late to run.

Trying to hold my breath, my heart and lungs thudding and wheezing inside my ears. I close my eyes and it's all about the sound. Just for a moment, despite the inner roar, like some secret ocean surf, I detect the tiniest sounds. Mice, disturbed after so long, scuffle indignantly away. A breeze in the big pines outside, their tall trunks creaking and swaying. The four-wheeler idling, a teenybopper version of my Harley, put-putting and loping in syncopated rhythm.

I open my eyes and look around. The box still there beside me. The back door barely supports the raggedy, sagging screen that now presents a sienna glow through its rust. Maybe I *could* run for it, leave the box, dance with fear, outrun the bullet.

A sound down the hall. A weapon being handled, its action worked expertly. The clip removed. The Glock—where I left it on the table.

Then quiet.

He must have moved, maybe glided like a snake. I didn't hear that. My heart rate is jacked up, banging against the redline.

The door to the room drifts open, slow, as if by a ghost. I see the boots first, just as I imagined. I look up. There's Louie. Perfect stance, two-hand pistol grip. Aimed square at me.

I wince, avert my eyes. Cower. I feel something warm trickling in my crotch.

Real soft, almost a whisper, he says, "On your knees, raise your fucking hands."

I comply like a robot. Too scared to think about it. He glances at the dark spread on my pants, dismissing me, and cuts his eyes left and right, clearing the corners. He steps in, deft.

Sounds keep playing in and out. You never know what a life-and-death moment will toss up in your soul. Mutations, beasts of unknown ancestry, things that wrestle up from the murk in your guts. Once you piss your pants, go pathetic, you either go downhill all the way or you regain some handhold of self-respect.

Let's play it out, I think.

Some beast inside me is crawling onshore, surprisingly calm, eyes blinking slowly, waiting. Louie is talking, "Now tell me exactly what's in the box."

That means I get a little more time. "It's . . . it's the *truth,* Louie. The stuff you've been worried about for fifty years. The links to what you and Carlos did. You want to know? I'll show you, one by one. It's the only way to be sure, right?"

The guy is unpredictable, off half a bubble. Maybe just toying, maybe wanting to know how much I know. I could tell him about the news photos. That might buy me time but sure as hell he's going to kill me. "All right smart-ass," he says, "Show me. Each thing. One hand up, one hand in the box. Eyes on me. Use your pinkies. That's it."

The box has been closed up for five decades. No telling what has taken up residence in there. Scorpions? Spiders? Snake, maybe? Something tells me coral snakes like places like this. One more assassin to worry about. Like I said, memory is fallible. I'm trying to remember what's in there. My *pinkies* will have to be my eyes.

My hand goes in. There is cloth, buttons, a shirt probably. It is balled up around something. I let it go and finger-walk further. Something stiff, cardboard? No, a brim, a hat brim.

I pull it out. A policeman's hat, mouse-chewed. "One of Dallas's finest," I say. I put it on the floor toward him. Actually, I bestow it, like a cursed offering placed at the foot of some bastard demigod. A long way from exacting justice, I am groveling before a killer demon.

My hand eases back to the box, stiff, like one of those toy-capture cranes in truck stops or Chuck E. Cheeses. Down it goes for another prize.

This time, it's paper. Also mouse taste tested. I pull it up. A sketch map. It just might be of Dealey Plaza.

The gun points to the box. He nods. *In you go.*

I finger-dive again, working for time, remotely aware I may have satcheled my drawers. I can't tell. I pathetically sniff the air, and then my fingers find a heavy, knobby metal brick. I pull it up. Louie can sense it's heavy. The barrel of his gun hones in, aiming at my soul. I pull my hand up from the box real slow. I'm holding a walkie-talkie.

Who knows if it, if anything, would work after all this time?

The offering pile grows.

His eyes and his pistol are unimpressed. Both stay cold set on me.

God, I'd like to have a conversation with him, find out the truth, buy seconds. My claw reaches in again and finds more metal. The pieces clink and the claw comes up.

Brass. Two spent rifle casings.

Louie's snake eyes get bigger.

He's gonna shoot me any second now.

I put my hand back in the box and let it search. Trying not to be desperate. I decide to talk. I go with the only play I can think of. My recent shtick. I might as well die shameless.

"You should fess up, Louie, do a book. Get a ghostwriter. I can help. I'm a writer. Do a tell-all. Make a million. Be famous. Really famous. I can help you turn state's evidence and get a walking deal. I . . . I can get you an agent. For real. You could do the TV talk show circuit. Book tours. Go public enough and they, *they* won't touch you. Maybe they're not even out there anymore." He's not taking the bait. "OK, just . . . just a couple more things," I stutter, bucking up and milking the seconds. My fingers grope blindly back to the shirt, trying to swarm into the folds. I won't have much time and I can sense the cat's paw increase in pressure on Louie's trigger finger.

I decide to ask what is probably the last question of my life. Right now. I want to hear the answer. "So, *you* killed my father?"

His eyes refocus for a second, get a kind of kindred glow. He fashions a smug, derisive smile, and finally speaks. "Yeah, I own his life. That makes us sort of related."

Drexl Spivey, maybe Joker, bullshit. All these guys live through movies. I feel the hot acid of pure hate.

Suddenly, a scrape against the tin roof. A pine branch stirred by the breeze. Louie looks left, up over his shoulder.

The side of the box blows out. Cardboard confetti fills the air and the bullet smacks the plaster in the wall next to his head. The noise clamps down my ears like manhole covers are dropped on them. Dust, bits of cloth, drywall, stuff leaking down from the ceiling obscure everything. I squeeze off another wild shot. The box bucks and gives up its sides. Another emphatic smack into plaster. I lift out the .38 pistol and try to aim at something while I'm falling backwards. Movement at the door, like a shadow behind a gray dust curtain.

He's gone.

I got no idea why he didn't shoot me. I say a prayer to God, to the patron saints of guns, along with Messieurs Smith and Wesson, and whoever manufactured this half-century old ammunition.

I stuff my new little helper in my pants, scrape up the sketch map and the rifle cartridge casings and put them in the hat, then stuff the shirt remnants on top. I check the contents of the box one last time.

I think of Louie out there. I grab all this dubious evidence in a double arm carry. I crash through the back door, carrying the screen with me, and light out for the woods. Just running. I'll take the perils out here. Poison ivy, water moccasins, copperheads, slimy seeps, soggy mudholes, slippery deadfalls overgrown with moss.

I can feel the adrenaline powering through my system, unleashing its wonders of strength, fear, and that wide-open feeling of being *alive*.

And maybe stirring up those long dormant SSRIs, selective serotonin reuptake inhibitors. I stumble on for minutes, maybe an hour, unable to outrun a swarm of mosquitoes. Somehow, somewhere, my little helper escapes and falls away. I'm defenseless. The woods become subdued and dark, as if waiting for the last yellow beams to creep up the canopy and fade into a vampire night. I blunder on, fearing Louie, the night, tasting the bitter fact of owning a life in peril. The trees hint at an opening, and I soon come out on a dirt path. A tributary of the old logging road. The grass is knocked down and fresh four-wheeler tracks line through the dust. The road turns a corner up ahead. I creep in the roadside brush and peer through to see if anyone's there. I catch a glint of chrome, then black metal. Scar. Gene's—*my*—pickup. I listen, then run for it, chuck everything into the shotgun seat. Lord, let this starter work.

At the gate, I fumble the lock, looking backwards, then swing the bars wide open and leave them that way as I gear-jam away.

Whoever, wherever Louie Diamond is, he won't stop. I'm running for my life now.

CHAPTER THIRTY-NINE

LOUIE—HAINTS

Louie grimaced. A conflicted North Louisiana guy—maybe one who'd just lost bets on *both* the Saints *and* the Cowboys. He pulls over at a Dixie Chicken parking lot and gets out. He whacks his baseball cap on his jeans and shirt, the plaster dust floating away in a cloud.

For all the world, another blue-collar stiff, laboring late and finished for the day.

Louie gets back into his truck, queues in the drive-through, orders the crispy three-piece combo. He pulls over to eat. His favorite meal. Just a moment to relish the hot grease and chicken, the rice and beans. He leans over and starts to open the warm box, savoring the moment.

He hears a *tink-tink* of neck chains. Cigar corrupts the air. Lusitanias.

The Little Man is back.

"Know your problem, Louie?"

Louie stiffens, peeved. *Fifty-some fucking years and he's still on my case.*

"First of all, you fucked up. Let the guy get away. With that stuff—you don't even know what all. Not so good." Then the kicker, "Like I been warnin', you slippin'."

Louie's eyes, antimatter viaducts, look over at Carlos. He sees disappointment in the dead man's eyes.

You slippin?

It feels like acid way down inside, but no way he'll show it.

"You other problem, kid, main one, maybe they're related: you don't believe—not in shit."

Louie starts to object. It never works in these conversations. He wants to say, almost sad-puppy-like, *'cept in confession, 'cept in you, Boss.*

Instead, he breathes deep. The Little Man is winding up.

"Nobody believes in shit. No more. Maroon, same way. Loyal, yeah, believe? No. Was a fucking lawyer for God's sake. What's your excuse, Louie?" Carlos doesn't pause for an answer. "Anyway, when I come over here, my family's Sicilian. Forget the Tunisia shit. They got beliefs, superstition, little old *nanna* stuff. He jams the cigar in his mouth, grips it tight in his teeth, and smacks the back of one hand into the palm of another. *Whack!* His hand emerges as a fist with the pinkie and index finger extended, stabbing downward. "*Stregare!*" He spits it out and continues.

"The day come, I need special help. I gotta do believing. Those fucking Kennedys, they gonna take me out! She give me this."

Carlos digs in his shirt and pulls out one of his two neck chains. On it is a red, highly polished, horn-shaped amulet. Exactly like the one Louie wears inside the leather gris-gris ball. "*Corno,*" he says as he holds it up. "Me, I know even this not enough. When you taking out enemies, worst enemies, you bring the best. We got people, you know, you the one, Louie. We got time and place. They let us know that. But we got to have the rest. *Fortuna.* We make our own, but we bring extra. So, I check around. Algiers, upriver, check the voodoo, all that shit. No way." He pulls on the long Lusitania, as if remembering how it came down. "Then I know this guy, up here in North Louisiana. Injun. Probably Redbone.

Anyway, I don't care, I call him Chief sometimes. Man and his kid. Injun says he's a . . . shaman. Like a *mago*. Not Sicilian, but same. I pay fuckin' serious money and he does this hoodoo shit and talks about Kopi-Kelli, something like that. Coyote-spirit, like the animal. 'Cept there's one big difference."

As Louie waits, Carlos looks into the distance, studies his cigar, lets the moment pause just to show how deep this shit is. The smoke curls into a cloud and creeps out in hurried wisps through the crack in the passenger-side window.

As if *smoke* had someplace to go.

Louie looks through the window. Through Carlos. The smoke seems to coalesce as it joins a gathering evening vapor.

Carlos shifts in the car seat and tugs on a second neck chain. He pulls out a little figurine, a man bent with feathers on his head playing a flute. Carlos looks at it reverently, shows it to Louie. Like it's a big fucking revelation. "'Cept this one you gotta believe, gotta keep the secret about what it, they helped you do. You talk, you let someone else talk, you get sloppy, maybe someone figure it all out, you know what happens?"

Louie shrugs.

The Little Man is pensive, solemn. "The spirits, they pulla the prank on you!"

Louie reflects, not sure what Carlos means. He thinks about all the talkers and snoopers he's taken out. The leads Caddo supplies. Getting easier with time. All the really important witnesses long gone. Caddo snoops, gets his information somewhere. Maybe he's talking to the government. Guy goes to the big JFK conspiracy fandangos, checks out who's left, fewer every year. What wiseass expert is new and doing what. Piece of cake. No slippin' there. *Then what's the problem,* Louie thinks.

Carlos is still talking. "The secrets, my friend, like omertà, 'cept it has to be kept forever, else the devils, the evil eye coyote things, come after *me*. Even now. I can feel the spell loose up. So the secret's gotta be put away, gotta stay that way *forever*." Carlos lets that imperative hang in the smoke.

After a moment, he points left: "Drive that way, Louie, down to the intersection."

It is getting dark. Louie pulls out, lets the truck roll down an overgrown, one-lane road. It stops at a crossroads with another dirt lane. The intersection, truck in the exact center, huddles in a gathering poltergeist gloom. Evening mist oozes in from the leering trees and kudzu that encroach on all sides. Carlos looks around, approving. "You used t'have a special knack, Louie, cutting the weeds, shutting up all those snoopers all those ways." Carlos looks over, looks Louie in the eye, quiets those black holes. The stare that no one—Giancana, Hoffa, Robert Kennedy—ever took lightly. "Now we got to finish—all of it."

Louie nods, anticipating, thinking, *Now this makes sense.*

Carlos is giving directions now, like old times. "Like closing time at the Gold Room, huh. No-Tell-Motel Time. Everybody out." He chuckles to himself and waits, as if Louie might need to digest this. "That means the wiseass Sarto kid, worse than his old man. The Injun too. Too bad, but he's gotta go, along with his spells. He's about to crack anyway. Spill his guts out there, maybe to this prick lawyer that just showed up. You do the lawyer's old man way back. You can't finish him? Don't fuck it up this time!"

Carlos toys with his Lusitania, rolling it between finger and thumb, letting the smoke uncoil and blossom. His voice is softer now. "You finish this all up, Louie, finish it tight, then you go away somewhere. Far. Money's where I said. Go live a little. Go believe."

Carlos gazes up and through the smoky headliner like he's looking at clouds in the sky. "We did good. Like fuckin' opera. The others did they part, but we did the deed. Ruby, played it out. The rest, even Garrison, keep the light away from us. Everyone keep the masks on. Fifty fucking years, you'd think the snoopy little mice would give up. Now finish it. *Capisce?*"

Louie utters the only words actually spoken in the last half hour. "Yes, boss."

He pushes a button, the passenger-side window rolls down, the smoke rolls out. Carlos is gone.

Except Louie thinks he sees him again, outside the truck, walking in the fog. His face turns back in something resembling . . . appreciation. Then the Little Man takes a few steps and simply disappears.

He's really gone, Louie ponders. *Gone in the crossroads, with the haints.*

Louie considers those last few weeds.

■

The Power Wagon hides a few cars back, follows Caddo for an hour. Caddo stops at a house, then gets into a half-assed yellow Toyota pickup with some other guy with a Fu Manchu and beard. They're heading toward Shed Road. Perfect.

Louie glances at his watch: 9:05. He follows, letting traffic thin, easing closer. They approach the railroad tracks and stop. He pulls up right behind them. No other car around.

All things are situational, Louie thinks.

The Toyota starts to move, then stops again. Guy's got safe driver instincts.

Down the tracks, like clockwork, the 9:11 locomotive blares its horn, its advancing headlight warbles. Dash clock says 9:12.

Louie eases the Power Wagon into four-wheel drive, sets the transmission into low, and rolls forward like a steamroller.

CHAPTER FORTY

BUS—DEAR JOHN

It's almost full dark. I'm driving around Bossier, erratic as a scared guppy, fast, slow, left, right, stop, go. I cross Texas Avenue for the tenth time and peer in the rearview for the hundredth—like I'll see the geriatric, relentless hippie fiend pulling up behind me any second, maybe glaring down from a Sherman tank with a super-charger. My crotch feels chapped, the pee dump in my pants still damp and burning.

What now? Call the police? FBI?

I remember I'm overdue to call Mary. I need her so much now, her clear, cool advice. My port and refuge in this storm.

I pull over and call. She answers the first ring.

"Babe!" I say.

"Hi." Her affect is flat as a squashed toad.

"You, OK? I've been calling."

"Bus, there's something I need to tell you."

This is happening too fast for me to have any guard up. I vaguely sense this is gonna be bad. I'm thinking about how I'm thinking. Those relentless nautical metaphors. I'm drifting into the rocks underpowered, main sails furled, helpless.

"Me too, something's happened. You go first. Sure, sure. What?"

"We're over."

"What?"

"I'm sorry. You've been great."

Just that quick. Just that complete. I'm speechless.

"It's . . . just the way it is. I won't be here when you get back."

Involuntarily, sappy stuff starts to come out of my mouth. "But . . . I thought we . . . why?"

"It's not somebody else. It's just . . . over."

Point-blank cannon shots into my sides. Gaping holes at the waterline. The dumbstruck, disbelieving, betrayed, flat-footed, sucker-punched waters pour into the breaches. I did not see this coming and now, in the space of seconds, I'm scuttled and sinking where I lie.

I don't think she said goodbye before she hung up, but I'm not sure. All I hear is those rushing waters. They will drown the sunrise, the moon, the sunset. All the hours of all my days.

I sit for a long time, replaying her words, cataloging the deceit, the false flags, the lies it took to get me here.

It's an hour later, maybe more, and I haven't sunk.

As my shrink said, I know how to wall things off. The emergency crews in my head are hard at work sealing the breach. They labor to a work song punctuated with exclamatory shouts of the B's and C's of political incorrectness. They close the gaps with timbers of anger. They seal their work with the hot pitch of anticipated paybacks.

I see that I'm a big talker, maybe a bluffing fool, when it comes to vengeance. All around me, however, red lines are getting crossed. Murder, betrayal. What's left? Physical torture? If I stay around here, Louie will find me. This is it. The back of the alley. I'll go get my stuff together. Then I will go home.

I will get the whole damn truth out of her. I will get paybacks.

I goose Scar into traffic on Airline Drive and weave down the street toward my brother's. In a few minutes, I bounce over a speed bump, tools and junk clanging in the bed, and pull in his driveway. Something looms in the headlights.

A cop car.

An officer is leaning against it. He jumps to a crouching stance, one hand positioned on the pistol holster on his hip, the other hand shading his eyes. He is covering for his buddy who is knocking on the front door. I kill the headlights and get out. My hands aloft. They tell me to stop, ID me, ask if I know Gene Ray. I hear extraplanetary words, surely not applicable to this world. "Your brother and his friend, Caddo Rockman"— *that's his last name,* I think, *weirdly appropriate*— "got hit by a train."

"A train?" I ask, like I might've said something more probable, like the arrival of a meteor or Thor's hammer. The rest is a blur of screeching tires and run red lights on the way to the hospital.

For a fleeting moment I ponder how disaster comes in threes. Or is it fours? Then I realize the day isn't over yet. Maybe not by a long shot.

Focus on your bro!

Running down the ER corridor, I can't stop even as I ask directions of passing staff. I barge into a room with what I think is the right number. There is someone, him I think, all swaddled up in bandages and IVs. He has one uncovered eye. He looks like he's somewhere between exquisite bodily pain and exquisite dopey bliss. I lean over him, whisper.

"Brother!"

His free eye rolls toward me, past me, then back. OK, he sees me. He gives a little battered smile.

I fake what I know, what I don't know. "You're OK. Doc says so. What happened?"

"Big truck. Behind us. Some guy in a baseball hat. Rammed us. Pushed us onto the track. Shed Road . . . just as the damn Mid-South was coming." He stops trying to reconstruct things. "Caddo?"

I show him a big shrug. His eyeball stops rolling, fades back into a spaced-out zone just as a man in a suit, a bit rumpled, like he wears it three times a week every week, comes up behind me. Central casting in real life. He holds out a badge, asks me to step into the hall.

I debate with myself and decide that less is more. I tell him pretty much nothing. He lets out that Caddo didn't make it. The train T-boned his side of Yeller. They pulled him from the wreck using Jaws of Life. The jaws worked fine for extracting a corpse.

The cop takes my info, looks at Gene, then leaves. I stand alone in the hall. I'm damn lucky to be here. My brother just as lucky. Caddo DOA. I know I'm being hunted.

Whatever that box in the cabin was, I opened it, and now the demons are pouring out. They look like hillbilly maniacs with scraggly ponytails and black voids for eyes. And harpy versions of Mary.

I go back into Gene's room and wait till he wakes up. I tell him about Caddo. My brother's a strong guy. He stays with it, tells me Caddo had been acting weird after we found the pictures at the archives.

"He kept looking at the photos. Troubled. Said something like, 'The spell's over. I'm ending it. Done carrying this. Kokopelli's gonna play the flute now.' Then he said 'The coyote's runnin.' Weird, huh."

"Dunno. I always thought Kokopelli was a humpback, a fertility god of the Pueblo culture. He's a far cry from the Kickapoos. So what's *done*? Anyway, you know him, not me, brother."

"Hell, what do we know about anybody, ever? He never talked much about his witch doctor, shaman stuff. Thought it was just another act in his one-stop shop. You know, bass player, Kickapoo Indian, wanderer clan, conspiracy buff, shaman . . ." He coughs, fades, then comes back. "Notary, realtor, dogcatcher, secret agent, get-along guy. Anyway, the picture file . . ."

The room door opens and Gene's kid and his family come in, fussing and giving him lots of TLC. The doc follows. Youngish guy, an aura of smooth confidence exuding from him like Sunday morning sunshine. Exactly the man you want on your case. We stand back as he approaches the bandaged wreck that is my brother.

After a moment's survey, the doc moves bedside. Everyone rallies around him. Just like I faked a second ago, the doc gives the skinny to Gene. "You are lucky, young man. No concussion, clean midshaft fracture to the right humerus. Understand you used to play the drums." He lifts his chin, smiles. "Me too. You'll appreciate that there's no apparent injury to the radial nerve. Cast and arm immobilization for six weeks. No sign of internal injury, just banged up. You can probably go home in two days."

I sidebar with my nephew. He tells me they're gonna take him to their house out in Monroe. He'll be watched over there. Safe as anyone can be.

I say my goodbyes, squeeze Gene's hand and he says a couple of words, finishing his sentence, ". . . file . . . on bed."

I head to the Countryside. Some part of me wants to just crash and sleep. But I can't. I don't dare. I drive through the lot a couple of times, which is even more conspicuous because, as usual, there are hardly any cars there. I finally pull up, leave the truck running, and unlock the door to my room. I push the door, letting it ease all the way open so no one can hide behind it. Empty. The maid has made it up. I grab my stuff, leave the room key on top of the TV and flee. I go to Gene's house and do the same door-swinging and looking-over-my-shoulder drill. The manila file with the pictures sits on his immaculately made bed. Like an offering on an altar. I stuff everything, the contents of the box, the pictures, into my saddlebag. I strap it on my ride. I fire up my bike, let it rumble, push the choke in. I'm ready. Just as I came, driven to get on the road. Cut and run. Head for the white line.

Until I realize I'm too damn scared to just head out. He'll be waiting out there, sitting patiently at some night crossroads.

Instead, I check into the Allighta Motel. Pay cash, ask for Elvis's room. The guy at the desk, a frizzled-out dude with a bad case of meth mouth, doesn't even comprehend the question. I end up with a room dumpier than the Hover Inn. I barricade the door with the chest of drawers, TV stand, desk, and chair.

My thoughts aren't even about Mary. The mental repair crew is working that one offsite. I think that somehow I gotta heel this killer dog on my trail. He's gotta respond to some master. Then I remember a little detail. My legal fail-safe. Sarto still needs one last signature on the patent assignment form.

And, if anybody does, he's gotta have the dog whistle.

CHAPTER FORTY-ONE

BUS—
SARTO MOTORS

I sleep late, jumpy every hour or so, even getting up a couple of times to peek through the blinds and give a shove to the barricade to confirm it's tight. Finally, I spend a half hour disassembling the barricade and another chunk of time reconnoitering the parking lot. I finally step out and linger in the doorway before inspecting my bike. The usual preflight check for the deeply paranoid.

I arrive at the Downs at noon, thinking free-form, Gene, Mary, Louie, the box, Marcello, JFK, strange ladies on the phone, the Dealey Plaza Oracle, and SSRIs. If I didn't care, which I sure as hell do, I could embrace this as a long, strange, laughable, tearful trip.

As to SSRIs, I remember I still get a digital newsletter from the Redeemer Clinic. The newest one says they have a grant to investigate Class V adrenaline surges—which, I assume, are big, like maybe they mimic the Fujita Scale for tornados or the Difficulty Scale for whitewater sports. The thesis for the study is that Class V adrenaline surges may operate as release agents for SSRIs. Like they're a decade or so late.

Anyway, I know the answer firsthand. Whatever is going on in my little internal chemistry set, it just got one hell of a kick start. At times like these, what's going on in your head, the thinking, defines the world—hell, *is* the world.

Mine is morphing fast. I can feel the edges peel back. My left hand is holding my cell phone. My right thumb is rolling up Caddo's number. Like I'm gonna reach him.

I'm so damn scrambled.

So that's the way we'll roll.

I glide up and sit, unannounced, at the same side door of the Downs. I park, locking my helmet to the bike frame. The goombah gauntlet is sitting there below a portable shade porch, loitering in folding director's chairs. A black Lincoln is parked next to them.

I try to act nonchalant. "Big shoot today?" I wiseass as I walk up, making the movie screen rectangle with my two hands.

Purple Pants, today sporting a light gray exercise suit with atrocious reflective green stripes, retorts with a pointed finger gun aimed at me, and a not-so-funny wink. He calls upstairs, then signals me to accompany him. I reflect that my fashion critique may be off. Maybe the pulsating green stripes, the color of a lime dragon, are just in my head. Suddenly the air is out of my sails and I'm pouring sweat as he looks at me with something like medical scrutiny.

"You OK?"

"The heat," is all I can muster.

He offers commiseration and his own weather forecast. "Big one supposed to be coming in. Missed us yesterday. You wouldn't know, 'cept for that." He points at a bank of dark clouds once more rolling up on the horizon. Out of the northwest.

I ask and he says his name is Renzo. I have a revelation that maybe he's a nice guy, one or two days a year. Christmas and his birthday. Maybe.

His associate comes up and whispers in his ear. He stops. The mood cranks from chit-chat to chill. Suddenly all *beezness*, he sizes me up as he opens the door of the Lincoln. "Get in."

"What about going upstairs?" I ask.

"Shut up and get in." His backups have me flanked, their gats out, held flush to their sides. Knowing these guys might be capable of *anything*, not sure what, or *whose* nerves I may have touched, I approach the car with the resignation of a death row inmate taking that last walk. I'd seen that shuffle for real as they led one of my clients into the chamber over at Canon City. The little half-steps to the abyss. Now my *own* feet shuffle.

The ride isn't "out to the country" as I expect. It is right back to town, to the old Sarto Motors sales lot on Texas Avenue. Still all closed, windows masked. Incongruous black Beemer there again. We pull up, Renzo nods to me, and I get out.

Mike is waiting at the door. He looks worried.

He doesn't talk, just turns and goes inside.

We go past a front counter and he unlocks a door. We go into a windowless office with a couple of tables. One has two glasses of iced tea flanking a plate of Florentines. The other bears a dour, old reel-to-reel tape recorder. The walls are lined with file cabinets.

He looks at me in a new way, like I'm actually somebody important, and says, "Listen, we each got a problem. Our mutual acquaintance has gone off the rails."

OK, I think, *I'll take understatement.* I blow out a relieved breath, try not show panic. "Yeah. I've got an idea."

"You got shit. Now listen. I've got an insurance policy, things I keep, so that whoever, whatever might come for me has to calculate that secrets can either die forever, or they get like those mummies. They eventually get discovered. Here's my mummy's tomb." He gestures around the room.

I look around. It's a boring, crappy, two-bit business office. He gives me a clinical appraisal.

"Look," he says, "I been thinking. I figure we should go with your book idea. And, maybe with IGT, I want to encrypt all the stuff I've got, put it beyond anybody's reach 'cept mine. I gotta own the keys. So I want this IGT stuff. Then we decide what to tell and not tell in your tell-all."

"First you gotta call off this dog," I say. Mike looks surprised, so I keep going. "He made his second big mistake. The first was my old man. The second, he tried to kill me. *And* my brother."

I'm back doing the tough locker-room talk now. I know it's a bluff. I don't have shit to take out on the field.

Mike finishes it. "I don't have a leash. Not for this guy. Nobody does. Nobody alive."

That, whatever it means, also means that Louie is out there on autopilot.

So I shift gears, curious for a moment, about what Mike has in this little room of secrets. "What other beans you got to spill?"

Mike blows out a breath, takes in another. Like a man with a lot to say and little time. By his side is a briefcase, which he snatches up and lays on the table. He looks at it reverently, as if it contains his mother's jewels. He clicks open the locks and lifts the lid.

Inside is a tiny, reel-to-reel recorder à la early James Bond, along with a set of black-and-white 8" x 10" glossies.

"You want some real *beans*? I've kept a few little trophies from Louie, things I couldn't part with. He sometimes collects . . . souvenirs and brings them back. Like he needs to report . . . to someone."

"Report on what?"

"Weed cutting, you think?" Mike lays out the glossies and hands me a magnifying glass. "Stolen from military records storage in 2005. In the early 1960s, U-2 pilots trained at Barksdale."

I've heard another side of this story, from Caddo.

"They made daily practice runs from here to Vandenberg and back. Along the way at 70,000 feet, they took their usual spy pictures. They were over Dallas at 11:20 a.m. on November 22, 1963. The acuity isn't good enough to see license plate numbers, but you can see a lot. Dealey Plaza is there. Kennedy's motorcade is maybe six blocks away. On the knoll, behind the fence, sits what is pretty clearly a white 1961 Chevrolet. Two guys are standing next to it. One has a white shirt, the other is dressed in dark long sleeves, a dark hat on his head."

Like a police officer, I think.

I'm peeking at the glossies, seeing the ridiculously fine detail on the negatives, the streets, trees, driveways, cars.

"Don't squint, it's bad for your eyes. Take my word on it. Louie brought it home, like a cat brings a mouse."

I finally set it down and let Mike continue his show. "Now, here's the prize. Like I said, my old man never bought insurance, but he believed in it just the same." He scoots the little spy recorder to the center of the table. "On this is his insurance policy, a conversation he had with Marcello. Maybe January, '64." He pushes the play button.

There is shuffling, as of muffled cloth on a mic. I know the sound of a wire. A voice begins. Marcello. "I fix that fucker. Boxed in, don't even know it. Everybody hate his guts. Goes in the trap and can't crawdad out. Twice they try, Miami, Chicago, they can't put it together. So then he's coming to my town. I make it work. Clean up the mess with Dutch's nephew real quick. Hoover, those Commission assholes, they all play dumb. So it's quiet, it's secret. Way it's supposed to be. Now, you and Pauli here need to keep your eye on Louie. He get carried away. Just let him do his business. Let the Chief and our other contacts be his eyes and ears."

Mike stops the tape. Leaving his index finger poised on the button, he gives me an arch-eyed appraisal. "My old man Pauli, you see, he's Italian, not Sicilian. So, he never knows if he's in or out. So he creates his own insurance. This is another part of it, January, 1975. He's wearing his own wire. Listen." Finger up, the tape rolls again.

"Pauli, sit down. [chairs scraping, clothes rustling, long silence] You OK, family OK? Your wiseass kid, he stayin' out of trouble?"

Mike smiles ruefully, pushes out a breath.

"Yessir, everything fine."

"You talk to Maroon?"

"No, he . . . he just called, told me to come here, the Country-side, this morning."

"Maroon, he says maybe I gonna be doin' time."

"Sorry, I . . ."

"Shut. What I want, you know? Listen. What I want is you watch over Louie."

"OK, what for?"

"Cause he got *cunja*, I put a spell with him. Someday maybe he's gonna crack. Go *impazzire*."

"Then?"

"Then what? Like that fucker Kennedy. Louie's a damn good shot, eh? You damn well know too . . . the gris-gris he wear, maybe he get tired of it."

"I got it."

"You got shit. Now listen what I said. Anybody snitch, anybody at all get close, he take care of them."

"Yessir."

"So, Pauli, here's your job: you watch him, keep him close. He goes off, you finish him . . . And one last thing."

"What's that?"

"He watchin' you too. He's a fucking *So-VANT*."

"Yeah, OK."

"I'm watching too. Always."

The tape sputters, crackles, ends.

Sarto looks at me, then around the room. "All this . . . What it needs is IGT—plug-and-play security in the cloud."

I have with me what he wants, an IGT device.

I lay the device on the table, keeping my hand on top. "You have it here. Whatever you say. Plug and play, sure, absolute security. Plus, you already got the IP rights, all signed and sealed. Except . . . one more thing. Absolutely nonnegotiable. Get Louie off my case. Forever. I'll be quiet. He stays away from me and anyone related to me. We call a truce. Get him to reason with your swell guys," I look over at Purple Pants blocking the door, "and put a choke chain on him." I add my own bullshit on top of this. "I got insurance policies too."

Mike appraises me. "No problem."

I'm trusting this because I got no choice. I just want to go home. We do the exchange, no handshake.

I'm halfway out of the chair, he quips, "And the famous book?"

"Fuck the book," I say. "Let it all die a lie."

He nods, then turns to Purple Pants. "Renzo, Mr. McIntyre's visit is over. Take him ba—"

The sound of a car engine, loud, in the attached garage. It coughs, starts with a rough, low-threatening snarl, then revs up over and over. A big, roaring, heavy engine. The room vibrates. Mike looks at the door to the garage, his eyes surprised and angry. I can see the doorknob quiver with each rev. He points at me, tells Renzo, "Get him outta here and take care of that loose cannon!"

Purple Pants steps behind me, lifts me up from the chair and escorts me to a side door. I leave, propelled by a shove, and turn around in time to see him give me the finger as the door closes. OK, Renzo's not a nice guy.

I'm in a closed alleyway, next to a dumpster. I walk toward the light and what I assume will be my ride back.

As I emerge from the alley, the sun is still a vicious beast. Its rays careen off chrome, glass, even the reflective stripes on jogging suits that clothe two dead bodies sprawled next to Sarto's Beemer. Their ongoing bleed-outs have run together to form a sluggish meander along one wheel. It disappears underneath, a blackish-red bayou sneaking into deeper shadow.

CHAPTER FORTY-TWO

LOUIE—UNLEASHED

Mike Sarto never allows anyone into the garage of Sarto Motors. It is locked and he's sure he has the only key. He is annoyed, maybe scared. He reaches for his keys, pointing for Renzo to go stand by the rattling door. As he stares, the knob turns. The door opens. There is a pop. Renzo turns, eyes big, his mouth a surprised grimace. His leisure suit has a dark spot on the chest, a nicely expanding boutonniere. He staggers, goes wobbly, then lurches and falls across Sarto's table just like you'd expect a three-hundred-pound piece of meat to do. The table flips up in the air, ass over teakettle. Propelling briefcase, James Bond tape recorder, iced tea glasses, ice cubes, papers, Florentines, into the air. Mike topples to the floor.

As the debris scatters and rains down, shattering, splattering, clanking, Louie is revealed. Just standing there.

"What the fuck?" Sarto yells as he tries to get up. He decides against dignity and crabs his way on all fours to safety beneath another table. He's panting like a dog. The bootheels following behind him. Summoning what authority he can, being as he's on his hands and knees, he says, "Whatcha you doin' you dumb fuck!"

The boots stop next to the table. *Coelacanth,* Sarto thinks. He ardently wishes he had a gun. He wishes so ardently he pats his armpit, just in case.

Louie bends down to look at Sarto. Louie makes a sad face, then mimics the voice of the old Italian grandfather.

"Time's-a-up."

■

A few moments later, Louie makes an adjustment to the open back of Mike's personal cell phone. Just enough tinkering to generate a spark when the phone receives a call, a certain call. He sets the phone next to the gas line which formerly fed the heater in the office of Sarto's garage. He turns a valve, hears the open hiss, feels the cold flow of natural gas, and scrunches his nose at the smell. An offering pile—files, reel-to-reel tapes—has been arranged next to the gas line.

He hastily steps away, opens the office door to the garage, and gets in the idling car. He clicks a remote. The garage door clanks open, stiff and unruly. Unopened for years, it cracks and groans like an arthritic old man rousted from bed.

Light pours in and bathes the sleek lines of the white '61 Chevrolet Impala. It shines, a best-of-show classic. A faded "Goldwater '64" sticker clings to the rear bumper, next to current Texas plates. The engine rumbles a perfect bass line. Louie is humming and singing. "Surf City . . . Surf . . ."

He gives a light touch to the gas pedal. The tachometer needle jumps to the redline and the mill roars the full-throated notes of a muscle car. He eases the gearshift into low and lets out the clutch. The Chevy rolls out, stylin' and eager to take to the road once again. *That's the way we roll,* Louie thinks, *follow the asshole to his bike, finish him, then Junction City here I come. Pull every last fucking weed.*

He punches the remote and the garage door crawls downward until it closes tight. Airtight.

The Impala is equipped with an eight-track tape deck. As it rumbles down the block to Texas Avenue, windows down, you can hear the Beach Boys' *Surfin' Safari* cartridge playing "409" about the big Chevrolet engine every hot-rodder dreamed of owning. It was still getting air time in Dallas on November 22, 1963:

Louie is braying along, off-tempo and murdering the lyrics:

> Git up and go, man.
> Nine . . . er . . . five gears . . .
> Can't catch me, man.

CHAPTER FORTY-THREE

BUS—THE DAVIS

After looking at the bodies, I break into a run and sprint for the next few blocks, making random turns, desperate for a place to hide. Fast, before he finds me. Any more running, any more Niagara Falls of adrenaline, and my SSRIs are going to emerge like a whirl-wind of flapping, mind-sucking bats. Then I'll go irretrievably "out there"—gibbering, postal, natal, perhaps unleashing a hysterical Twitter rant.

Or I'll be dead.

Gimme shelter! Someone! Somewhere!

I got an idea.

I notice taxis are short-cutting through the street to get back to the casinos.

I flag one, make it out to the Downs, and insist the driver wait until I get my bike running.

Next stop is a hardware store.

A half hour later my bike is parked in the back of a Southern Maid Donut Shop on Texas Avenue. I look up and the sky has thickened into a brooding, vaguely green cover that will usher in an early darkness. I wait until the storm and night are imminent. Hefting saddlebags and stealing glances over my shoulder, I carry the oversize Ace Hardware bag and do my best imitation of a secret agent running. Stealthy jog, stop, ready stance, look left, look right, continue. After a couple of blocks, I'm there.

The Davis Theater. I walk the perimeter fence. The wind is gusting, the cold front coming from the northwest and mixing with soggy air up from the Gulf. The makings of a violent storm. I step through knee-high grass, broken wine bottles, unknown urban debris piled up like shuddering tumbleweeds on a Texas fence line.

I trace the entire property. I test the gate, rattle the heavy chain and lock. If, and how, Bruce gets in and out of here, by what rabbit hole, is a mystery.

Scaling the fence, with the razor wire coils on top, isn't in the cards. I return to the shadows along one side, open the Ace Hardware bag, and remove the bolt cutters. They do a nice job on the fence links.

The ornate front door of the theater, just behind the ruined ticket kiosk, is locked solid. Like a fool, like I didn't just cut my way in, like this is a *house*, I knock.

Having committed to this odd formality, I knock again. Actually, it's more of a frantic pounding. I yell "Bruce. Bruce!" I've got nowhere else to go.

I'm on my fifth or sixth pounding when I hear something behind me. I look at the kiosk, the dirty windows all around. I see Bruce's head rising up above the counter. Seemingly disembodied, he's looking at me. He stands all the way up and we silently regard each other. He has the look of a pissed-off homeowner interrupted by the solicitations of an encyclopedia salesman.

I say, "I need help."

He purses his lips, precursor to a *no*.

I implore, "Help me!"

He scratches his nose and wild hair, signaling an imminent loss of interest in me, as if he is about to descend to tinker with whatever urgent business he conducts in the realm below.

Finally, I beg, "Please!"

I must be getting good at the begging. He looks around to check on who might be with me. Then he gives a come-hither gesture with his finger, unlatches the kiosk door so it cracks open, and descends from view once again, his eyes staying on mine till they dip below the counter.

In the distance I hear a chain being rattled, slid across metal. I swing open the battered little kiosk door and look down and see a hole, perhaps an old sewer entrance. From its edge, ladder rungs disappear into pitch dark. A faint hiss and tang of funky steam seeps up from the hole. I regard the abyss and think, *better this than Louie.* I embrace my saddlebags, squeeze in, try to shut the bulky door, and grope with my foot for the rungs. Once at the bottom, I see ahead a flashlight banking swaths of light along a utility tunnel. I stoop and crab toward the light, banging my head and elbows on pipes of unknown purpose, entering a realm of unknown fates.

I could never retrace the tight turns, forks, and ascending set of rungs that bring me into a utility room behind the single movie screen of the Davis Theater. I do notice it is clean. The canvas is taut and unstained.

Bruce is waiting there, the flashlight putting a sinister glow on his whiskered features so that he resembles a man made of bark, bearing a clump of Spanish moss on his face.

He gestures with the light, showing me the way to the side of the screen. I go there, and he turns to an electric control box on the wall. As he tinkers with it, I hear a series of clicks, switches, then a bar being pulled down to bring forth electric power . . . and a wonder.

From above, I hear a whirr. Like an ancient alien engine revving up, the lights flicker and a disco ball far overhead begins to rotate. Bizarre colors play across the inside, the rows of seats, the big screen up front. Psychedelic light show time.

Neon Charlie's world is back. Across the room, the projector stabs a cone of light through the air and the screen erupts into a countdown sequence: 4 (crosshairs), 3 (profile of a chieftain, not unlike the late Kickapoo Diner sign), 2 . . . 1. Credits begin, signaling the start of reel one of a movie. It's not *Rodan*. It's one better. The original *Godzilla*. *Ah so, Gehzirra*! as we used to pimp the Japanese pronunciation, with squinted eyes and teeth bucked, long before political correctness censored American mores.

Bruce raises his arms, his rheumy eyes shimmering with reflected light, and he becomes a vagabond Oz.

"Pay no attention to that man behind the curtain! Ha! Take a seat." I do, ten rows back, middle. Done with puttering backstage, he eventually sits beside me.

I try conversation. "So, the Neon Charlie story is all true?"

"Who knows what's true? All I know is I wormed my way into *here* . . ." he looks around, the admixture of lights playing off of his homeless man attire, "and . . . found . . . *this*. The old Magician of the Bossier Strip maybe left it. His own personal Bat Cave. Sealed up with his hopes and dreams."

Bruce jumps up and goes to cut off the zany disco lights. He returns and we sit, stare up, and watch Raymond Burr, later to become the TV character Perry Mason, witness the monster roast Tokyo and explain it all in sci-fi babble.

I don't know how long this happy mood will last, so I just say what I got to say. "At the Country Joe Concert. They came and took you away."

Bruce looks at me. "I can't wind that part back. Up to then . . ." He does the I'm-up-here-you're-down-there thing with his arms. I know I'm still on the bottom rungs of cosmic consciousness.

He drifts away for a moment, then returns to the general vicinity of the here and now. "Anyway, thank God for Reagan. They let us all go. Out from the Cuckoo's Nest."

I start talking over the movie, blathering really, not sure he's comprehending any of it. About young Mike Sarto (that gets a vague nod), the car, the joyride, the box, the cabin. I get to the point. "There's a guy out there. Looking for me. He's gonna kill me. I need to leave these." I lift up the saddlebags. "I need to stash these somewhere."

Bruce gives me a *whatever blows your hair back* look. He leans back, his head resting on the chair back. His eyes relax into a nest of lines and furrows. The real Bruce, spot-on in the present, arrives and muses to me and the air. "Bus, we had a destiny. We'd rule. You remember? It all evaporated. How'd we go wrong? 'I am an American!' Ha! I still don't know what that means. It all went wrong because we're free to screw it up. And we do."

He's letting me off the hook that's been imbedded so long and so deep it's become part of me. I look over. "I wish I could've saved you."

He smiles, showing a couple of missing molars. "Hell, you know where I ended up? After I got out? Driving a truck for that guy Owsley, the fugitive LSD manufacturer. His production lab was hidden in a semitrailer. I drove the rig."

I think about that, envision Bruce crisscrossing America, a roadie for Owsley's peripatetic LSD light show. We grow quiet, enjoying the movie like kids again.

The end of *Godzilla* finally draws near. The greatest Japanese mega-monster, king of the *kaiju*, dying and croaking out plaintive calls of distress.

A shadow moves by the screen, stage right. I know what it is.

"He's here!" I whisper. I drop between the seats. There is a flash and boom from up front. The shot thuds into my seat cushion. The click of an electric switch and the disco ball starts up. It rotates and splinters a harsh white strobe into a thousand fragments. I'm pulling at Bruce. "Get down here!"

Suddenly I can't get my breath.

Flashback, SSRIs, Owsley's Gift, whatever, and what the hell, I'm back there.

My view of the world morphs into fish-eye perspective. It is the Country Joe Concert all over again, except instead of the pigs with riot helmets, it is Louie. He is here, somewhere.

Cage match with a killer. And he's got the gun.

Bruce squirms back up and looks around. Whatever Louie is shooting tonight, it is loud and has a stunning, armor-piercing impact that can cut through walls or a dozen seat backs like they were feather pillows. The first of a two-shot volley flutters Bruce's shirt sleeve in stroboscopic stop-action and cuts through a dozen seat cushions behind us. Choreographed clouds of dust erupt over a line of seat backs that bend and return in chorus-line unison. Bruce screams and pulls away. The second bullet rips into the seat where his heart would've been.

I hear the next bullet smack into the wall, eating up drywall and clanging off pipes. The next second I hear water, like a hose spraying out of the wall.

I pull Bruce down all the way to the floor, grab his collar with one hand and the saddlebag with the other, and begin to crawl along the aisle. I expect Louie to calmly walk up at any second and finish us off. Two hapless guys huddled in their grave.

He doesn't. Maybe he's thinking of my little surprise in the cabin. Right now, I'll take any respect I can get. I drag us along like a beetle tugging a prize beyond its capability. Blood is starting to ooze down Bruce's arm, the floor feeling slippery and sticky as I dig with my boots to get traction.

We get to the far end of the aisle and I dare a peek over the seats. I see why Louie didn't come finish us off—he doesn't have to. The screen is alive with a pulsing, backlit glow. Either a radioactive variant of the Blob has descended upon us, or Louie has set a fire that grows by the second. It blocks our escape. Smoke is seething up and rolling along the ceiling, making a kind of polychrome sheet lightning as it engulfs the rotating disco ball.

The first tendrils of acrid, tear-pulling smoke reach me. I vaguely remember the long ago thuds of cherry bombs and stench of smoke bombs. The kid madness of it all.

I'm not sure if there is a way out at the front of the theater. Bruce is helpless. More scared than hurt, he looks at me with eyes that, once again, implore *save me*.

For just a moment, I roll over and lie on my back and let the pieces coalesce. The Davis has come alive with a dark and demented resurrection of the past. Explosives, screams, smoke, spraying waters, bizarre lights. Raw adrenaline-fueled flight. The fell air replacing that innocent kid madness.

Behind the screen, an explosion and sparks like the Fourth of July accompany the loss of electricity. The place sinks into a Halloween darkness of night with a fiendish, orange jack-o-lantern thing roaring its approach. The movie screen displays a leering, gap-toothed pumpkin face, worthy of the world's scariest B-movie, just before it erupts into angry flames.

Louie is gone and he has unleashed this monster movie thing that will exact recompense for our childhood excesses and misspent lives.

I roll back over and get my grip on Bruce and the saddlebag. I get up, one leg at a time, and drag us up to the theater door, waiting for the sudden surprise of a bullet blowing out my chest.

We clear the swinging doors into the lobby. The smoke is crawling along the ceiling with us. I run to the main doors and shove, feeling the chain outside clank and hold. Only one window is not completely boarded up. I tear at the plywood, bending and wrenching, until it falls to the floor. The concession counter stands, as if ready to vend. I scrounge behind it and find an unopened, five-gallon can of popcorn.

Perfect. Neon Charlie was a detail guy. I lug the can over and hurl it at the glass.

The window, hardly safety glass, shatters outward as a spray of fresh air rushes in, eager to feed the fire. The air is wet, ozone-thick, smelling of thunderstorm.

I try to knock out the glass shards from the frame. Our escape route looks like a gaping shark's mouth.

The saddlebags go first. Bruce is on his feet and I lift him and shove him out the window. I follow. It is raining hard, the roof of the Davis boils columns of smoke that twist and coil in the wet air. Flames have found rents in the roof, giving an orange underbelly to the smoke.

Louie has to be waiting close by, black-hole eyes framed by a pyromaniac's glee. I sense the direction of the hole I cut in the fence. From there to my bike. I look over and Bruce has my saddle-bags. I gesture for him to follow me. He does the same, urging me towards some other escape route known only to him.

Once more, we are at the crossroads. Places, where and when, for inexplicable reasons, we take different directions. Bruce and I stand for a further moment in the rain, looking, acknowledging our divided paths, our once-luminous and now ruined visions of ourselves. He rakes his eyebrows and scrooches a shoulder to ask if I want the saddlebags. I nod a quiet *no*.

The last I see of Bruce is a drenched figure, bloodstained arm and saddlebags over the opposite shoulder, loping into the darkness.

PART FIVE

INSIDE THE LINE

"Shale County Line, crossed so long ago.
Life was gonna be fun, easy and slow.
It all went so fast, then I knew it well
A thousand lines I'd crossed, a thousand tales to tell
Thousand tales to tell
SC Line, SC Line."

Smiler's Cramps, "SC Line,"Vinyl Dreams Cassette,
Robin/Mercury 1968

CHAPTER FORTY-FOUR

BUS—WHITE LINE REDUX

I get to my ride. It is uncovered, drenched, but it starts. A faithful steed patiently waiting. I half expect a muscle shiver to flow through it. I mount up and we rumble through streets of gusting horizontal rain and overflowing gutters.

I suppose speed, even caution, doesn't really matter. There are beings, like Louie, who can tunnel the stormy night unseen, gliding on tenebrous wings that eclipse time and distance. Such a being will always be ahead, straddling the white line, a demonic spider resting its papillae on the taut signal strands of some vast, invisible, and unfailing web.

I head north, helmet on, visor down, my body cringed against the rain. I eventually stop at an all-night gas station with bright lights and a canopy. I pull out my tool kit and disassemble portions of the bike right there. I search for a GPS bug. Seat, fenders, battery compartment, gas tank. Nothing. I'm back to magic, the hoodoo feeling, neck hairs as compass needles.

Outright fear tells me one thing. Avoid I-20. I will continue north, ride out the squall lines, and get the hell out of Louisiana and Texas.

The rain finally relents and the wind eases to a breeze pushing at my back. A warm southerly up from the Gulf. Texarkana is but a blur and soon I'm into Tribal Nations territory. I hug the Oklahoma state road system and, hours later, pay cash for a room in Comanche.

CHAPTER FORTY-FIVE

LOUIE—DEALEY PLAZA

The car had been parked all night on a quiet side street. The driver had gotten out twice to pee on the sidewalk, had chucked his empty Chick-Fry sack onto the sidewalk. Had slept until now.

Louie checks his watch, straightens up the seat back, adjusts the rearview, clicks his seat belt buckle. It is ten 'til ten.

He listens. No voice. The Little Man is really gone. A moment, unsteady, as if his soul had a dizzy spell. Then it all clicks back. This moment, this now, this job to finish, this . . . weed. A whole sprout of them. And the plan is, well, not just situational. This is pure improv.

He turns the key. A thing of beauty, the way the 409 mill jumps to start. Effortless, smooth, its eager quietness belying the four-barrel carb, bored and stroked up to 4.13, the cylinders yoked and teamed for 120 horses of raw power.

Louie slips the white Chevy into gear, thumbs an eight track into the deck. The King begins to sing, drowned out by Louie's butchered rendition.

. . . It's now or not ever . . .

Gravel crunches, the hood noses into light traffic. Six blocks to go.

He turns onto Main. Five blocks to go.

Soon it'll be too late . . .

He can see the top of a tent. Down by the knoll. Crazy pennants streaming from some sort of flagpoles. He downshifts, his foot still on the gas pedal, RPMs kicking in, the engine growls.

A right turn into Houston. The Depository straight ahead, the corner window high up. Yeah.

I been waiting for this time.

The Chevy bucks down the single block, ready to run. He turns left onto Elm, the trees to his right, looking down to Dealey Plaza. To the tent sprawled on the slope of the grassy knoll. Lots of people, neatly arrayed on folding chairs. Like an old-time revival. Preaching the Gospel of Lost Truth. He can see a stage, somebody at the podium. Another guy in a wheelchair, no, one of those scooters they hawk on TV.

He downshifts, floors the gas, burns rubber. Smoke erupts from the tires. Squeals. The crowd can hear something, they look in his direction. Some start to scatter.

Smoke torrents from the rear tires, the Chevy's nose wants to lift. Speedometer rockets past forty . . . fifty . . . jumping the curb. Onto the grass. Aiming right at the wheelchair guy.

. . . now or not never . . .

The crowd parts as the Chevy plows ahead, tossing mangled folding chairs into the air, crumpling tent poles, and tearing the tent into a streaming shroud flowing along with the careening car.

CHAPTER FORTY-SIX

BUS—
JUNCTION CITY

Fourteen hours of sleep.

The rest fuels enough energy for another push through neglected roads. I catch the tail end of a news report. Dallas. Hit and run. Sixteen hurt, two dead, one victim in a wheelchair. Cell phone pic of a speeding car with a tent flapping from it. I make it back to Colorado late that night. I fill up in Salida and gauge my next stop.

■

Seven in the morning. High-altitude cold. Nine straight hours of riding. Wind, vibration, the endless tension of leaning the bike into tight road curves, cramps from the hand grips. I'm exhausted. Punishment to get here at this exact moment.

McClure Summit. I sit astraddle my bike, looking to the quickening glow in the east. A few pink clouds float between snowcapped peaks. They seem like prized ships carrying the merchandise of a new world. The moment is close. I pull off my helmet and nestle it on the gas tank, the gryphon's talons encircling the top.

The sun is just behind the peaks.

A millisecond of green light, like the exquisite slice of an épée across the face of the world. Crimson flows like blood into the clouds. I am headed home to a world bearing one more wound.

■

The front door to my house is unlocked. The security system is off, but I hear the doggie alarms. They tell me Mary is home.

The kelpies come tearing into the foyer. Whimpering, huddling close to me. They're agitated and scared. Something is off. I yell her name, with the possessive tone of a happy husband returning to a happy wife. Make believe hard enough and . . . who knows?

I go room to room and realize it's just the four dogs here. Her purse is on the kitchen counter. I check the garage. Her car is gone. She's gone.

I call her cell, which erupts with a catchy tune from her purse. I wait another hour before I call Rick Van Pelt.

He's there in fifteen, followed by others. It is two hours before the investigating detective and a forensic tech leave. I take the dogs to the neighbors.

Rick stays in the background as the investigating detective, a young guy, goes through lots of questions. How long I've been gone? How long it took to get here? What was I doing in Louisiana? In . . . where? . . . Bossier City? Go over that again. What about this journal? Detective Van Pelt gave it to you? Yeah, we'll check with him. It's missing? How? What was in it?

I'm fudging on answers, knowing all the while I'll screw this up. A felony is probably lurking here, amidst the lies. Too many questions, too many improvised answers, too fast.

How do I explain the mess I just ran from? You can't. Just help them find my wife and skip the distractions.

Rick comes over, tells me he's heading to the station. Then he stops, turns back. Script perfect, here comes the MacGyver.

"I checked with Bossier PD. Your brother, Gene Wray, was in an accident? Tangled with a train? Passenger died? Did you know that last part?"

"I only know what my brother and the cops told me."

"They also said some kind of arsonist was loose on the town. Burnt down a place called . . . the David Theater. And Sar . . . Sartisian Motors. Those ring a bell?"

"No." Too flat. I follow up. "Rick, what do you think?"

"Something's wrong. I'm worried. You worried?" He has this scrutinizing look. I'm in his zone of worry.

"Hell yes, I'm worried sick. That's why I called. She'd never head out without her purse and her cell. Her jogging stuff, her cross-trainers, all here. Leave the dogs? No way."

"OK, we're on it. Stay in town, OK?"

"Right."

Then he does it again. Double MacGyver. "Speaking of arson, we just got a call. A white '61 Impala, Texas plates, down by the river, burned out so it's just an ashtray." His face is one big question mark.

My expression is one big fake shrug that barely covers the fact that I'm speechless.

I wait for the call from Louie. I could have spilled everything to Rick, but that would put the focus on me. He would have taken me in for more questioning. I can't let that happen now. It would disrupt the streams of fate that even now are sweeping Mary, me, and Louie into the same Class VI, impossible cataract of destiny. A cosmic keeper hole so deep and intense that all sins will be boiled up and escape will be by miracle only.

Just to compound things, I can feel the free ride coming on. Like a desert storm, psychedelic rain skirts and purple haze lightning play on the horizon. A freshening breeze and raindrops and mesquite smells swirl in my head. The psychological rainstorm will unleash runoff, gather and coalesce until it becomes the flash flood of fate I'm thinking of.

Then, it lets go. The storm dissipates.

I sit, a bored zombie, and stare at the TV. Reality shows, each its own absurdity, roll by.

At five in the afternoon, the phone rings. I make no recording of the conversation, but it imprints. I can play it back like a tape, like I'm reading a transcript:

Me: Hello.

The voice on the other end is a man, but eerily high-pitched. Like a living voice mimicking an old analog tape. I've heard recordings of a certain Senate hearing. A Cajun-Italian drawl. I realize who this—or they—are.

Carlos: Hi. How you fellows today? All right, Louie gets you took care of. Oh—here, someone like to talk to you.

Me: Yessir, thank you, Mr. Marcello.

Mary: Bus, oh God! Don't talk! Listen! He . . . he's right here. He gave me a note. He wants the box, all the stuff . . . the news pictures, the negatives, the hat, all of it. And . . . hold on . . . he says . . . the codes. I don't know what he means.

Me: Where are you?

Mary: I don't know. Bus, I'm so sorry.

Me: Put him back on.

Mary: . . . He's shaking his head. His note, it says, eleven tonight. At the desert spot. Dud, no Dude Stomp. Says you'll know. Bring all the stuff. Be alone or I kill her first. Bus, God, I'm scared! Help me!

Me: Ask him . . .

Dead line.

So, full circle. Dude Stomp. Hardly anyone knows that name anymore. Except, of course, me. And Louie. It's a long-gone cattle gathering point, probably once a rough corral and chutes, next to a railroad stop. A little sign, the one in my office, used to be there.

Hanging on a post. Everything else, all but the rails turned to dust. Memories barely live out there. The McCarty Gang, cohorts of Butch and Sundance, rustled cattle in that area. Now there's not even a cactus or buzzard nest nearby. It's just off the westbound frontage road along I-70, the original Highway 50 asphalt still intact. Forty-five miles from Junction City.

The spot where Louie murdered my father.

Then I realize what she just said: the "news pictures" and the "negatives." The Gold Room pics? Those weren't in the box. How in the hell does he know about them?

Caddo. RIP. Maybe getting ready to fess up, maybe playing all sides.

I remember an unmarked dirt road that norths off from the Stomp toward the byzantine canyon lands of the Colorado River. I've hunted out there, gathered Anasazi artifacts. It becomes a track, then a 4x4 trail following a dry steambed into broken country. Ambush country. A night scope and he could blow my face off from a quarter-mile away, maybe farther.

My old man's voice echoes back, whispering, "*Careful son, no backup.*"

Something dumb inside me thinks that, in the end, Louie won't sit back and rely on a rifle, on distance. He could, I know he's damn good at it. But I fancy that this time he'll prefer close work. He wants to see the stash of evidence, wants me to inventory it in front of him once again, then he wants to finish his play. He thinks Mary is his key. He thinks I've got unalloyed love for her.

Well, it's a helluva lot more complex than that.

She's bait for both of us.

I'm not gonna call in the PD, or the Shale County sheriff, or tell Rick—hell no—I'm just gonna go. This is the time, and I'm ready to re-meet this guy, proper like. Who gets killed in the process, me, him, Mary, is incidental now. Let the play begin. It's *Hamlet*, and you gotta work yourself to the real pivot point of vengeance. You gotta appreciate that vengeance has a lot of collateral damage. It's messy. It's incomplete.

And, to mix literary strands, no matter the outcome, the Faulkneresque moment is here. The moment, the thing that's great and profound. The NOW.

Four hours to go. I pull a ring of keys off a hook hidden in the back of my closet. I study them in my hand, as might Saint Peter. Once held, they cannot be given away. They bindeth and looseneth.

This time the plot is going to get played all the way out.

The keys jingle as I hold them before I unlock a cabinet in the garage. I swing open the metal doors and start to get ready.

Maybe I've never been good at anything except locker-room talk, but we'll see.

CHAPTER FORTY-SEVEN

BANNER'S NOTES

Yours truly is hiding. A madman is on the loose. His 1961 Chevrolet tripped a toll road on E-470 outside Denver. As Jim Morrison said, *killer on the road, his brain is squirming like a toad*. I've lost track of Louie. I can't get online for long. My former employer is probing relentlessly. To find me, suppress, and eliminate me. And Bus.

In the meantime, I've gone omniscient. Metadata analysis doesn't look for anything in particular at first. It just follows all the ant tracks. Then you can assess the patterns, make connections, and drill down. I've discovered two things about Bus. One he sure as hell will want to know. It's about Mary, her secret. The other is his secret, something he sure as hell doesn't want anybody to know, ever. Something he's kept hidden.

They've got more capability to find me than I have to hide. My time is short.

CHAPTER FORTY-EIGHT

LOUIE—THE FINISH

Cinching his gloves, Louie checks the blindfold, puts the other plastic ties in his pocket, says to Mary, "Stay like that. It's gonna be awhile. Pee in your pants if you gotta, just don't move. I'll be watching." Mary's muffled response, through the duct tape, is a garbled but emphatic "Huugh-UUU!" He smiles, cuffs her upside her head. *Bitch.* She's chewing, trying to bite through the tape.

Louie dithers for a moment, the tape roll being back at the Subaru. He moves off to take his position and he wonders if the Little Man is still on his case, naggin', whisperin'. Just like that, he hears a voice. "You-a sure?" Louie gets ready, finally, to let his boss have it. He turns like a whiplash, hands choke-ready to reach out. Empty air. *He's toying.* Louie pivots to his left, looking around like the henpecked, beta side of an odd couple. He pivots again, then just shouts it to the air. "I do my fuckin' job!" A pause, Louie breathing heavy. "Always. Always! Fuck your omertà shit!"

If the Little Man is anywhere around, that shuts him up. It definitely shuts up the difficult broad. He can tell, the way her head is cocked sideways, that she's listening, trying to figure out who the second guy is, where he came from. How truly psychotic this situation is.

You don't wanna know, thinks Louie.

CHAPTER FORTY-NINE

BUS—DESERT REDUX

Ten thirty at night and I'm at the Stomp. Sure enough, there's a sheet of yellow legal paper tucked beneath a rock in the middle of the dirt turnaround. I go where it says, north, yellow headlights playing off the sagebrush like I'm a ship in a rolling sea. Shadows, ravines, cattle guards, mesquite clumps, all ebb and flow for the next five miles. Whatever his plan, this bastard must have a back exit, maybe just disappearing into the canyons. Not hard for a country boy, even for a southern transient out in this red rock and cheatgrass moonscape. I can see that I'm in an arroyo, the swirl of stars eclipsed by the hard black lines of cliffs.

I dip down into a draw, gun the four-wheel drive, and dig clouds of dust that surround me as I churn to the top. I stop to let it clear, snuff the dust out of my nose, and, as the cloud drifts away, I see her.

She is kneeling maybe twenty yards away, blindfolded, and dead center in the road. Her posture tells me she's trembling, frozen like a mule deer in the headlights. I see a slash of silver—duct tape—across her mouth. The tape is maybe coming apart, gnawed as if by some animal chewing for its life.

Her head turns to each side. Like me, she knows there is a universe of possibilities swirling in this moment of time and space. She knows she is probably lined up four-square in exquisitely fine crosshairs, illuminated by a green night-is-day glow in a professional sniper's scope. There is an uncaring finger on that trigger, and its pull is deathly light. She is a baby's breath away from death.

For that matter, so am I.

I sit there, my dad's .38 revolver, the one he last used out here, on this same enemy, nestled in my crotch. I assess the limited information I can glean: middle of nowhere, Louie's got the advantage. I got no backup. But he has two, maybe three weaknesses—he wants the stash of evidence, he (hopefully) wants to work close up, and, most important, he thinks I give a rat's ass about Mary.

He could be anywhere.

I leave the headlights fixed on Mary. The last of the dust drifts away . . .

For just a moment my psychedelic helicopter is lifting off, slowly rotating up and looking down at myself, at her. A whoosh-whoosh rotor sound slows and meshes with my own heartbeat.

My whirly descends, lets me back off with myself.

And the world clicks back to blunt reality. Hard, cold desert air. My unfaithful wife. A killer out there.

A familiar black ballistic cloth bag lies next to me. I open the door, put one foot out for traction, and give the bag a heave. It arcs into the headlights like a slow, dying bat. It plops, tufting a spray of dirt.

All in one move, I kill the headlamps and exit the truck in a roll. I get up and start sprinting back down the road in a bent-over, zig-zag sprint.

If he doesn't nail me first, he sure as hell knows I'm getting my ass out of here. Just above the wheezes roaring out my lungs and my thudding boot clumps I can hear Mary yelling through the

KNOLL STEPHEN HILLARD
244

remnants of tape, "Buhsszzs? Buhhzz!" I don't stop. To hell with her. Let her know that ditched feeling.

A good half-mile or so back down the road, I fade from a dead run to a labored hitch of a jog, to a hands-on-hips walk. I just hope he didn't set up behind me as I drove in. I stop, get my wind, and turn. A lone cottonwood stands next to the track. It waves gently in the air, a coral fan in a silver current of undiluted starlight. Its presence is a sure sign of an intermittent water source and game crossing.

I reach behind the tree, find what I'm looking for, and then take to a trail that winds up the cliff face and wobbles back north by northwest.

Being hunted, succumbing to sheer terror and fright, is noisy business. Being a hunter is slow, quiet, patient business. It's almost an hour before I get to the overhang.

I take off my baseball hat, let the breeze cool the sweat in my hair, and crumple the hat as a gun rest. I set it on a ledge in front of me. I lean back and look up at the bottom of the overhang. An expanse of pictographs. This spot is all but invisible from the arroyo just below, and the ledge has protected the rock art since it was scraped into the sandstone by Anasazi hunters centuries ago. Hunters, like me. Kindred spirits in their recognition of the interflowing nature of the world. Fellow takers of the psychotropic sacrament. In their case, peyote, buttons from an obscure, low-growing cactus. In mine, the residue left from Owsley's long-lasting mind-trip specials.

Just as it was when I first found this spot, a dozen years past, the ground is littered with flint shards. This was no doubt a view site and an armory for hunting parties. They rested, scanned the country, worked on their flint points, and communed with their gods through their art.

An excellent scorpion image, the size of two hands, is just above my head.

My armory tonight is not evidentiary proofs, not flint-tipped arrows. It's my Remington .270. Named "Buck Killer" by my kids as they annually stood in awe at the body brought home to hang from the garage joists, Buck Killer was like me—old, scarred, pitted, but, with luck and easy breathing, still capable of deadly accuracy. A reach that is flat, true, and long for a hand of death.

The scope is Buck Killer's second, a two-year-old 6x Armasight that I pray has stayed spot-on since last sighted in for night hunting coyotes. The illuminated reticle and high transition will light up the night like it's noon under a green sun.

Thinking about it, I'm sure he's got something better.

I thumb the electrics and let the barrel ease forward. It moves low and slow and horizontal, like a viper's head. I blow out a breath and position my eye to the scope. It shifts and discovers the green-glow country. Here all things are unsheltered from the merest finger pull that can visit destruction from a quarter mile away.

The trick, as ever, is finding the target. At the pace I learned from my grandfather, hunting for fossils, for arrowheads, for deer, my eyes scan with deliberation.

Light from the star-sprent sky bathes the world. I methodically examine discontinuities of form and shadow. I pick a cluster of pictographs on the far canyon wall, then move on.

I stop. A single antler prong pokes from behind a boulder. It moves slightly. The buck is bedded down on a cliff-hanging ledge hidden by rocks and junipers. He is nervous. The night wind bears to him the stench of man. He can sense that two predators stalk this night.

Louie can't be that close to him or the buck wouldn't be there. I raise my face and study the landscape once more. The Book Cliffs loom on the horizon.

Below me, the creek bed winds its sandy path. It approaches from the right, advances left, then turns at a corner marked by a tall cliff face packed with window-like shadows. The bed of the creek doglegs left and curves back below me. I've seen this layout before.

Dealey Plaza. The cliff face is a spot-on, sandstone reincarnation of the Texas School Book Depository. Down to horizontal strata with eroded depressions to match the rows of windows. The sixth floor is etched, clear as a postcard on the Oracle's table.

Below me is Elm Street. I am positioned exactly as if I were on the grassy knoll. Zapruder with his 8mm camera would be to my left. I can almost sense the presidential procession approaching.

I reenter the world of the scope and find Mary, kneeled and bowed on Elm Street just below me. The angle is shallow. Easy shot. I study the side of her face. Tear tracks cut the dirt on her cheeks. She bears the aspect of a penitent, kneeled in a church of celestial candle fires. Awaiting the footsteps of fate. Awaiting her execution.

Feeling what it's like to be told *it's over.*

The bag lies ten feet in front of her.

I poke my view in all directions and return the crosshairs to Mary. This time I let them settle on her. As a target. Heart-lung shot, or head? I decide on the chest. Being decent and all. I thumb the safety off. So easy. So *just.* A slight pull . . .

My finger tightens. My capacity for retribution is open and so-o ready. I steady the crosshairs of annihilation on her and straighten my trigger finger, relaxing it so the following pull will be smooth. *Silky*, like Mary describes fluid NBA moves.

I fleetingly imagine her strung up and hanging upside down from my garage joists, neighbors aghast. I stay poised that way for a long time before letting my right hand drop. I pull back, shaking my head.

Maybe I should have listened to her. Stayed inside my little garrisoned world. Now having taken the keys in hand, the terrible loosening has happened: wounded ancestors, my old man's white-line fever, fated president, back-of-the-alley Mafioso, acid flashbacks, roadside killers, friends forsaken, cheating wife, Lucas lamps, and . . . *strictly junior high.*

And, of course, one hell of an assassin. Somewhere near. Waiting to kill me.

It dawns on me that I, we, are all just momentary reshapings of the past.

I shake my head, lift my eyes, and look over the rocks again.

I stop breathing.

Louie is approaching Mary, maybe thirty yards behind her. He is walking slow. He has a rifle at ready. *Bastard!* He carries a little pool of star shadow beneath him. His own dark magic.

He is on Elm, coming my way.

I go to the scope and see his facial expressions. He seems to be enjoying the atmosphere. He turns to his left, his mouth moving, as if talking to someone, as if in an intimate exchange with, say, Jackie. Or himself, or Carlos. Hell, who knows? He is almost head on, oblivious to me. Exactly where JFK was when Louie blew his head open like a pumpkin shoot. Now I am Louie. He is looking at Mary, at the bag, at Mary. The crosshairs settle on their mark, three inches below the collarbone, then I decide to go for the headshot. Sorta poetic. I line up above his right eye, settle, then the sight shudders slightly. The truth for me is, if I'm *really* going to pull the trigger, to kill, the shakes take over. Well, I am, and shakes and all, here we go. Buck fever. The crosshairs jiggle, then yaw and pitch, fighting me.

He stops, deerlike, sensing something. His antennae for presence, for danger, are exquisite. He is all business now. He stops, raises his rifle and draws down on Mary. I sense the ritual mechanic, the gathering of steadiness. He is finishing things. One more weed to pull. He will shoot within the next second.

My aim slides down and to the side, losing him completely. I gasp and bring it up to his shoulder, then just above him, and let it descend like the prow of a ship in a heaving sea.

The NOW is here.

The two shots are almost simultaneous. My rifle bucks. My ears close up. I have an after image, his muzzle flash, the shudder of impact, maybe his skull coming undone, the head snapping backwards, suggestion of a dark spray to the rear. I resist the little mental arm pump and stare down. His body is sprawled, one leg weirdly askew, cocked up on a rock. Like JFK's leg propped up on the window edge of the Lincoln convertible as it sped from Dealey Plaza.

I jack out the casing, hearing it bounce in the rocks somewhere below me. I look for Mary and scramble out of my perch. I jump some boulders and make a dead run down the slope of this other-world knoll.

I vaguely remember picking up his rifle, tossing it, before walking over to Mary. From there the horror goes all red.

CHAPTER FIFTY

BUS—JAIL

Until the past few weeks, my experience in jail has been clinically tame—a drunk tank night as a kid, a three-day DUI stint as a mortified adult in Alaska's notorious Wildwood Prison (again, another story altogether), and innumerable visits to incarcerated clients, including the two death row inmates over at Pueblo.

So it is with mixed fascination and horror that I find myself getting accustomed to the lidless, stainless steel toilet abutting the stopperless stainless steel sink in my little cell in the Shale County Detention Facility. I have already acquired an innate clock for meal times, the relished "change-up" moments of the day. I feel a Pavlovian anticipation for the faraway clanks of doors, the whish-whish of the food cart wheels, the rattle of metal trays, the trustee's gruff bark—"Meal time!"—calling us like dogs to our kennel doors. We, my fellow guests and I, all eager to see and smell these odd lots of sustenance from the outer world.

Of course I'm, as they might say, a high-value prisoner on both sides of the bars. On the inside, I get no special perks, but I'm quickly sized up as a willing jailhouse lawyer. My fellow inmates line up in the rec room to get practical advice on their situation, their public defender, the way plea deals work. No one gives me shit. Outside the bars, my keepers want to make sure I'm safe for my ultimate trial and hanging. Works out both ways.

Every day after breakfast, after the somewhat sad reversal of events—the gruff "Trays!" the stacking of metal, the whish-whish away of the cart, the last door clank down the hall—I sit and look at the walls. Isolation isn't the inside, it's the absence of the outside. It's birds and walking and puffy clouds that aren't there—and the blunt fact that your fate is being decided by persons and events outside impenetrable walls. *Out there.*

They let me read the *Monitor* every day.

Things come and go out there. Mary's funeral. A big event, several hundred fascinated mourners, enough to double as my lynch mob. For my part, I'm strangely ambivalent. I'm sad, I'm sorrowful, I blame her. Meanwhile, life is out there. The Junction High Tigers win their football opener. Business goes on. Hydee Thomson sells a big property, rakes it in.

My three kids come to visit. Of course, I failed to duly report in to them at the end of that week. They got the news via phone calls from Carrie Williams, my partner and suddenly my lawyer, right after she visited me in jail. Before they saw my mugshot on the Internet, saw a face-drooped, mouth gaped, mad-eyed, presumptive felon. The picture made the mugshots of Nick Nolte, James Brown, and Mickey Rourke look like choir boy photos.

Anyway, my kids throng here. They implore with their eyes. Their spouses look dubious. They all hold pictures of my grandkids up to the imbedded wire Plexiglas. Voices through the phone are flat. I wonder how, by what fate, I led myself here.

My dismal reflections this morning are broken when Carrie arrives. I am escorted to meet her in a windowless consultation room. My preliminary hearing on charges of murder, first and second degree, is set for next week. Bail was denied on the basis that, having been *out there* on my bike for ten days, I am somehow a flight risk.

I'm not optimistic about the hearing. I judge it unfortunate that the prosecutor at this point is "Tiny" Sohertz, a man fattened by donuts, Slurpees, fast-food burgers, and under-the-table largesse. Worse, a man dulled by the cynicism that, in time, barnacles nearly all journeymen in the criminal justice shipyards. Worse yet, he is a man long beholden to those city fathers who want my scalp. The prosecutor isn't James Cressen. He will win the election and he will undoubtedly recuse himself from my case. The judge is from Sedgwick County, out on the plains of Eastern Colorado. He has been brought in because of the notoriety of my case across the Western Slope.

The armory of proof can be arrayed so things look pretty bad for me. My .270, fresh from firing, was found in a "sniper's nest" among some rocks. It is specially equipped for long-distance, nighttime killing. No shell casings are found. Mary's body bears an entry wound next to her left shoulder blade—not inevitably lethal, but a shot-in-the-back nonetheless. Distance, forty yards, plus or minus five. A shot no doubt fired by me, using the dead man's rifle after I "ambushed" him. A clumsy attempt to deflect guilt. She was murdered in an almost bungled, pitiless execution. Her blood all over me as I held her, perhaps finally aghast at my crimes.

There is also one helluva motive. I left some pretty edgy, pretty politically incorrect messages on her voicemail. I also admit what I know others, her friends, her unknown lover, must know: she Dear-Johned me five days before her death. After receiving her blunt message, I drive day and night 1,200 miles to get back to Junction City. I pay cash along the way to insure no credit trail. I call my friend Detective Van Pelt to set up my "gee-I-just-returned" alibi.

The dead man, Mr. X, is, I explain, a guy named Louie Diamond, one-time associate of Carlos Marcello, coconspirator and murderer of JFK.

That gets the eye rolls going.

My old man's journal, the roadmap to my story? Also gone, no copy, no record except a purported digital file in the cloud

secured by an unfindable, unbreakable security platform called
I-Gig-Tam. A patent under that name exists, assigned to me,
but the so-called experts trying to figure it out say it is either so
general or so weirdly complex as to be deemed improvidently
granted. Detective Van Pelt can vouch only for recently returning some documents to me, as my father's heir. The father was a
heroic cop, murdered in the line of duty, whose shoes the defendant could never hope to fill.

Medical records, even without Amalie Adams' privileged notes,
show the defendant has a drug-related instability. Someone told
them about the Mayonnaise Conspiracy.

So the prosecutor's closing is all there: Bus, an antiauthoritarian
gadfly of a lawyer, is a "ticking time bomb" who "snapped" over
his wife's understandable decision to leave him. Whatever the role
of Mr. X—friend, paramour, whatever—we'll never know. What is
clear is that Mr. X and Mary McIntyre were set up for an ambush.
Probably lured up there somehow. Mary trussed and gagged as
bait to lure in Mr. X. Mary's Subaru is found a quarter-mile further
up the draw.

They say the setup worked exactly as I planned it. The man
killed from a coward's distance. Mary executed at "close range."
The defendant, Bus McIntyre, is truly the Lone Nut.

The evidence, for the purpose of the hearing, will be sufficient.

I read the account of my "JFK Mystery" written up in the *Monitor*. The impression, "preposterous," is all but declared in the coverage. The *Monitor* reporter is all over it, even goes to Bossier. My
brother is billed as a "former musician" recently involved as the
driver in an accident with a train. An accident that killed his passenger.

Whoever Mr. X is, he has no records, no archived fingerprints,
no presence in any database. A big zero, except I killed him. From
seventy yards. A fairly long distance, a coward's shot totally incon-
sistent with self-defense.

So the armory of evidence yields prosecutorial weapons that fit: jealous husband kills wife and her mysterious paramour. Any other details are unimportant. Premeditated double murder.

The note at Dude Stomp? Gone with the wind. The phone call from Louie? Pay phone. The conversation? My imagination.

And the Maltese Falcon, the black bag with the JFK murder proofs? The bag was filled by me with magazines and the *Junction City Monitor* from last Sunday. The real stuff is in some other universe, with a long-gone Bruce and those saddlebags on his shoulder. No evidentiary revelation and no legal footwork is going to save me from my fate.

Wearing a funny look on her face when I enter, or rather shuffle, in leg chains into the consult room. I expect Carrie to chastise me one more time about spilling my guts at the scene, where I directed the cops on the scratchy, disturbed 911 call from the cell in my pickup. Spontaneous honesty? Belief in justice? Come on, boss.

Instead, she is beaming. She checks the room for obvious bugs. Why, I ask myself, would they be more obvious than the little black grill in the ceiling right above the metal table bolted to the concrete floor? I gotta admit, however, I've developed an even deeper paranoia about spying. Wearing iron bracelets makes you keen on your suspicions.

I'm patient and she finishes her professional recon. She sits across from me, her lawyer's tote bag strategically on the floor by her side. She spreads her hands. "You feel like you're being railroaded? Like a lynch mob is out there?"

It's strange to hear her say this. I know for a fact that her great-grandfather was lynched by a mob in Calway, Mississippi, in 1927. He made the mistake, being a black man of no means other than his own hard work sharecropping, of looking at the mayor's white daughter. The attempted rape accusation, never proven, was moot by the time the mob finished.

I preemptively offer bad news.

"I think Tiny's going to go for the max. He's got heavy hands laid on him."

"Well, here's the news. Tooey got a clue. He's been on a digital tear and . . . "

"What kind of clue?"

"Well, you know he's really good."

"Sure, tops, so what?"

"Someone bypassed every digital security system in the office. They left no trace, except a simple message on his screen."

I raise my hands and eyebrows. I'm lost.

"Tooey found some other heavy hands. Your friend, Hydee Thomson, has laid those hands on more than just Tiny's career prospects."

"I don't get it. Like what?"

She slides over to me a printout of a computer screen.

"Like your wife, Bus."

The text on the screen says:

Mary and Hydee are a number. They doth conspire.

I'm stunned beyond speech, until the depth of the deceit slams into me. "She . . . she was getting it on . . . with . . . with him, my enemy?"

The thought is gagging, how they both could conspire to bring me down. Then it dawns on me. "I think this makes things worse, more motive for me to kill her."

She smiles, makes a note, puts her pen down. "Except for one thing."

I hike my shoulders, squinch my eyebrows. "What?"

She lets it out, like a gift. "*Mrs.* Thomson. If she finds out, she will go so nuclear it'll put Kim Jong Un out of the proliferation business. She'll take Hydee down, keep all the companies she's got, and rip away half of whatever he's got left. Plus his balls. If Hydee goes down, so do a lot of other folks in this town. Besides, Junction City has only a few blue bloods left, and she's one of them. They don't cotton to being tied up in scandals."

"So?"

"So, it's already afoot. We let Hydee know this morning. He talked to Tiny this afternoon. Your case just got weaker for the prosecution. Burden of proof, who fired the second shot, whatever. They offered to make a deal an hour ago."

I balk at the word "deal." I want to stare at both sides of this coin, try to divine the odds that will decide my fate. "What about Tiny's rock-solid, career-making case? Maybe we could beat it? Wh . . . why not?" I know my eyes, my demeanor. They say scared, uncertain. I've sat in her chair and delivered plea bargains before.

She exhales, assumes the dutiful air of a lawyer explaining the legal cosmos to a dithering client. "Look, your rifle killed Louie. Louie's rifle killed Mary. Your own admissions at the scene," she sighs here, "plus the forensics—trajectories, bullet fragments, blood spatters—all confirm those facts. The core question, the only question, is: who killed Mary?"

That hangs in the air. The very question sufficient to cast a gloom of guilt. She resumes, "Your fingerprints are on both weapons. Louie's are on neither. He was wearing gloves. A draw there. You both had gunpowder traces. Timing on that is imprecise, but he just might have been out there shooting prairie dogs earlier, maybe plinking for the hell of it. Another draw. Maybe a shrug from the jurors. The rifle he was found with? It was stolen from a trailer in De Beque, thirty miles from here. The owner didn't know it was missing. It could have been gone six months or a day. Maybe helpful? Probably just another shrug from the jury."

I'm not feeling good, this coming from the one person who stands between me and a probable life sentence.

"The reason they may shrug off *any* helpful evidence . . ." She stops, looks at me, sees my emotional state, and reaches into her briefcase. Out come two bottles of water. I stare at them. I realize my throat is parched. She offers one. I guzzle as she gathers herself to continue the delivery of bad news.

"The reason none of that is helpful is *you*, Bus. Tiny will look across that courtroom, deliberately extend his arm to level and point his fat index finger . . . at *you*. They will follow his aim. He will present you as an experienced, clever, ruthless criminal defense lawyer. Someone that likes getting things their way. *You* had a revenge motive. *You* are familiar with forensics. *You* stole the rifle. *You* staged the evidence to frame Louie as the bad guy. *You* bound Mary. *You* set her up for callous execution. *You* stalked them." She pauses. "He will keep that accusing finger poised in the air and let silence sink in until it becomes a damning, indelible fact." She slumps, leans back.

I'm feeling queasy, as if a bell on some distant hill—hell, some knoll—is tolling away my existence. "So what do we have?" I ask.

Sitting up, hands open on the table, looking me straight in the eye, she delivers the message she came here to present, "We have lightning in a bottle. An alignment of planets and stars. It won't last. We know they put pressure on Tiny. They want a deal. That's huge. We haven't had the preliminary hearing, so the public doesn't know all the facts. That gives the prosecutor some flex. Their case may have holes we don't know about. Also, and this is important, they don't know if you will testify at trial. Maybe you've got some real evidence on Louie." She raises an inquiring eyebrow at me.

"Finally, I'm willing to make a bet." A knowing look glows on her face, "Detective Van Pelt, if put on the stand, will testify that the raw, physical evidence, the sheer forensics, are equally consistent with both the prosecution and defense cases. That would be a serious torpedo of reasonable doubt circling out there for Tiny to worry about."

Carrie takes another half hour to go back and forth with me. I am still resisting, fretting, pondering the odds at trial. Finally, she does the indispensable thing a good lawyer has to be able to do: tell her client "no." As in "no trial." She makes a call to Tiny to iron out some details and test his bottom line. After all, with two murders in the county, some price, as they say, *just gots to get paid*.

"And the hacker?" I ask before I forget.

"Tooey's stumped. Somebody good. The main thing for now is that the information is true. Worry about your guardian angel later. Time to resolve this case."

A deal is offered. I take it. The coin of my penance is a plea to manslaughter in the second degree with a one-year sentence. Effectively that means I'll walk from here into a halfway house in three to six months if I'm as polite as I plan to be. I'm defrocked, my law license suspended. That is a nonnegotiable part of the deal. A handful of salt from Hydee and those city elders.

I agree to keep quiet about Mary and Hydee. Mrs. Thomson will never know, never hear careless whispers from me. Jim Cressen will dutifully stay on the sidelines. Tiny Sohertz will get a promotion. The *Junction City Monitor* will let the story die with a few dispirited follow-ups.

Life goes on.

Secrets stay secrets.

Lies become truth.

CHAPTER FIFTY-ONE

BUS—SPRINGTIME

George Orwell's opening line in *1984* said it perfectly:

It was a bright cold day in April, and the clocks were striking thirteen.

The breeze today is mild, the crocuses are up, and the sun is shining. I am walking through downtown Junction City, free as a bird, with no bracelet and no GPS tag. Free as a man can be that has a parole check-in time at 6:00 p.m.

Across Main Street I see Hydee Thomson, still in golf attire, going into his newest business venture, the Mesa Partners Bank on Main Street. He looks at me, we assay each other's status, and surprisingly he nods as he goes through the revolving door. On to his next entrepreneurial milestone in the life of this modest Middle America town.

I stop by my old office and peek into the reception area. "Mail?" I ask to the air. My cheery effect vaporizes like a dandelion in a blast furnace when I see Carrie. Her face is heated, her finger is pointing, first at me, then at my personal office door.

I go in and she directs me to the client's chair. She takes the high-end, Corinthian leather swivel behind my desk. Just so our roles are clear. I look around, seeing my old self from a distance. The professional accoutrements, the unused books, the flimsy facade hiding a wrecked career.

The gravity of her voice cuts through before the words. "'Cause if you're not straight with me . . . can't help you."

I'm lost.

She continues. "Anything else in your past you would like to tell me about?"

"Like what?"

"Oh, someone killed. Bombs?"

I gape, stunned, feeling my deepest foundation stones shift beneath all the rubble. In their wake is revealed that last, deepest, most locked dungeon inside me.

I resist the way guilty people often do, by essentially admitting culpability. "Tell me what you've got."

She glowers like a schoolmarm staring down the dumbest kid in the class. So I don't embarrass both of us, she says, "Aspen. 1968."

That's it. She knows.

"OK, I . . . I . . ." Nothing comes out. I've not spoken of this out loud, well, forever. Not to Mary, not to . . . damn!

Amalie must have spilled the beans. As much as I told her anyway. Against the patient-doctor, the shrink-nut privilege. Colorado rules of evidence something or other. Her notes, on her precious, tedious, maddening little iPad. Easy to hack. I should appreciate that by now.

I don't bother to ask. I just tell the tale. Carrie leans back.

That high, cold, long-ago night on McClure Pass, riding the Vincent Black Shadow. Fall of 1968. Lots had changed since my acid trip in the '67 Summer of Love. The world caught a case of madness, me with it. Hick rube to acidhead flower child to Che-spouting revolutionary in little over a year. Students for a Democratic society. Weather Underground. Strong right arm of the proletariat.

I ramble on how it, the madness, was everywhere and unstoppable. France and Mexico with student-led strikes. Prague Spring erupts. Tet happens and Cronkite declares the Vietnam War unwinnable. North Korea captures the *Pueblo*. Johnson bows out of the election. MLK, RFK assassinated. Cities burn. Columbia shut down. Chicago Democratic Convention riots. Russia invades Czechoslovakia. Black Power salutes at the Olympics. Burning draft cards. *Planet of the Apes*. Captain Kirk kisses Uhura.

All that rambling context, but in the end it's a simple story: On that night I'm a courier. I am ferrying dope and money to a Weatherman safe house outside Aspen. Actually, it's not so safe. When I arrive I see a dozen cases of DuPont 50 percent ditching dynamite crammed into the living room. Enough to vaporize a city block. I make my delivery and watch four bearded hippies smoke dope and try to make bombs. With them is a kid I know. Named Phil Noonan, baby face, wire-framed glasses, headband, suburban kid from Junction City. My roommate back at Colorado State in Fort Collins.

On a kitchen table are strewn packs of Zig-Zag rolling papers, smoldering roaches from half smoked joints, overflowing ashtrays, beer cans, and more bullshit than you can handle with a scoop shovel. These guys have never worked a hands-on, tool-ready job in their lives.

They have metal tools, fuse, and blasting caps interspersed with all the other crap. One of them is toking up. They are idiots.

I'm looking at the caps. They are what really set the dynamite off, make the whole thing go bang. Volatile, unpredictable little devils that can blow apart in a blink.

"Here," I tell them, methodically clearing the pliers and wire cutters away, gingerly putting the padded case of caps back together. "You don't . . . *ever* . . . use metal tools with blasting caps."

In one hand I hold a shiny tin blasting cap, thick as a no. 2 pencil, couple of inches long, tubular end open to receive the fuse, which I hold in the other hand. I demonstrate insertion of the fuse in the cap.

"The trick to holding these together is to crimp the end of the cap around the fuse. No tools. No metal. You do it with your teeth."

They are watching me, bug-eyed, in a *far-out-wow* sort of way, as I demonstrate.

There is a Russian roulette intimacy, a high-consciousness moment, when you take a blasting cap—this inherently unstable thing that in an instant can explode your head like a gunshot melon—put it into your mouth, settle it between your molars, and slowly bite down. Hard. Until you feel it give, like it's alive. Feel it settle around the fuse.

The crimping done, I pull my accomplishment out of my mouth, hand it to the nearest beard, and grab my Storm Rider jacket. One of them is shaking his head, picking up the pliers, saying, "No fucking way, man."

That's it for me. I ask Phil if he wants to go. He says, "Yeah, wait a second and let me go to the head." I fidget, I watch the fools at the table tinker with extinction. I can hear, feel, a clock of stupidity ticking down to disaster. Ticks. More tocks. No Phil. I busy myself with jacket buttons, upturned collar, bandana tied around my face, wool cap pulled on, goggles just so. No Phil.

I lose it. I cut and run. I leave Phil.

Twenty minutes later, I'm on the road to Glenwood Springs. I notice something in my rearview, hear a low thump in the air, and look back at a boil of glowing smoke rolling up in the night sky a few miles back.

I don't stop. I see the aftermath on TV, read the papers: "Radical Bomb Factory Explodes in Aspen. 'Identifications Impossible,' sheriff says."

Right then and there, I pretty much go straight. Clear out every bit of weed, every piece of paraphernalia from my basement apartment. I settle into being a solid, beer-drinking, foosball-playing, girl-chasing, apolitical, low-profile student at good ole Colorado State.

But I still dream about crimping that fuse. And Phil sitting on the john as I rumble away.

Carey is asking, "The FBI interviewed you?"

"Yes, a few weeks later. Not much to it. I tell them Phil left school, dropped out, never came back for his stuff. Maybe joined a commune in Nederland. Nothing unusual."

"You lied to the FBI. You transported dope. You gave aid to bombers using stolen dynamite. You conspired. People got killed. You could be up shit creek."

"Statute of limitations?" I ask, pretty sure of the answer.

"None. Not for this."

"So how'd they, you, find out?"

She shows me a single-page FBI interview form dated November 1968. From my little talk with the local bureau agent. "Subject appears to have no knowledge," it concludes. Good BS by me. Phil goes on the missing person list and is never heard from again.

Then she hands me a second page, a notation on top says, "Snowmass Corner Explosion. Forensics Inventory—October, 1968." The page has a low-power microscope picture of a scorched but unexploded blasting cap, probably, miraculously, blown clear in the explosion. On it are a clear set of teeth marks.

"I suspect, if anyone ever checked, that those marks still fit your left molars, Bus. No one back then would put the pieces together. Today, if so inclined, they could."

I think about my teeth, briefly flirt with getting that molar pulled this afternoon. Walk-in dentist office in this town? Then I realize it's too late, too many dental records.

"You mean someone already did. So I've got this Sword of Damocles over me?"

"Yes, well the FBI reports and this picture showed up—again on Tooey's computer—long enough for him to print copies. A message with it said, 'This has been DRZ'd from every source. Gone forever. Good luck.' Then it *all* disappeared. No trace of it, or who sent it. Perhaps someone is watching out for your ass, my damn lucky partner."

It feels like a pardon, but I got no one to thank.

Nonetheless, I feel selfish relief. Phil, another abandoned victim of my selfishness, another mental prisoner to which I'd chained myself, is released.

And at last I understand the stupidity of locked gates.

This will take time to absorb, but, somewhere in this mess is a direction to where I go from here.

Two hours later, the thoughts are still turning as I continue my downtown walk. The time is appointed and I enter the door at 217 Main. Back in the 1960s the building housed the town's first and only psychedelic head shop, The Mirkwood Forest. The irony is small but rich, as it now hosts the regular meeting of the Flashback-ers' Club. My old chair has a pillow on it, as if saved for me. We go through our discussion, honoring the protocol of anonymity.

The speaking moment rounds the attendees and gets to me. They all lean in, figuring I'll spill my guts. Who killed whom? Why? How? Carrie's advice sticks today. I shift to something else, straight from the heart.

"I know each of us believes, has experienced, a world *out there*. Bigger and beyond ourselves. Dimensions, minds, spirits, forces only dimly glimpsed."

I look at each of them in turn. "More so by us than others."

Their eyes glisten as they each agree. Our little band of explor-ers, psychedelic brothers. They know more is coming.

"I have been spied upon, dissected really. But all the spies and machines in the world can't see what's inside me. Inside you, inside all of us. And . . . I have a guardian angel. I think it's a lady. I don't even know her name. She knows me. She reached out. More than once. She saved me."

I'm getting misty now. "I hope she's OK. I would like to thank her. That old-fashioned way. So it means something. In person."

CHAPTER FIFTY-TWO

NEWS ARTICLE

(Not reported in the United States)

JUVENTUD REBELDE

UNIÓN DE JÓVENES COMUNISTAS

APRIL 22, 2015

TRANSLATION:

A Cuban vessel, the *Domingo Expresa*, exploded and sank at Ensenada de Marinela yesterday under suspicious circumstances. The incident occurred next to the Marinade Guerra Revolucionaria. The body of an unidentified woman was found. There were no survivors. One witness described a small missile hitting the vessel.

An official from the Ministry of the Revolutionary Armed Forces described the matter as "suspicious." "This was not an accident," he said. He went on to say, "This has the earmarks of an American drone strike. We know that such devices are released and retrieved by submarines of the United States. Such provocative intrusions on Cuban sovereignty are cowardly and illegal. Very soon we will capture one of these spy robots and embarrass the US imperialists."

The matter remains under investigation.

———

CHAPTER FIFTY-THREE

BUS—LAST WORD

As I am finishing this book, I realize it's not about JFK or Carlos Marcello at all. It's about the echoes we all are, sons of fathers, children of parents, descendants of never-met ancestors. Unknowing bearers of perspectives, quirks, even emotional frames and scars borne by those before us.

I never, with one exception, heard from Bruce. Nor has my brother seen him in the back alleys of Bossier City. I think he's out there though, and finally, we're OK.

The exception was a package that came from Los Gatos, California. It held something last seen as I stuffed it into the saddlebag that was fuming smoke in the rain, held by Bruce as he went right and I went left in that storm. The mouse-chewed, 1960s vintage Dallas Police Department hat hangs now on a hook in my lawyer's lair. Someday soon I'll ask my friend Van Pelt to do a cold case DNA test on it. Next to the hat hangs the framed letter written by Dalton Trumbo, overseen by a frame holding my new Certificate of Good Standing from the state bar association. My license was restored early, based on a petition from my legal peers, a good word from the new DA, James Cressen, and the one condition that I devote 100 percent of my time to pro bono work over the next two years. You bet. My shingle is back, with the name of the firm changed to Williams, Escamilla, and McIntyre.

I sold the house and cleared out every bit of Mary's stuff. The kelpies were adopted out ensemble to her best friend.

My new house has, of course, that inevitable, invisible upper story. On its ramparts the pennants still flow in quiet defiance of whatever rough beast may broach the seawalls and lurch toward my keep. My inner psyche is, I suppose, always on defense.

I'm sure nothing remains of my mad dash to the white line, to Bossier City, to shattered funhouse mirror pieces of the truth. Save one last page. I found it stuffed in some estate documents from my old man. It was destined for his journal, typed on that same old Remington on the same paper. It reads:

    Where are they now, the men of Spain, the men
    who heard the drumbeat and the skirl, the men whose
    politics and cause is ever confusing, whose lives
    were angry and whose hopes were high?
    Did these men who wear the three-point star become
    bitter and do they walk the dark night ever trying
    to explain their reason and their cause? Has the
    trefoil turned to brass? Or is the ring of laughter
    still strong and does illusion still march with the
    sound of a different drummer, have they told their
    sons of Segovia, of Madrid, and of the taste of wine
    at Castillo?
    It is perhaps saddening to think of the men of
    Spain, for like us all, time dims the past, and
    the wild intent is now only a glimmer, but one will
    always wonder--where are they now?

The question, forever unanswered, still haunts me. However, I know that feeling. I'll always know that feeling.

EPILOGUE

After the worst winter in thirty years, May 2016 heralds what some experts predict will be a Goldilocks summer in the Northern Hemisphere. Not too hot, enough rain to give hope to the drought stricken, a mild outlook for Tornado Alley. Rock bands and C & W acts will tour. Hot dogs will sell. Stock markets, now corrected, will rise with gusto. The Red Sox will lead their division and football fans in Austin will dream of a revival.

Meanwhile, the world's communications system is humming at optimal levels. Sagan-flops of data flow every nanosecond.

The disruptions today are minor: a blip in one Atlantic undersea cable, variously explained as a routine maintenance cutover, as the Chinese putting in another tap, or perhaps an Iranian sea drone engaged in disruption. Elsewhere, Nigeria is down again.

An inside joke is circulating within the NSA. Seems they have been watching a guy named U-Jin Wo, a lieutenant in North Korea's notorious cyber sleuther Unit 21 as he, in turn, pores over the entire collection of Hillary Clinton's missing emails. The joke is that he's at the back of the queue. Every spy outfit worth its salt, and then some, had long ago raided Hillary's home basement server. The one purchased at Best Buy and put together by the Geek Squad. The only people in the dark are the US public and the flustered members of the House and Senate Intelligence Committee.

Subpoenas get nowhere.

Hacking gets results.

As always, layers upon layers of intrigue.

As always, the machines get smarter and smarter.

All in all, a smiley face on old Skynet.

Like invisible remora fastened to its underside, this vast data flow is being read by thousands of parasites. The NSA's Corellian-class data syphons in Texas, Oregon, and Maryland are humming with energy as they gather, filter, assess, and package it into actionable sequences through various schemes. They also store it. All of it. Warrants, court orders, treaties—pesky questions from congressional committees be damned.

As nature has tiers, so too does the world of spies. Everyone spies on everyone. Level upon level upon level.

Thus the encrypted phone call of Tector "Big Tone" Vannet, originating in a corner of the 1872 courthouse overlooking the dusty, tree-lined town square in a county seat in South Texas, is being monitored by multiple listeners.

"This damn line better be secure. I paid and you promised, Ochray."

Big Tone pronounces the congressman's name like it is a bad vegetable. Corpulent in girth, suit jacket off, tie loosened, sweating through his Dior white button-down so it shows the wifebeater underneath, he suddenly stops. This he rarely does. He's about to chew someone out, which he always does.

"Who gives a shit about legal shit! Nobody gives a shit. Listen, Ochray, you need to get this under control."

Vance is so agitated his immensity seems to be levitating up from his chair. "Your project was supposed to get ahead of the curve. Clean up any last weeds. Now this little renegade bitch of yours is still out there. Alive. She's kidnapped our project. Get your people to reign this in. And you stay bought or you'll be bumped back down so far you won't get a job cleaning toilets in Austin."

From the secure phone in his office in the Longworth House Office Building, United States Representative Ochray, unable to think of a rejoinder, much less say it, is wheedling. "Uh, yes, but . . ."

Vance is now standing. To his side, the wall sports a white flag with a single black cannon. Below this are the words "COME AND GET IT." A phrase still meant for all enemies of Texas and thus Big Tone, as he stares down at the town square named after his great-granddaddy, Tector Vannet.

On the opposite wall is a plaque that reads:

Two can keep a secret if one is dead.

Vance ponders the message, then continues. "We got a good thing going down here. Nothing to be ashamed of. Lyndon gave my granddaddy that bridge in return for delivering this county in '60. At least that's the story, and it's legal enough for Texas. It's one of two privately owned bridges that cross the border. That's how come I get to charge a toll. NAFTA made me, and lots of people associated with me, rich. Rich people down here own land. Lots of land. If you own lots of land in Texas, sooner or later, there's going to be oil. The last oil boom down here was the biggest in the history of the state. It'll be back. You know why I'm telling you this?"

He waits exactly one second.

"Of course, you don't. It's because a man's name—and you wouldn't understand this because you're a white-trash, no-name trailer rat—the name means a lot. You lose that, people think you're weak, think they can *pr-ry-y*."

He pauses, then resumes with a voice that quivers with spittle and frustration. "*In-VES-ti-gate!*" He gestures to the air, a finger and thumb coming together, the hand pulling away. Like pulling a loose thread that might unravel a whole tapestry. "So I'm not about to let anybody besmirch my family's good name. What he really did to earn that bridge, that's a lost secret that is nobody's business. You're gonna make Sonny-Jesus sure of it! Get rid of her for real!"

■

Allen Bernsmith, project director of KNOLL, sits in his cubicle facing an array of screens at the Texas Cryptologic Center in San Antonio. He is reflecting on the fragility of his career, his inclination to shoot first and ask questions later, the picture of his mentor—a scowly, smiling Dick Cheney—and a younger version of himself taken a decade ago at a fund-raiser. He fidgets as he eavesdrops on Big Tone Vannet scolding Congressman Ochray.

The delay to break the encryption is 3.7 seconds. The end product is flawless, capturing the inflections of their voices. He could run this through a veracity filter, but there is no need. Banner McCoy somehow survived. She is now especially dangerous. A personal threat to everything he has built, an affront to the responsibility given to him. Soon the clunky machinery of overlapping bureaucracies, of politics and spies, will render a phone call, perhaps a visit, perhaps a summons up to the sixth floor. But why wait for a call from up the chain of command when you can just listen in on their every step? Stay ahead of the game.

He knows this game. The forthcoming imperative is already a done deal, thanks to orders from someone, from somewhere far up that chain.

Clean out all the weeds. Once and for all.

He sits, musing about the implications. *Just maybe, someone might consider me, ole Double-Dis himself, to be a weed.* A vague, troublesome thought. He is distracted by a beep from a screen on his far left. It shifts to information that would be ignored by most of the world. He watches as the satellite image focuses on a cloud of dust just as a minor seismic event is recorded in a USGS office in Junction City, Colorado.

■

Richard Reitman, inventor, failed entrepreneur, founder of IGT, trains his binoculars and watches across the five-mile width of Sinbad Valley as the dust cloud boils up. It obscures the vertical slot that is the sole entrance to the valley. Three counts later the sound, a gruff bark followed by a train of rumbles, reaches him. He can see that the dynamite charge was perfect, cascading boulders and an entire five-hundred-foot slab of rock down to bury the narrow defile along Salt Creek. The dust cloud climbs up and up to the top of the valley rim

Now the door is sealed, he thinks.

He glances at the computer screen, the searcher drone's GoPro view, and leans back, enjoying the view from the rock steps of the old outlaw cabin. Obscured in trees and commanding a view of the entire valley, the tumbledown structure once sheltered the gang that, in various combinations, would be known as the McCarty Gang and the Wild Bunch. He spies weathered initials carved on a rock in the wall: "RLP." It would include Robert Leroy Parker, aka Butch Cassidy.

Unless they come after him by helicopter, he knows where they will have to try to enter the valley. The south cliff face, where, in the 1880s the first prospectors had winched buckboard wagons and terrified mules, kicking and braying, down the vertical drop of a thousand feet.

A rough trail was later excavated along Salt Creek. Cattle could be rustled and then run in and hidden on the mesa rim. Sew-Em-Up Mesa they called it. Rustlers would simply cut off the brands and sew up the wounds.

Bus McIntyre, who owned the little ragtag spring and ranch on the valley floor, let Richard stay in the ranch house as a caretaker.

Now he would be beyond furious. Blowing up the only entrance to the valley? He just wouldn't understand. Nobody would understand.

■

Of all the hidden feeding frenzy that is the digital spy world this day, the most unnoticed node sits in a secure room in a windowless warehouse near the Russian-friendly resort at Varadero in the Republic of Cuba. The cyber intrusions originating from here are as undetectable as any accomplished by the NSA. They are via the Glass Box.

The young lady, Banner McCoy, routes everything through IGT. She is selective, her handlers are patient. Each weighing the balance of control: invaluable data access, selective bits of strategic information, life, death. She won't defect. She won't surrender the keys. She will confound them all.

Of course, she had only two minutes' warning to get off that boat. Which still leaves a real bad taste.

She hits "Enter" and gigs of encrypted data—documents, emails, internal memos, her own analysis—flow into the web from thousands of captive servers. It flows through Tuckerton, through the TCC, through a silk-fine fishnet of NSA surveillance tools. Three newspaper editors, one each in London, New York, and Junction City, watch as it downloads and reassembles in plain English on their personal computers.

■

I can see the auction room on video feed. On Wilshire Boulevard in Beverly Hills fifty people are seated in plush, red upholstered folding chairs at Julien's, "Auction House to the Stars." A bank of phone operators and online representatives is along one wall. I am a remote bidder, but not as Columbus McIntyre. They accept Bitcoin.

Business this day has been brisk.

From The Trilogy Collection catalog of Julien's Auctions 2017 were life-size orcs, swords, and sword shards, shields, axes, rings, wraiths, Elvish bows, and Palantirs. They have sold well. The last few lots are anticlimactic, styled under the heading of "The Hollywood Pen: Artifacts of Screenwriters."

The auctioneer announces the next item:

> The Lot 477. An original version of the script by Dalton Trumbo for the film *Executive Action*. The script has handwritten annotations by the author.
>
> This item comes with a 10" x 8" manila envelope, its original seal still intact. The envelope cover says "Research Notes. Do Not Open. D. Trumbo."
>
> May I have your bid?

My bid is already entered online. I click on "Submit." The live feed rewards me with recognition of my bid. "Five thousand dollars is the opening bid, ladies and gentlemen."

Seconds tick by. The auctioneer, eager to wrap the day, says, "Going once. Going twice . . ."

I will win this, and I will dig out what Dalton Trumbo was working on, the secret he left out of the movie.

I'm never going to accept a locked gate again.

ABOUT THE AUTHOR

STEPHEN HILLARD grew up in Bossier City, Louisiana, and Grand Junction, Colorado. He received his BA in political science from Colorado State University and MA in philosophy from Columbia University before obtaining his law degree from the University of Colorado.

While at Columbia, he was a National Woodrow Wilson Fellow and volunteered as a tutor at Rikers Island Prison. He was managing editor of the *University of Colorado Law Review*.

Mr. Hillard moved to Alaska and began his legal career as an associate and then partner in the international law firm of Graham & James. He went on to become managing partner in the Alaska office of the highly regarded Los Angeles-based law firm of Munger, Tolles & Olson.

While in Alaska he worked extensively with Alaska Natives, ran the largest minority-owned broadcast group in the United States, and pioneered the participation of minority-owned businesses in the ownership of federal spectrum licenses.

Mr. Hillard returned to Colorado to form Council Tree Communications, a private equity investment fund. He founded the company with the goal of increasing diversity of ownership in communications. Mr. Hillard has been featured in the *New York Times*, the *Denver Post*, the *Rocky Mountain News*, the *Hollywood Reporter*, *Variety*, the *London Guardian,* and the *Wall Street Journal*.

In addition to *Knoll*, Mr. Hillard has authored or coauthored (with Joel Eisenberg) five novels, including *Mirkwood*, *The Lost Chronicles of Ara: The Mirkwood Codex*, and *The Chronicles of Ara* series. The latter has been purchased by the Ovation network and is in development as a TV series. A graphic novel, *Farway Canyon* (coauthored with Dennis Nowlan), is in development as a TV series with Anthony Ferrante, director of the *Sharknado* movies.

Mr. Hillard and his wife, Sharmaine, continue to make substantial charitable contributions to educational and social institutions. In 2015, he was the first non-Latino to be recognized for the Lifetime Achievement Award by the Denver Hispanic Chamber of Commerce.